THE LAST DRAGON

USA TODAY BESTSELLING AUTHOR

GENEVIEVE JACK

He's lost his royal title. She's lost her family's fortune. Can a gamble on each other pay off?

He's a dead man walking.

After three hundred years, Marius must face a world that has moved on without him. Haunted by nightmares about the horrors he endured in the underworld, he's desperate for distraction. He finds relief in the exhaustion that comes when a dragon named Harlow, the alluring daughter of a washed-up Paragonian aristocrat, agrees to train him to fight.

She's flirting with danger.

Life as Harlow knew it is over. Her family was lucky to escape execution for their former support of Empress Eleanor. Now she's just thankful to be alive and that her keen talent for pit fighting has earned her a job training Marius. The money is the only thing keeping her family afloat, but growing close to Marius could be hazardous to her health.

Together they'll battle ghosts of seasons past.
When echoes from his time in the underworld keep pulling Marius back into the violent domain of the dead, can Harlow help him break his ties to the past before death reclaims what it lost?

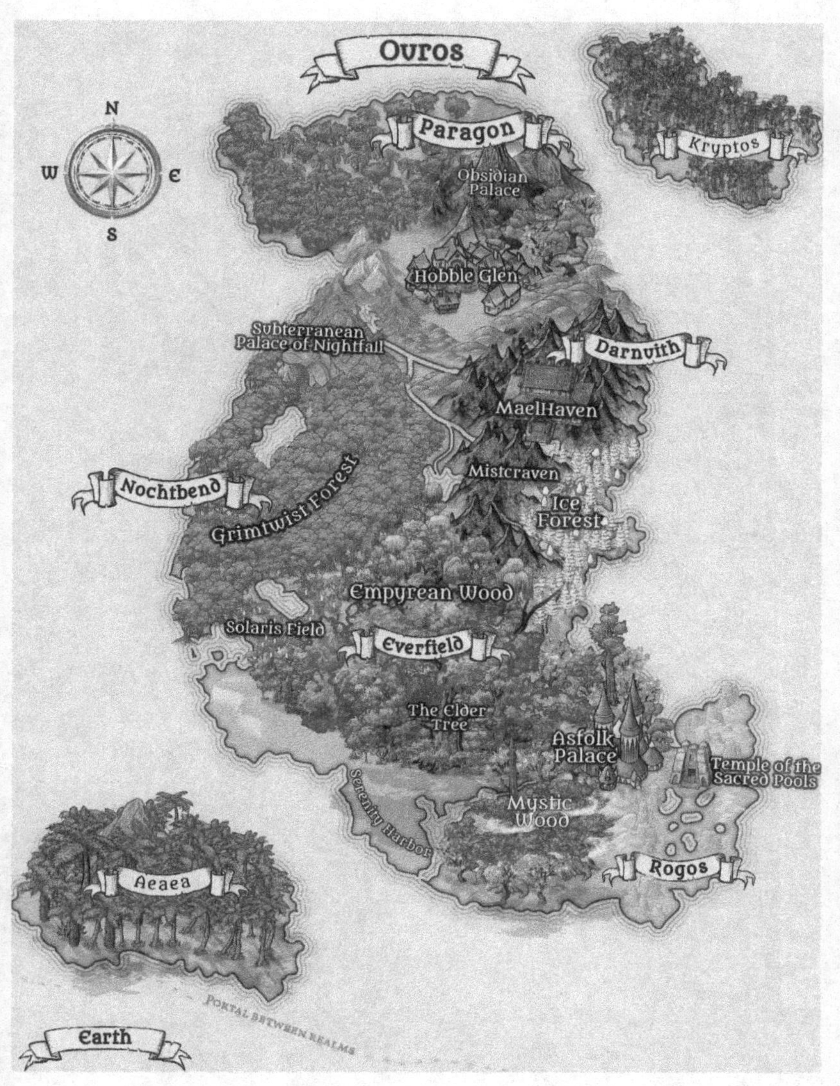

Ouros
Paragon
Obsidian Palace
Hobble Glen
Subterranean Palace of Nightfall
Darnvith
MaelHaven
Mistcraven
Ice Forest
Nochtbend
Grimtwist Forest
Empyrean Wood
Solaris Field
Everfield
The Elder Tree
Asfolk Palace
Temple of the Sacred Pools
Mystic Wood
Serenity Harbor
Rogos
Kryptos
Aeaea
Portal Between Realms
Earth
N
S
E
W

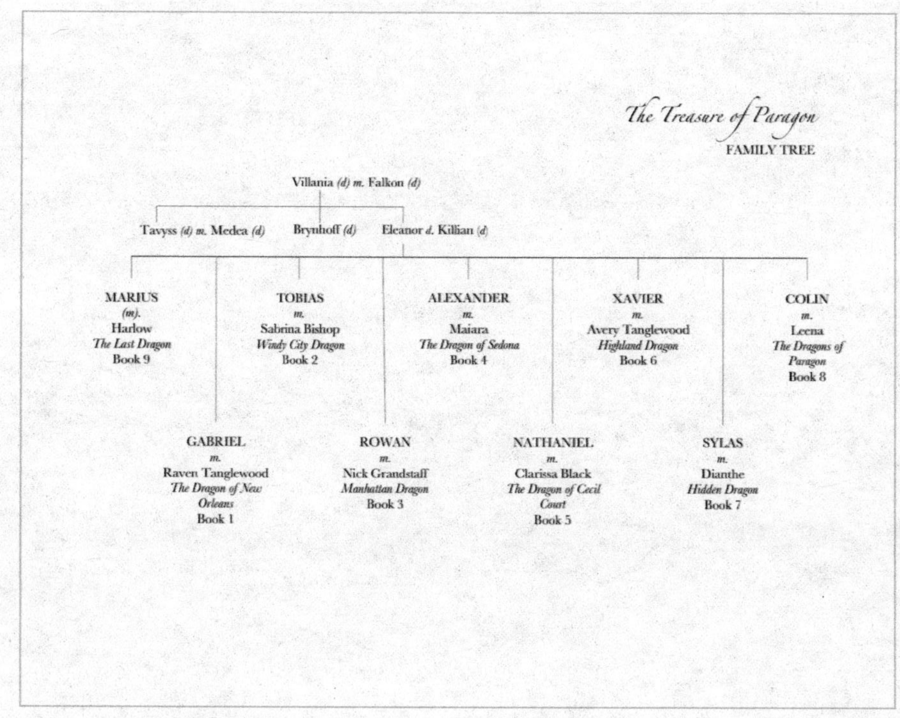

The Treasure of Paragon
FAMILY TREE

Villania (d) m. Falkon (d)

Tavyss (d) m. Medea (d)   Brynhoff (d)   Eleanor d. Killian (d)

MARIUS
(m).
Harlow
The Last Dragon
Book 9

TOBIAS
m.
Sabrina Bishop
Windy City Dragon
Book 2

ALEXANDER
m.
Maiara
The Dragon of Sedona
Book 4

XAVIER
m.
Avery Tanglewood
Highland Dragon
Book 6

COLIN
m.
Leena
The Dragons of
Paragon
Book 8

GABRIEL
m.
Raven Tanglewood
The Dragon of New
Orleans
Book 1

ROWAN
m.
Nick Grandstaff
Manhattan Dragon
Book 3

NATHANIEL
m.
Clarissa Black
The Dragon of Cecil
Court
Book 5

SYLAS
m.
Dianthe
Hidden Dragon
Book 7

AUTHOR'S NOTE

Dear Reader,

Love is the truest magic and the most fulfilling fantasy. Thank you for coming along on this journey as I share the tale of the Treasure of Paragon, nine exiled royal dragon shifters destined to find love and their way home.

There are three things you can expect from a Genevieve Jack novel: magic will play a key role, unexpected twists are the norm, and love will conquer all.

The Treasure of Paragon Reading Order

The Dragon of New Orleans, Book 1
Windy City Dragon, Book 2,
Manhattan Dragon, Book 3
The Dragon of Sedona, Book 4
The Dragon of Cecil Court, Book 5
Highland Dragon, Book 6
Hidden Dragon, Book 7
The Dragons of Paragon, Book 8
The Last Dragon, Book 9

CHAPTER ONE

Ash snowed from the inky black sky, sparks of bright red fire lighting up the otherwise endless darkness. An otherworldly growl came from somewhere in the woods beyond the cave. Thick, dense woods filled with sharp claws and slashing teeth. Hunters. When they killed, they stole more than your life. Life was meaningless here after all. What those monsters took was far more chilling than just life.

"I'm so hungry. We have to try for the temple." The voice beside him was a low whine. If a rat could speak, it would have that voice. But the other man was right. They needed food or they'd become weaker and weaker, unable to die but also unable to move unless some other soul took pity on them and carried them to the sacred place. It was the only way to move on.

"We go together," another voice said, this one lower, more confident. Killian.

Marius couldn't see the other man in the darkness, but he knew his face well, knew that he could trust him. They were connected somehow, from before. How exactly, he couldn't remember. That piece of history had been buried by pain and darkness a long time ago. So long ago. A lifetime. Maybe, if he had time and enough light to see the man, he'd remember. Not that it mattered. Every day was about survival. There was no room in his mind for anything else.

He gripped the hilt of the sword hanging at his side in a black leather scabbard. The other man tapped the heel of his spear on the cave floor.

"I'll help too," the rat man said.

But Marius understood that only meant he'd follow behind and keep a safe distance from any violence. The man had never even found a weapon for as long as he'd been in this strange, desolate place, and the only reason he had fighting leathers was because Marius had found him some.

Killian didn't respond. An exploding ember lit the sky beyond the cave. "Now!"

Marius sprinted toward the temple, weaving between trees at breakneck speed. A screech rang out behind him, and he whirled to find Killian facing off against a winged beast. The thing's skin was gray and leathery, its head covered in rows and rows of eyes, and its lipless mouth unable to close fully due to the length of its many teeth. It slashed a multijointed limb through the darkness.

Marius swung his blade, lopping off the thing's claw before it could tear into Killian. He spun, ducked, and thrust at the hunter. A metal-on-metal screech sounded as his sword slid into the thing's steely flesh.

And then he woke up.

Marius blinked at the thing in front of him. He was no longer in the land of ash and fire. He was warm and well-fed, surrounded by shiny obsidian. On the floor in front of him was a suit of armor through which he'd stabbed a sword that was not his own. It wasn't even an actual weapon. He realized in horror that it was part of the sculpture, the sword that the suit of armor had been holding.

"Uncle Marius?"

He spun to find Princess Charlie standing behind him in the hall, her platinum-blond curls a tangled mess and a stuffed animal clutched in her arms. What did Raven call it? A teddy bear. That was it. The girl loved her bear. He couldn't get over how much she'd grown this past year. Her development was rapid even for a dragon. Then again, she was only half dragon. The other half was witch like her mother, Raven. It was still to be seen how the two species would manifest in the child. She'd yet to shift and had no ring as he and his brethren did.

"What are you doing up?" He silently thanked the goddess that he hadn't hurt her. He could have. Might have stabbed her in his sleep as he had the suit of armor. "Your mother and father would not like to know you're out of your bed in the middle of the night."

The little girl rubbed her eyes with her tiny fists and ruffled her strange feathered wings. "I heard you."

Marius looked right, then left, down the hall. If anyone else had heard what he'd done, they hadn't come to help him. "I'm sorry I woke you, but you should have left it for the guards to sort out. What would you have done if I'd been something dangerous?" He was, in fact, extremely dangerous. Again, his stomach tied itself in knots at the thought he might have hurt her.

"I knew it was you," she said, confused. "Or I wouldn't have come."

"How did you know it was me? Anyone could have made this noise." He gestured to the destroyed suit of armor.

Her little nose wrinkled, and she wiped a hand across her forehead, sweeping platinum curls from her eyes. "That's not what I heard. I heard you screaming inside my head." She pointed at her temple. "I came and woke you up so you wouldn't be scared anymore."

Ice formed in his veins. He swallowed. That wasn't normal. "You woke me up because you heard me in your head?"

She nodded. "I used my zappy zap."

"What's your zappy zap?"

"Mommy said I shouldn't talk about it."

"You can tell me because you used it on me," Marius said. "I already know about it."

Charlie's brow furrowed as she thought about that for a moment. Then she clapped her small hands together.

A shock flowed through Marius, making the tiny hairs on his arms and legs stand on end. "That's a fun trick."

"Mommy says I'm not supposed to use it unless I'm in danger."

"You have a very smart mommy." Marius held out his hand to her. "Come. I'll tuck you in."

She slipped her tiny fingers into his, and they padded toward her room. "What was your bad dream about?"

"I don't remember." No way was Marius telling a— What was she in earth years?—seven-year-old child about his dreams. He seriously needed to start locking his door. He'd never forgive himself if he accidentally hurt her.

"I saw a monster." Charlie's slippers scuffed across the floor.

"You could see what was happening in my head and hear me scream?"

She nodded.

"Does that happen to you often?" Marius asked.

"No. One time with Aunt Avery, but her dream was pretty. Sunshine and blue sky."

Marius sighed. "Great," he mumbled. He'd have to tell Gabriel about this. Charlie clearly had some psychic abilities he and Raven weren't aware of. "I'm sorry my dream scared you, Charlie, but it was just a dream. Nothing real. If it happens again, try to push it out of your mind."

She stopped in front of her room and giggled. "It doesn't scare me, Uncle Marius. You killed that monster. Killed it dead. You would never let it get me."

He kissed her on her head, noticing how his hair, now completely lacking color, almost matched hers, although her eyes were blue while his were a pale silver. And her perfectly smooth and unmarked skin was a warm golden tone, not pale and covered in symbols as his own.

He gave her his most assuring smile. "I would never let anything get you, Charlie. Not on purpose. But I'm afraid if I'm having a bad dream, I might bump into you on accident and knock you down. I'd be asleep and not know you were there."

Her young face grew serious. "I'll send my zappy through you from far away."

That made him smile. "Good idea. Okay, Princess, into bed." He lifted her into the plush four-poster and pulled the frothy pink blanket over her. She tucked her teddy bear under her chin and closed her eyes.

"Uncle Marius?" she said before he could leave.

"Yes?"

"Mommy says that bad dreams happen when something isn't going right in your life and your brain is trying to work it out."

"Hmm. I'll keep that in mind."

"Maybe if you fight the monsters in your real life, you won't have to fight them in your dreams."

He studied the little girl and then placed a kiss on her temple. "Good night, Charlie."

CHAPTER TWO

"Fifty on Validar in the second match." Harlow slid her dragmars through the slot under the window to the bookie. She'd counted out the silver coins carefully before placing her bet, leaving enough in her purse to make it home if the unexpected happened. The bookie counted her wager and acknowledged its correctness with a quick nod before scribbling the bet in his ledger. He handed her a receipt.

"You do know that Validar is on the board at twenty-to-one odds?" Adradys, doormaker to Paragon and previously her father's biggest business rival, stood in line behind her, wearing a vilt suit in a dark sapphire blue that matched the ring on his finger. Although he was around her age and extremely wealthy, Harlow rarely interacted with the man. Adradys was not an ugly dragon. In fact, his tall, lean stature was pleasing to many women, as was his eye for fashion. It was just that Harlow was not one of those women. To her, he'd always seemed a bit fastidious and high-maintenance. Not to mention, Harlow had always found his personality unbearably pretentious and self-aggrandizing.

"Oh?" she asked vaguely.

Raising his chin, he added, "Validar lost his last three matches, Harlow. You might as well have thrown those fifty dragmars into the volcano. Does your father know you're here? Do you even understand how betting works?" He chuckled haughtily. "If you'd like, I can explain it to you."

Harlow plastered a smile onto her face. Adradys wasn't a regular at the pits. He couldn't possibly know that she'd been attending matches since she was a young girl or that since the new king and queen of Paragon had stripped her father of his business license—punishment for his support of Empress Eleanor—her gambling habit was what was keeping clothes on their backs and food on their table. He also was clearly unaware that Validar had lost the past three matches because he was nursing an injury that hadn't healed correctly.

Aside from beheading, there was no way to reliably kill a dragon. But immortality was not without its problems. Dragons healed swiftly. So swiftly, in fact, that a broken bone would knit back together in a matter of minutes. The problem was that four matches ago, Validar's leg had been broken by Drakkar, who'd remained standing on his thigh while the bone mended. Because the fracture healed while the bone was misaligned, he'd been fighting with an uneven gait the past three matches.

But Harlow happened to know he'd recently visited a healer in Rogos who had reset the leg and healed it properly. Validar was back to his old self, which meant he most certainly would win this match. But that didn't mean Harlow couldn't benefit from some sparring of her own.

She fluttered her lashes and stroked the long, caramel-colored hair that waved against her shoulder. Harlow was a patient dragon. As much as it would please her to unleash her tongue on the man, Adradys was a piece on the social playing board of Paragon. Given her family's current position, she couldn't risk alienating him. He could still be of use. "Would you care to sit together, Adradys? Perhaps you could offer me a few pointers."

"It would be my pleasure." He placed his bet on Validar's opponent, Mayhem, and then offered her his arm. She took it and strolled with him to his private box overlooking the arena. Normally she'd be in the standing-room-only section. What a stroke of luck!

"How is business?" she asked casually. A man like Adradys would want to talk about himself, and she wanted to please him. She had a favor to ask, actually, and buttering him up first seemed to be a good idea, especially since he was about to lose a great deal of money on his bet.

He patted her hand. "Business is booming. How kind of you to ask, considering my success is due to your father having to shutter his doors."

"It's not kindness. I'm genuinely curious. I never shared my father's politics, and I'm just happy to be able to continue to live in Paragon after what he did. Still, it's been difficult for him. He's a talented man, and although his punishment fit the crime, it is such a waste of a good door-maker, wouldn't you say?"

"True. Darium was talented. It *was* a waste, especially when the three of you were forced to move from the Firedrake district. Where are you living now?"

She looked down at her hands. As embarrassing as it was to admit, there was no use in denying it. Everyone knew they'd lost their fortune. Her parents had always been horrible with money and hadn't saved a thing during their centuries of wealth. "West of town."

He screwed up his face as if he smelled something bad. "You can't mean Swilton? How do you stand it? The smell alone..."

Swilton was the slums of Paragon. Property was cheap there because it neighbored a vilt farm. A pit nearby processed the creatures' waste and ensured the entire district always reeked of sewage. She couldn't help but draw the connection between his suit, the finest vilt, and the stink that likely clung loosely to her clothing.

"We get by." She raised her chin. "It's not what I was expecting, but a dragon of grace makes the most of it. I am thankful for a roof over our heads. I've adapted."

He scoffed. "I am truly sorry for you, Harlow. None of this was your doing. If there's anything I can do..."

"Actually, there is."

He turned his full attention to her. "What's that?"

She gave him her brightest smile. "You could speak with my father. As you said yourself, he's extremely talented. The palace took away his business license but not his right to work for someone else. It seems obvious to me that you could help each other. If you hired him, he could bring you his contacts and his talent. And I'm sure he'd take anything you'd be willing to offer." It was humiliating to ask, but she didn't care. She'd humiliate herself every day of the week if it would help them rise even slightly above their current circumstances.

He scowled. "Your father is two centuries my senior. He never took me seriously before the revolution. He is talented, but what makes you think he'd even want to answer to me? Has *he* suggested to you this is something he wants to do?"

"No, not exactly," she admitted. "But he needs something to do with his time, and working for you makes the most sense. If you would just speak to him..."

The announcer's voice rang out, and the crowd got to their feet and clapped as Validar and Mayhem entered the pit at the center of the coliseum below. She stood and clapped with Adradys. When she sat back down, his shoulder brushed hers, and she had to stop herself from shrinking from his touch.

She stared down at his hand resting on his knee. Door-making required strength and manual dexterity, but you'd never guess it by the softness of his hands or his perfect manicure. Even dragons developed calluses over time. His hands spoke volumes about his priorities, the first of which must be his appearance. Was he wearing makeup? She couldn't see a single pore as she perused his face.

"I'm going to help you, Harlow," he said, and it came out exactly as if he'd meant *I've decided to save you, damsel, to prove to you the hero that I am.* "I've always held you in the highest regard."

She smiled just as the horn went off and the two warriors below them started to fight. She turned her attention toward the ring and the two shirtless dragons, wings out, circling each other below.

"Oh, it's time," she said excitedly, scooting to the edge of her chair to get a better view.

"Excellent. Now, as I mentioned earlier, Validar was a terrible bet on your part because—"

With perfect balance, Validar snatched Mayhem's punching hand out of the air, twisted it behind his back, then used a low stance to set the other dragon off-balance. Mayhem attempted to roll to his feet, but Validar was there, his agility better than it ever was. His right wing snapped toward the ground and ripped through Mayhem's torso from left shoulder to right hip. Mayhem howled and didn't even attempt to get back up. The matchkeeper counted down from ten.

Jumping down from his platform, the matchkeeper took Validar's hand and raised it toward the sky. "And we have a winner!"

Harlow leaped from her seat and clapped her hands. "Ooh, I guess I won? Goddess, I must be lucky today."

Adradys stared at her open-mouthed.

"It must have been your company, my dear friend," Harlow said to Adradys in the sweetest tone she could muster. "And to think, you didn't even have time to explain the game to me." She grabbed his hand, pumped it twice, then kissed him on his cheek. "We absolutely must do this again."

"Yes," he drawled.

"I'm off to collect my winnings." She gave him a light-hearted wave over her shoulder as she slipped from his box and headed for the bookie.

Hours later, winnings in hand, Harlow trudged to her new home in Swilton on the west side of Hobble Glen. Exhausted as she was, relief flooded her when she saw the simple cottage. The only indication that a former socialite family lived there was the front door. It had been designed by her father and was still one of the finest in Paragon.

Doors told a family's story. No family in Paragon would purposely go without the heirloom. The pattern of gems inlaid into the wood represented her heritage. She ran her fingers over the spiral of square rubies that symbolized her father and the interconnected spiral of oval aquamarines that matched her mother's ring. Harlow's amethyst rectangles decorated the door in a spray between and below her parents' jewels. Other stones spiraled out from theirs, tens of thousands of years of ancestors, most lost to wars or battles unknown. Her grandparents and great-grandparents had been killed in a battle with Nochtbend before the time of Eleanor, thousands of years before her birth. But here they were, remembered in emerald, diamond, citrine, and jade.

The door represented their history. The door was their legacy.

At one time, her father Darium was the premier doormaker in all of Paragon. No one of any means would have chosen Adradys's craftsmanship over his if they could afford it. Back then, Adradys was known for mass-produced, cut-rate doors for those who couldn't afford her father's quality or chose not to invest in a high-end door. How things had changed. Adradys had a monopoly on the trade now, and new families had no choice but to go with his repetitive designs.

Harlow understood that her mother and father had enjoyed a close relationship with the Highborn Council and had benefited greatly from Eleanor's reign. They were once the center of high society. All that was over now. Their social status was as ruined as their economic one. The door was one of the few things they'd been allowed to keep.

Heavy and ornate, the absolutely stunning masterpiece was completely out of place now that it had been moved from their mansion in the exclusive Firedrake district of Hobble Glen to the hovel in the slums of Swilton. The tiny place seemed dwarfed by the door. Harlow was surprised her father had been able to install it on the weak hinges.

She pushed inside and took a seat at the small, wobbly table at the center of the room. Her father was there. He was always there. He barely left the house anymore.

"Did you win?" her father asked from his chair, his gaze flitting to hers.

"A little." She pulled out a fistful of silver dragmars along with a few precious gold tallons and five bronze spencies. She spread them on the table but did not mention the additional dragmars she kept hidden in the lining of her purse. As much as she loved her parents, she needed something for herself. She had dreams, and her parents had a way of spending every dime she gave them. She suspected they'd try anything to regain the status they'd lost. They didn't realize that not only could they never get back in the game, the entire board and all its pieces had moved far out of reach. The game they needed to play now was a completely new one for all of them. It was called survival, and so far, they weren't pros at it.

In fairness, they were all lucky to be alive. A lesser king and queen would have had their heads.

"There's a few hundred here. Enough for the market."

Her father's brows bobbed. "Thank the goddess." He rose from his seat and joined her at the table, a flicker of hope in his expression.

Harlow had been obsessed with the games since she was a child and knew every competitor in the pits. Truth be told, she enjoyed fighting. A close male friend had taught her and often sparred with her for practice. Not that she'd want to pursue it as a career. The pit fighters lived a hard life and usually ended up working in the quarries eventually.

Competing in the pits was forbidden to females anyway. Female dragons were rare. Only about one in eleven eggs matured into a female by the last statistics she'd read. Which meant that a single dragon of her gender was more valuable than any amount of money. Every female dragon carried the societal expectation that she would eventually participate in perpetuating the race by marrying and then producing whelps.

She'd never had any interest. Not that she was against it per se. She wanted children someday. She'd just never met a male she wanted to have them with.

What interested her these days was betting on the fighters. She'd developed a knack for wagering on them. She could take one look at a competitor, at the lines of their muscled limbs, at how they balanced their weight between their feet, and know if they had what it would take to win.

Her favorite champion by far, though, had been Marius —before he'd died, of course. Back in his youth, he mopped the floor with almost every other dragon in the kingdom. Oh, she understood that since he was a prince of Paragon, no one else was allowed to win his matches, but that didn't stop his competitors from flexing their machismo and trying their best to prove they would win if they could. Harlow would grin at their vain attempts and watch Marius bury their faces in the gravel.

She'd been so excited to hear he'd been resurrected, although she'd never met him in person until the coronation. Oh, how her stomach had flipped with exhilaration that night. He'd been positively enchanting in person. To have been who he was—a champion, a prince, a would-be king—and then lose everything... His return to society was undeniably brave, but the grace and dignity he applied to the situation was nothing short of noble. Rare in a dragon.

Every time she thought about it, her heart thudded out of admiration.

"Harlow, did you hear me?" Her father's face came into view.

Startled, she blinked at him. "No, sorry, I was working some numbers in my head. What did you say?"

"There's something I want to talk to you about. I think it's time for you to get serious about taking a husband." He folded his hands on the table. "You can do better than this. You deserve better than this."

A groan escaped her lips. "I'm not interested in marrying anyone, Father. I've met every individual with money in this kingdom, and none of them is my fated mate."

All the softness drained from her father's expression, and his ears reddened. "Get your head out of the clouds! True matings are rare. It's folly to wait for that magical connection."

"You and Mom are mated."

"Pure luck."

"Even if I were willing to settle for a common marriage, it's not exactly easy to meet an appropriate suitor since the war. Everyone knows we were on the wrong side of things. I'm not holding my breath one of the new rich will sweep me off my feet."

Her father ran a hand through his hair. "That's only because you don't understand your power, Harlow. Not only are you a female but a beautiful one at that, and refined. You've known what it is to have money, know the expectations of the elite. That's valuable to any mate. Men want a woman who can manage their home with grace and elegance."

She rolled her eyes toward the ceiling. "Sounds incredibly dull."

He laughed cynically. "Dull?" He gestured vaguely around him. "What exactly is this? These four walls are about as dull as I've ever had it. And the smell! Mountain, Harlow, if I were you, I'd be anxious for something better."

She raised her chin. "Aww, Dad, it's not so bad. This is the simple life! It's how most people lived when we were basking in the advantages of wealth. We have a roof over our heads and food on the table." She rounded the table and stood behind him, rubbing his shoulders. "Have you thought about getting out of here more? Maybe finding work?"

He tipped his head back and stared up at her in surprise. "What would I do? The only skill I have is door-making, and I doubt Adradys would hire me. The man hates me. We were bitter rivals."

She kissed him on the forehead. "Maybe he'd surprise you."

He sighed heavily and swept the money from the table into his hand. "I suppose I should go to the market. No food in the house for evening meal."

As he stood from the chair, she took him in. Dragons were immortal, but they weren't invulnerable. Thin. Sallow-skinned. The dark circles under his eyes had grown. His wings were tucked away, but she was certain they would hang listlessly from his back if they were out. He hadn't been eating or sleeping. Clearly, he was depressed. He needed something to do, a purpose. More responsibility than the occasional trip to the market.

"Where's Mom?"

"The Silver Sunset."

The popular tavern was her mother's favorite haunt lately. "Again?"

"Every night this week. I'm afraid to see the tab. We most certainly can't afford it."

She closed her eyes for a beat and then hooked her arm in his. "Well then, I guess it's just you and me. Let's go to the market. I'm famished."

CHAPTER THREE

Marius's back hit the ground, and he skidded across the gravel, wings thrashing under him to slow his momentum.

When he finally came to a stop, his brother Colin leaned over him and clicked his tongue. "Maybe we should move this back inside. The training room has padded floors."

"I'm done with padded floors," Marius growled.

Colin reached down to help him up, and Marius knocked his hand aside and scrambled to his feet. He was sure there were stones tangled in the back of his white hair. No matter. A familiar itch signified his abrasions were already healing.

He lowered himself into a fighting stance. "Again."

"Can't." Colin glanced at the clock on the wall of the fighting arena. "Out of time." No doubt the Master of the Guard had more important things to do than help his brother relearn what he'd lost. He snapped his feet together and bowed.

Marius bowed back and allowed his shoulders to relax.

He dragged in deep, cleansing breaths. Exhaustion sniffed at his heels. He had to fight the urge to sink to his ass in the middle of the practice arena.

"You don't have to do this," Colin said.

"No?" Marius's voice was edged with sarcasm.

Colin shifted on his feet. "I think you're expecting too much from yourself. You're working out like you plan to fight in the pits again." His brother laughed incredulously. "Goddess, you were dead just over a year ago. You must realize the experience has altered your body composition. I was impressed when you lost the cane."

Marius jerked and bared his teeth. "Would it be wrong to want to fight again?"

Colin sputtered, and Marius realized he was holding back a chuckle. "You're serious! Why? Marius, you don't have to do it anymore. You have a job in the palace. You have a purpose."

"Adviser to the Council of Elders—sorry, *Ambassador* to the Council of Elders. Gabriel gave me that title once I put the crown on his head. Right. That keeps me busy all of an hour a week. I'm bored, Colin, and restless. You don't understand." He kept secret the positive effects the fighting had on his strange nightmares. The truth was that on the days he trained with Colin, they stopped. He supposed he was so exhausted when he fell into bed at the end of a day filled with training that his brain was too tired to dream. And he was more than happy to work himself to the point of pain if it would keep the monsters away.

All levity drained from Colin's expression. "All right," he said tentatively. "You're a dragon, Marius. Theoretically, you have no limits. I have no idea what you've gone through or what lasting effects it has had on you, but I do know this —if you truly want to compete again, you need to do more than spar with me. I don't have the time or focus to take you to the next level."

"Who can?"

"I'm not sure yet."

Colin strode to the attendant's office. The man who usually worked there had stepped out, but Colin found a piece of paper in his desk. "Until we find someone, I want you to do this routine every day." He sketched a list of exercises that started with a twenty-mile run from the palace to the hills beyond Hobble Glen. Marius wasn't sure he was strong enough to make it to town, let alone through it and beyond. Then, according to Colin's notes, he was to perform another series of exercises before running back. The list looked impossible.

"Is that all?" Marius frowned.

"Work up to it. We'll keep sparring like this before Guard training. Meanwhile, I'll keep my ear to the ground for someone to help you."

He took the list from Colin with a hand he tried his best to stop from shaking. He needed rest after a thirty-minute sparring match. This list of exercises would take him hours to complete—*if* he could complete it at all. Still, he was thankful to have it. If he thoroughly wore himself out each day, perhaps he could rid himself of the nightmares for good. Bonus if the distraction reduced the strange visions that randomly plagued him.

He needed this, needed a way to settle his mind, and the only way to do that was by pushing his body to the limit. "Thanks."

Colin stared at him a moment with those piercing gray eyes, then gave him a nod Marius had seen him use on new recruits. That nod was weighty with encouragement, high expectations, and challenge. Without further ado, he strode out the door toward the field where the Guard trained.

Funny, Colin was his younger brother. He'd beaten the dragon in the pits on more than one occasion. How things had changed.

Marius stopped at the hydration station and guzzled water, staring at the practice ring. The private training space was smaller than the public one in the fighting pits. If he couldn't win against his younger brother here, he'd be doomed there. He imagined himself flat on his back in front of a stadium of judging eyes and laughing mouths.

He gripped the paper tighter in his hand. Placing his cup into the receptacle, he left the building and started to run.

THE FIRST DAY, HE DIDN'T EVEN MAKE IT OFF PALACE grounds. He had to stop at the gate to catch his breath. The guard in the booth came out to ask if he needed help, and Marius lied, actually invented an excuse that he was surveying the wards for the queen to save himself the embarrassment of having to explain that a five-mile run—an easy jog for a dragon—had almost made his heart explode. He ended up walking back to the palace and collapsing on his bed for an hour.

The next day was better. He started before practice and made it to the gate and back at a run. But the effort left him unable to hold his own against Colin. His brother slammed him into the stones over and over again. He couldn't even accuse his brother of being overly aggressive. On the contrary, his intuition suggested Colin was holding back. To his brother's credit, when at last they bowed and went their separate ways, there was no judgment, disappointment, or condescension in the dragon's parting words. Those gray eyes held nothing but the same challenge and encouragement they had the day before.

He kept going, farther every day, until he'd almost reached Hobble Glen before he had to turn around. Only he wasn't strong enough to run all the way back, and when he finally reached the practice arena, he was late. Colin wasn't there. Someone else was, though, and it was the last person he'd expected to see. Avery.

At the center of the ring, the queen's sister wielded a sword that looked far too big and heavy for her petite frame. Somehow the iron danced for her, though, carving patterns through the air as she executed perfect footwork and battled an imaginary opponent. She stopped and sheathed her weapon as soon as she noticed he was there.

"Hi," she said, thrusting her chin in his direction. "Colin had to go. He asked me to hang around to tell you he'd see you back here tomorrow. Oh, and also, don't be late again. He's too busy and will drop you from his schedule. Honestly, I'd get your ass here. He looked pissed."

Marius wiped a hand over his face, his skin still slicked with sweat. "It was a mistake. It won't happen again."

"Dude, what happened to you? You look like you've spent the morning fighting for your life. Do you need me to fetch a healer? Or I can help you back to the infirmary. Maiara can help."

He shook his head. "Not sick," he said breathlessly. He walked around her and folded onto the observation bench, his backside slapping hard as his legs gave out. He couldn't have popped back up if he tried. "Just badly out of shape."

Her brows furrowed, and she stared at him for a moment. "Fuck. I didn't know it was possible for a dragon to look like he was having a heart attack, but you do, Marius. You really do!"

He raised an eyebrow in her direction. "Thanks for the tip. Turns out being dead for three hundred years is hazardous to your level of fitness."

"Are you sure you don't want me to fetch Maiara?"

"No. I don't need a healer. Just a moment to catch my breath." He glanced away from her, loathing the heat that blazed toward his ears. If he had even an ounce of energy, he'd excuse himself and make a hasty retreat to his room. No one should see him like this.

She chewed her lip. "Hey, sorry I brought it up. Just... as the only mortal in this place, it's surprising to see someone else with any vulnerabilities."

He looked back in her direction and had to pause at her contrite expression. Being married to Xavier, she must realize that dragons didn't love to have their weaknesses pointed out. His stomach contracted with a laugh meant to put her at ease. "I'm glad something good has come from my pain." He grinned and patted the bench beside him. "Your penance is to keep me company until I'm rested enough to make it off this bench."

With a good-natured laugh, Avery took the seat beside him and stared across the empty arena. He didn't know the woman well, although their encounters had always been positive. Her mate, Xavier, was the toughest of warriors, even when they were children, and was spending his days helping Colin train the Guard.

"When do you and Xavier go back to Earth?"

"At the end of the month... I mean moon cycle. I can't get used to your terminology." Avery leaned back and stared up at the overcast sky.

"Soon, then."

"Soon." She pushed up the arms of her training sweater.

Marius couldn't miss the red-and-black spiral tattoo there. It matched one that appeared on various places along his torso. He nodded toward it. "Do you feel that anymore?"

She glanced at him and then down at the tattoo, seeming to piece together what he was talking about. "I thought I might ask you the same thing eventually. I didn't want to be insensitive, but—"

"But we are the only ones to have them," Marius finished.

"We're the only ones who've been brought back from the dead." She seemed to catch herself because she shook her head. "Actually, that's not true. Raven brought Gabriel back from the dead, and he doesn't have one."

"What do you think they mean? What's different about us?"

She raised her brows and scoffed. "I have no idea. Raven doesn't even know, and she has the entire golden grimoire in her head."

He stretched his legs out and crossed them at the ankle. "Charlie told me you've been having nightmares."

"Charlie's a precocious little peanut, isn't she?" Avery raised a brow. "I wouldn't call what I'm having nightmares, but they are strange. I think I'm seeing where I was when I was... gone."

He cracked his neck. "That's what I'm seeing." He lowered his voice. "I remember."

She ran her thumb over the symbol. "I'm immune to magic, so it can't be the symbol that's causing the dreams, at least not in me. I asked Raven to try to remove it. If she can't do it with magic, I think I'm going to try the human way and have it lasered off."

He glanced down at himself. His entire torso and back

were covered in them. There had to be hundreds. He envied Avery. She might free herself of the mark, but he doubted anything could remove the scars the past three hundred years had made in him. "I hope whatever you try works."

She seemed to pick up on the darkness that had crept into his voice because she sighed and said, "I'm sure Raven will figure out what they mean and help you with your nightmares."

"She hasn't yet."

"She's been a little busy establishing a new government in Paragon and everything."

"True." Marius pushed himself off the bench. He felt like an asshole for bringing it up. "Thanks for the company, Avery. Xavier's a lucky dragon."

"You're welcome," she said, but she couldn't keep a spark of worry from her blue eyes. "Marius, I just know things are going to work out for you. Look how far you've come already. Just give it time."

He gave her a reassuring smile that he didn't feel. "All I've got is time."

CHAPTER FOUR

"**W**hy is this place such a wreck?" Harlow brushed plates and glasses aside on the table to make room to count her winnings. The floor hadn't been swept since she'd done it the previous evening, and there was nothing on the stove for dinner again. The fire in the fireplace desperately needed another log or it would give up the ghost.

Her father shrugged, his eyes empty. Dragons didn't age, but his slumped shoulders and sagging mouth made him look positively ancient. "I've never been good at housework. I wouldn't know where to start."

She leaned back in her chair and sighed. "Dad, we don't have servants anymore. I'm gone all day at the pits. I know this transition has been hard for you, but you're going to have to learn to do it."

He blinked, grimacing as if the thought of it might push him over the edge of whatever mental precipice he was perched on. "Perhaps you and your mother could help. You'd do a far better job than I would."

She held up a fistful of dragmars. "I *am* helping. I'm

keeping us fed. And Mom hasn't been reliable in months. You need to talk to her."

"She won't listen to me."

"Where is she?"

"The Silver Sunset... Again. Every night this week."

Harlow gritted her teeth. They had no extra money for casual drinking. "What do we have left in the pantry for dinner?"

"It's empty." He stared at the fire. Its dying light added to the overall bleakness of the moment. It would be better if it just burned out. As dragons, they didn't need it for heat, and she was starting to wonder if they could afford it for comfort.

"What happened to the food we bought yesterday?"

"Your mother came home for lunch."

"Why didn't you go back to the market?"

He waved a hand in the air, looking dejected. "I never know what to buy when I go alone."

"Dad..." She was losing him.

It wasn't particularly surprising that her father was in a dark place after the year they'd had. He'd lost the career he loved and the business he'd built from the ground up. With it went all his creature comforts, his friends, his support system.

He hadn't always been like this. Harlow had vivid memories of a man who'd once been adored by his employees and customers alike. He'd been a good father as well, denying her nothing before their fall from grace. Which was why it was twice as hard to see him like this. Darium was a man who built things and made people happy. How had he become this dragon who felt too helpless to even lift a broom?

She swept her winnings off the table again and into her hand. Mind made up, she strode for the door.

"Are you going to the market?" he asked.

"No. I'm going to the Silver Sunset. I'm going to get Mom and bring her back here so that we can all talk about our responsibilities. If I'm at the pits earning money all day, I can't also cook and clean."

He didn't protest her leaving. She wondered if there was any fight left in him at all. By the time Harlow reached the Silver Sunset, her frustration had grown into a monster she could barely contain. The walk hadn't calmed her down one iota, and she burst through the door and into the tavern with enough force that heads turned, even her mother's.

Lemetria was sitting at the bar, surrounded by dragon males, none of whom Harlow recognized. That was the thing about being a dragon. Immortals didn't age. One might assume she and her mother were the same age if they didn't know better, and because dragon females were rare, any in an establishment like this would garner plenty of attention.

"Harlow?" her mother slurred. "What are you doing here, darling?"

Harlow crossed the bar in three huge steps, elbowing a patron out of her way, and yanked her mother off her barstool. "You need to come home now!"

"Why? What's the matter?" She blinked wide eyes at Harlow as if she truly had no idea what was going on. Everyone was staring. The bartender seemed especially concerned and shot her a warning glance.

"Come outside with me to talk." Harlow tugged at her mother's upper arm.

Lemetria gave her a disarming smile. "Wouldn't you rather have a drink? I can introduce you to some fine young men. I wouldn't say any of them are marriageable material, but they might be fun to practice on."

"Eww." Harlow bristled. "Mom! Outside now!"

"Oh, all right." She huffed and followed her out into the late afternoon sun. "Now what seems to be the problem?"

"The problem is, you have a husband and a house, and both are falling to pieces. You need to come home with me." Harlow folded her arms over her chest.

Lemetria snorted, her hand waving wildly through the air. "Who says? Darium is more than capable of taking care of himself, as are you. Just look at you. You look delightful, darling. Living in Swilton hasn't knocked the bloom from your flower at all."

"Stop trying to charm me, Mother. It's not going to work. Dad is not okay. He's in some sort of deep depression. He barely moves from his chair. And the house is an absolute wreck. There's nothing to eat."

"If you don't like it, Harlow, do something about it. You can shop. You can clean." Her mother flipped a hand in the air and raised her chin as if she couldn't be bothered with what was happening in her own home.

Harlow huffed. "No, I can't. I'm busy earning the dragmars to pay for the gallons of tribiscal wine flowing down your gullet every day."

Lemetria growled, swaying a little in her drunkenness. "Well, isn't this an ungrateful surprise? How many years did we support you, Harlow? We gave you the best of everything when we had it." Her eyes flicked back toward the bar. It took a lot to get a dragon inebriated, but Harlow did not miss the red in the whites of her mother's eyes or the haze of distraction in her pupils.

Harlow released a deep breath. "Mom, I *am* helping out, but it's more than one person can do. I need your help.

Dad needs your help. I mean *really* needs you. He's not himself. Please come home."

For a second the clouds parted, and her mother looked at her as she used to, with love and empathy. She reached out and placed one hand on her shoulder. Harlow thought for sure she'd made it through to her, that she'd come home now and be the mother she needed her to be. But the softness in her face changed to something hard and cruel.

"Harlow, our situation is utterly hopeless. I admire you for trying to make a life for us in that horrible place. I do! But it's a losing proposition. Do yourself a favor." She pinched the bridge of her nose. "Find a man who will marry you. With your looks, you could have anyone you set your mind on. You'll never want for anything. Leave us behind. We're never making it out of Swilton, but you might." She turned, straightened her collar, and walked back into the Silver Sunset.

All the air whooshed from Harlow's lungs as if she'd been socked in the gut. Both her mother and her father had suggested the same thing, that she should save herself by finding a husband. She staggered to a nearby bench and sat, leaning her elbows on her knees, mindfully drawing in a breath. Her hands trembled as she buried her face in them. She would not marry for financial gain. The thought of having to cook, clean, and spread her legs for someone she didn't love just to live in a bigger house seemed utterly ridiculous to her. She'd flee to Rogos before she'd entertain the idea.

The bench groaned as someone flopped onto it beside her. Labored panting met her ears, and the scent of smoky male sweat filled her nose. Not unpleasant. Woodsy, like the forest, with a hint of dark spice. Brow furrowing, she removed her hands from her face and sat bolt upright.

"Marius?" She said his name softly because the male looked as if he might die if she startled one extra beat from his heart.

He seemed to see her for the first time, his strange silver eyes widening slightly as he tried to sit up straighter and pull himself together. "Harlow!" The arch of his brows told her he hadn't noticed her before. His cheeks reddened, perhaps from embarrassment or from whatever physical exertion had brought him to this point of near death.

"Are you okay? You look like you need a healer." She inclined her head in the direction of the apothecary across the street. It had once been Aborella's but now was run by a witch named Blingsworth, who'd moved from Darnuith after the war. He wasn't nearly as helpful as Aborella had been but was good for the occasional tonic.

"Fine. Just fine." He wiped a hand over his face and smoothed back his white hair toward the ponytail at the nape of his neck. He straightened on the bench. Goddess, even in his current worn state, the man was incredibly attractive. That face was all angles and cheekbones, and a woman would have to be dead not to take notice of the muscles that had formed on his arms and chest. When she'd seen him last, at the coronation, she'd found him fetching, but now... It looked as if he'd packed on a hundred pounds of muscle since that night. Sweat had soaked his tunic, and it clung and molded to his pecs and biceps.

She crossed her legs at the ache that began at the sight, then cleared her throat to dislodge the thickness that had formed there. When she spoke again, her voice came out like a squeak. "What brings you into Hobble Glen?"

The question wasn't a particularly hard one, but he blinked at her as if he wasn't sure how to answer it. Was it the way her voice had sounded? Goddess help her, he could tell she was smitten by him. Humiliation threatened to knock the air from her lungs again.

"I... Uh... I..." He looked away from her, taking interest in his shoes.

She licked her lips and waited. When he didn't answer, she tried her best to make a joke. "Is it a secret mission for the palace? Are you working with the Guard now?" Aaaand she was a complete idiot. What if he was? He was the brother of the king after all. Now he was in the awkward situation of having to sidestep her question if she'd hit too close to home.

"I'm sorry," she blurted. "You don't need to answer that. I was trying to be funny."

The corner of his mouth twitched. "It's that obvious I don't belong in the Guard, eh?"

She flustered beside him. "No! Not at all. I just assumed as the king's brother you'd be on more exciting missions than to Hobble Glen, not to mention that if you *were* on a mission, you couldn't admit as much to the likes of me. I didn't mean to put you on the spot."

He snorted. "I'm not on a mission." He wiped his hands on the thighs of his breeches. "If you must know, I'm... exercising."

She balked, giving him a once-over before she could stop herself from being so brazenly rude. "Exercising? Here?"

"I'm attempting to run to the base of the Dark Mountains and back," he said evenly, pointing one finger toward the hills beyond Hobble Glen. "I didn't make it."

She couldn't hold back a snort. "Why? That can't be more than twenty-five miles. Must be easy enough for a dragon such as yourself."

He glanced away, and the truth hit her like a ton of

bricks. The cane... He'd used a cane at the coronation. It hadn't seemed odd to her at the time, considering he'd been recently resurrected. But it had been a full year since then. Was it possible his body was still recovering?

"Not as easy as you might think." His face fell.

Goddess, she was a steaming pile of vilt dung. Horrified at her own rudeness, she stared, open-mouthed and utterly speechless.

CHAPTER FIVE

*F*uck! Marius hated that look on her face. Her damned chin was practically on the dirt. This was a disaster. Socialite Harlow would no doubt spread the news about his physical inferiority to every ear in Hobble Glen by the end of the day. Of all the people he didn't wish to see him like this, she was at the top of the list!

"You're doing really well," she finally blurted, and to her credit, the sentiment sounded genuine. The soft, encouraging tone of her voice had him turning to look at her straight on. "I just now put it together. When Eleanor killed you, your body turned to dust. You aren't just recovering. You have a brand-new body. You have to train it again like you would if you were just starting out."

"A child," he mumbled, disgusted with himself. He looked away, shaking his head.

"No." She shifted on the bench beside him, and he wondered if he was making her uncomfortable. "Not like a child. Like a phoenix."

He folded his arms. "Don't do that. Don't try to placate

me with compliments. I'm not the heir apparent anymore. You don't owe me anything."

She laughed. "If you think I'm blowing smoke up your ass, you don't know me at all."

"I *don't* know you at all." He snorted. "We've met at a few functions. Hardly enough time to form an opinion."

The smile she'd held in place since he'd sat down faded. "Maybe. I suppose you're right, although it feels like I know you. I still remember exactly where I was when you won your last championship."

"I'll let you in on a little secret. It was fixed. No one was allowed to best me because I was a royal."

She shook her head. "Most of those matches you would have won anyway."

He narrowed his eyes on her and snorted. She didn't look or sound like she was patronizing him, but the comment was entirely unexpected. "What makes you think so?"

She raised an eyebrow and turned to lean her back against the bench. "Your balance was impeccable. So many dragons make the mistake of planting their heels. It gives them a more secure base, but with the weight of their wings, they have to sacrifice agility. You always stayed on the balls of your feet even when you were tired. It was your secret to reacting quickly. Even if you weren't the fastest competitor, you would react the fastest because you were already halfway there. Always moving, always ready. Not a single champion from the past ten years has had your balance."

Marius was intrigued. He didn't know many females who enjoyed pit fighting, and even fewer who truly understood anything about the strategy behind the sport. "How do you know so much about fighting? Learn it from your husband?" If she'd watched his matches way back when, she must be married with a few whelps by now.

"Never married. Never mated." She lifted her chin as if the statement made her proud, although it was highly unusual for any dragon of her age to still be single.

Marius took in the woman beside him. He didn't run in social circles anymore, but she was undeniably attractive, and before his death, she was a popular socialite. Her family's money would have been a draw, as would her looks. "Do you even realize how strange it is you're unmarried, or have I been gone so long that Paragonian traditions have changed?"

She seemed to contemplate that for a moment, her soft smile secretive. She tangled her fingers in her lap before answering. "Traditions haven't changed. It just hasn't happened for me."

They sat in silence for some time. Marius couldn't keep his eyes off her. He tried not to stare, but his gaze kept drifting to her side of the bench. She was beautiful, yes. Striking caramel-colored hair and amber eyes. But that wasn't what fascinated him. Her family was once one of the wealthiest in Paragon, yet she was wearing a common, simple dress with frayed cuffs. Odd. Why had she never married? Would it be rude for him to ask?

The clock tower at the end of the square started to chime. He sighed. "Fuck."

"You have a filthy mouth for a royal heir."

"Former heir."

"You still live in the palace." She raised an eyebrow in challenge.

"I'm an ambassador to the Council of Elders."

"You have a filthy mouth for an ambassador."

"I'm just disappointed in myself. I'm late again for training. My brother told me if I was late one more time, he wouldn't coach me anymore."

"Which brother?"

"Colin."

She whistled through her teeth. "The Master of the Guard. Damn. You messed up a gig training with the Master of the Obsidian Guard? Yeah, you fucked up."

"Now who has the filthy mouth?" He leaned his head back and looked up at the sky. "In my defense, this is the farthest I've run in this body. I underestimated how long it would take me."

Her smile faded, and she leaned toward him. "I wonder if we might help each other." Her thumb scrubbed nervous patterns over the back of her opposite hand.

"What do you have in mind?"

Harlow's eyes twinkled mischievously. He wished he knew the secrets flitting like ghosts through her expression.

"What if *I* train you?" She tapped her chin three times and then pointed her finger his way. "And you pay me one gold tallon per day to do it."

For someone like him, living on an ambassador's salary, a gold tallon—a hundred dragmars—wasn't a lot of money, but he snorted anyway. It was such a strange proposal. "Now why would a woman like you want such a position?"

"That's my business." She glanced toward the Silver Sunset. When he didn't respond for a beat, she added, "We live in a patriarchal society, Marius. Can't you imagine why a woman might desire her own income, one her father knows nothing about?"

He could imagine. He slanted her a wry grin and asked, "What makes you qualified to train me?"

She chuckled. "I've been a regular at the pits for almost

five hundred years. I've even trained a bit, if you must know, although they won't let me fight, obviously."

"Exactly. If you've never even competed—"

"I know how to fight."

"But you've never fought in the pits. Whoever taught you probably went easy on you." He was needling her, but he couldn't let it go. For some reason, he wanted to test what she was made of.

"Let's settle this," she said tersely. "You are concerned that I do not have the skills to train you. I put forth that I do. You'll never believe me unless I prove it to you. So let me prove it to you."

"How exactly do you plan to do that?" He leaned in closer, lids heavy. She smelled good, like water lily and a cool night breeze.

"Name the time and the place, and I will fight you. If I win, you train with me for the fee we discussed. If I lose, I'll go home, patch up my dignity, and never bother you again."

For some reason, that thought sobered him. He enjoyed speaking with Harlow. It would be a tragedy not to be bothered by her in the future. "I might hurt you."

"Dragons heal quickly." She tipped her head to the side inquisitively.

"Tomorrow," he said. "Come to the private training arena at the palace. I'll give your name to the guardhouse."

She beamed at him in a way that made his skin feel warm. "You're on." She stood and straightened her dress. "Do you need me to call a carriage to take you back to the palace?"

He shook his head and pushed himself up from the bench, stifling a groan. "No. I'm fine now."

The curve of her lips suggested she was aware of the aches and pains he was still feeling despite his efforts to hide them. But she didn't mention it. With a wink, she said, "Good to know. I wouldn't want you to be sore for our match tomorrow."

HARLOW ADJUSTED HER DRESS OVER THE TRAINING outfit she wore underneath as the carriage she'd rented pulled up to the palace guardhouse. She wouldn't get far wearing her training clothes anywhere, but dressing like this made her feel hot and confined. She had on too many bulky layers for the tropical climate of the kingdom.

"Harlow, meeting Marius," she said to the guard through the window.

The young dragon inside the tiny house nodded and slapped the seal of the palace on the side of her carriage. "Please proceed."

They started to move again, rounding to the back of the palace where the curved stone walls of a private training pit came into view. By the Mountain, the wealth! Her family had once been affluent, but even the wealthiest of her Firedrake neighbors hadn't boasted a private fighting pit. The facility was magnificent. Nothing short of extravagant.

Her heart thudded in her chest. Was she really going to do this? It had been a long time since she'd practiced pit fighting. Yes, she had a friend, a former champion, who'd trained her and practiced with her occasionally. She understood far more about the sport than most males. Still, Marius had the height and weight advantage. He was at least twice her size, and she was out of practice. This could go terribly wrong.

The carriage came to a stop in front of the arena. She helped herself out and paid the driver his fare, tipping generously from her precious stash of hidden dragmars. Inside was a facility far nicer than the Paragonian pits, although slightly smaller. A reception office stood off the main hall with a schedule of practice times. Marius's name filled the current time slot, and she paused a moment to appreciate his even scrawl. His handwriting was pleasing for a dragon male, but then, she supposed, he'd been schooled as a child to speak and write elegantly. He was to be king, after all.

Across the hall was a locker room. She silently wished she'd known it was there. She could have used it to change out of her dress instead of wearing her fighting clothes underneath. Next time. If there was a next time.

The next room was a workout facility with weights and a running track. She audibly gasped when she saw the ring itself. It was a smaller circular space than the one in the pits but in far better condition. The floor was carpeted with pea gravel. She'd learned during her years of training that this was preferable. Dragons were incredibly tough and healed quickly, but injuries still hurt. If she was thrown, she'd skid harmlessly across the gravel. A fighting ring of stone or packed earth would grip and tear at her. Indoor rings sometimes had padded mats, but she knew that was too much to ask for here. Besides, she'd heard the benefits were negligible when it came right down to it.

Marius wouldn't coddle her. He'd try to win. She'd have to bring all her skills and more if she was going to convince him to hire her.

"I wasn't sure you'd come." Marius stood behind her, watching her with the profound interest one might give a dancing animal.

"Why? I said I'd be here. I want this, Marius, and I'm going to prove to you that I'm a worthy coach."

"Hmm." His gaze traced over the frumpy lumps of her dress.

"I'm not going to fight you in this!" She started unbuttoning her dress at the neck.

His eyes grew wide, and she couldn't help but notice another part of his anatomy paid attention as well. "The locker room is there." He gestured with his hand and looked away from her.

Harlow paused, the corners of her mouth twitching when she realized the misunderstanding. He thought she was undressing in front of him, and he was interested. Her stomach gave a little jump at the thought, and she was suddenly aware of him, not just as a competitor but as a man.

Should that worry her? She decided it didn't. If anything, their mutual attraction was to her benefit. She'd learned to fight from a man. He'd likely never fought a woman. She was not above using that to her advantage.

"I'll be quick." She winked at him, then drifted toward the locker room. Oh, she could have explained that she was fully dressed beneath her outer layer of clothing, but what would that serve? She emerged moments later in her fighting gear, surprised and disappointed to find they were no longer alone. A dark-haired woman with a sword stood with her back to Harlow at the center of the ring, speaking to Marius. As Harlow drew closer, she turned.

"Avery Tanglewood," the queen's sister said by way of introduction. She extended her hand. Harlow pumped it twice awkwardly and gave her a friendly smile. Shaking hands wasn't a popular gesture in Paragon, although it was practiced occasionally by transplants from other kingdoms.

"It's a pleasure to meet you again. We spoke briefly at

the coronation, but I'm sure you don't remember me," Harlow said.

Avery's eyes narrowed. "Oh... You're the old doormaker's daughter. I remember."

An expression she couldn't quite read passed over the other woman's face, and Harlow had to take a steadying breath. Everyone knew about her family and her father's past. Avery probably didn't trust her. A pit formed in her chest, and Harlow's confidence melted into the ground. She wished she had her dress back.

"You probably are wondering why I'm here," Avery said. "Marius asked me to act as matchkeeper. Have to make sure it's a fair fight, right?"

Marius rolled his eyes. "Ironic, considering it's already unfair."

"Why's that?" Avery asked.

"Because she's a female!" he said as if it were perfectly obvious.

Harlow bristled.

Avery's gaze swept between her and Marius, and she gave a low chuckle. "As your matchkeeper, I find nothing unfair about this contest. Take your places." She backed away and stepped onto the matchkeeper's platform.

Harlow cracked her neck and gave her arms and legs a quick stretch before taking her position at the center of the ring. She thought she was ready, but when Marius took his place across from her, she wasn't sure. He'd removed his shirt, and everything she knew about pit fighting was crowded out of her brain by the magnificence of the man standing in front of her.

When she'd seen him at the coronation, he'd been thin and pale, still using a cane to walk. No more. His hair might be white and his eyes silver, but his skin was now a healthy golden brown. Dragons could use illusion, but she'd always been able to tell when men layered it on. If Marius was enhancing himself, he wasn't doing much.

And the symbols... Goddess, they were beautiful. Dragons couldn't normally be tattooed because their flesh healed so quickly and thoroughly that their skin pushed out the ink before it could become a permanent part of them. But these tattoos had appeared when Marius rose from the dead, and they were magical. Harlow tried not to gape at the intricate patterns they painted across the muscles of his torso.

Harlow had never seen a dragon male with anything like them, and she desperately longed to trace them with her fingers. Not only were they exotic, but they shimmered when he moved, making it impossible to ignore any beautiful flex of muscle that was happening in his chest and abs.

His silvery-white wings arched over his shoulders. "See something you like?"

Her gaze shot up to meet his. *Crap*. She'd been staring. Ogling, really. Her mouth felt dry. She swallowed.

He smirked.

Her eyes narrowed. Oh hell no. Two could play at this game. Slowly, as if a good stretch brought her all the pleasure in the world, she unfolded her wings.

Harlow had stood facing the sun for a reason. She'd always been complimented on her looks. She was naturally thin and enjoyed staying fit, and her caramel-colored hair and amber-hazel eyes were rare in a dragon female. Eye-catching, she'd been told. But she knew her wings were something dragon males found extremely erotic. Every one of her past partners had mentioned them. They were gold with flecks of deep amber the same color as her eyes. Her scales reflected a spattering of light around her as she stretched them out to her sides.

Now who was ogling whom? His eyes widened and his mouth gaped.

She scoffed. "See something you like?"

"Something I'd like to strangle," he said under his breath.

Avery cleared her throat to get their attention. "The rules are simple. There are two ways to win. The first is to knock your opponent out or injure them to the point they cannot rise from the ground within ten seconds. The second is to force them from the ring and keep them outside the boundary for ten seconds." She pointed at a dark ridge of wood that circled them, about three feet from the edge of the ring. "No beheadings. Excessive use of talons near the neck area may result in a disqualification. All other moves are permitted."

The same rules as always. No surprises.

"At your ready..." Avery raised a red flag.

Harlow tipped onto the balls of her feet, bent her knees, and raised her hands and her wings. Fighting stance. Marius did the same. She noticed immediately that he was favoring his left leg. It was slight, but she picked up on the subtle imbalance. She could use that.

Avery released the flag. "Fight!"

CHAPTER SIX

Marius didn't want to hit her. On the contrary, he desperately wanted to fuck her. His dragon had taken one look at those golden wings and rushed against his skin. He wondered if they'd feel as silky as they looked. A vision of her above him filled his mind, those wings like a sunrise, her full breasts bouncing with his thrusts, her luscious red mouth—

Pow.

Her right hook landed against his left cheek with such force he spun around and skidded face-first into the pebbles. *Ouch.*

"Just stay down, Marius," she said. "We can end this now and start training tomorrow. My fee is a mere hundred dragmars per day. I can make you a champion."

He narrowed his eyes. Was that laughter he heard in her voice? By the Mountain, it was. He'd love to spend more time with Harlow, but not like this. Not... emasculated. He wanted her respect, not her pity.

"Six... five..." Avery's voice counted down in the background.

With one beat of his wings, Marius lifted from the ground and spun toward Harlow, avoiding the kick she'd thrown and dipping low to jab toward her gut. She spun out of the way, skimming along the side of his arm while yanking his wrist forward, setting him off-balance. At the same time, her leg swept into his right knee.

Fuck. He tumbled forward, tucked in his wings, and somersaulted across the ring. He caught himself just short of out of bounds. Popping off the gravel, he turned toward her again. He circled at the outer boundary, watching her now as he would a true competitor. She was good. Really good. He could dismiss that first hit as a lucky blow. He'd been distracted. His fault. But that last move was a sophisticated counterattack. Not only had she seen through his fake and avoided his blow, she'd used his momentum against him and successfully targeted his strong side. Which meant she'd detected the slight imbalance in his gait.

She, however, had no such imbalance. She practically floated over the gravel, her hips low and even. She looked ready for anything.

He surged forward, faked an uppercut with his right and hooked his left toward her head. It was like he was moving in slow motion. She bent backward, her wings flaring parallel to the ground, and his punch landed harmlessly in the air above her. She snatched his arm and kicked up into his gut with her right foot, throwing him over her head. He somersaulted again, scrambling to his feet in time to see her recover like she was a puppet on strings. Her back had almost brushed the ground, and somehow, despite throwing his superior weight, she hadn't fallen. She was ready again, watching him like a hungry predator.

Narrowing his eyes, he analyzed her stance, her prior moves. As he circled her, it was clear she was attempting to keep a gap between them. He had the longer reach. He had the size advantage. Clearly, her strategy was to use her slighter and more agile frame to dodge his attacks and strike while he was off-balance. But her strikes weren't as powerful as his, and she was half his size and less than half his weight. If he wanted to win this, he'd have to get in close and keep her there.

He rushed in. She tried to dodge, but he caught the talon of her wing with his. She landed a blow to his gut. He absorbed the pain and used her position to lock his other wing with hers. Unable to pull away, she let her feet dance between his, alternating between his ankles and his knees. Goddess, she was good. She successfully tripped him twice, but because he was locked with her, when she righted herself, she righted him as well.

He punched into her sides, her face. This time, he didn't hold back. She blocked every blow, but he could tell she was tiring. This type of close fighting could drain even the best fighters. She twisted and stomped, but he used his larger talons and size advantage to keep her entwined with him. If he went down, she would too.

He saw the moment that very idea sparked behind her eyes. Her arms locked around his neck, her legs around his hips, and she fell backward.

Marius instinctively broke their fall with his elbows, not wanting to crush her no matter how badly he wanted to win. He lowered her softly to the gravel and settled between her thighs, hard as a rock in an instant. Their gazes locked. Her lips were so close he could taste her breath. She softened beneath him, her fingers digging into the back of his hair in a way that was nothing short of carnal. He lowered his lips toward hers.

"Seven... six..."

With a powerful thrust of her hips and wings, she flipped him onto his back, straddled him, and pinned his wrists beside his head. Her golden eyes twinkled in the afternoon light. He started to resist. He could easily flip her back. But she ground her hips against his. With one subtle tuck, she rubbed along his cock, and the hard tips of her breasts brushed his bare chest. And just like that, all his will to win leaked out and soaked into the ground like spilled wine. His inner dragon stretched languorously, hoping for a belly rub.

He could move. He could win. But goddess, he had no desire to. Was that feral heat flashing in her eyes? He slanted her a languid, wolfish grin and raised his hips to grind against her.

"Ten!"

She was off him in a heartbeat, arms raised. She jumped into the air, whooping her victory. He frowned and tried to imagine an icy bath to cool his throbbing erection.

Avery grasped Harlow's hand and raised it above their heads. "I declare Harlow the winner!" As Harlow squealed her victory to the heavens, the witch's gaze caught on his obvious erection, widened, and then darted back to Harlow, who seemed completely oblivious to his plight. Avery cleared her throat, cheeks flushing. "Now, if you'll excuse me, I need to find Xavier." She rushed from the pit without another word.

Thank the goddess. He adjusted himself in his breeches and brushed pebbles from his clothing, watching Harlow through heavy, hungry eyes. She stopped jumping for joy as he neared. Her smile faded. Her eyes were warm honey and her lips parted, begging to be kissed. But before he could get within an arm's length of her, she strutted toward the locker room.

"We start training tomorrow!" she called. "I'll expect my payment up front." She disappeared, leaving him hard, sweaty, and alone.

FOR THE LOVE OF THE GODDESS, HARLOW WAS GOING TO burst into flames. She changed quickly into her dress and hastened to her waiting carriage, thanking her lucky stars that Marius had vacated the arena. Holy dragon fire, the chemistry between them was off the charts. She couldn't remember ever wanting someone like this. If he was hers, she'd have run her hands over his chest and traced every one of those symbols with her tongue. She'd reach into his breeches and learn exactly what that hard length under her would feel like in her hand.

And that was enough of that! She mentally slapped herself. This project was about training a fighter and making enough money to buy her independence. The last thing she needed was to muddy the waters with sex.

No way could she train that closely with him again, though. She'd end up a moaning mass of need. Which meant she was going to need help. And she knew just where to go to get it.

She knocked on the sliding door between her and the driver. "Take me to 13 Bellweather Lane in the quarry district."

"It'll be an extra dragmar."

She did a quick calculation in her head. She'd have to walk or fly home, but it couldn't be avoided. She nodded at the face beyond the window. The door slid shut and they were off.

Twenty minutes later, she pulled up to a simple home

in a row of similarly simple homes on a quiet street lined with jewel dust and the occasional trundle tree. She paid her driver. It occurred to her that she should have sent a falcon. What if he wasn't home?

Lifting her skirts, she navigated the weed-obscured stepping-stones to the front door and knocked. Inside, a baby started to cry. Harlow internally kicked herself again for not sending a falcon. She'd forgotten about the baby.

When the door opened, an exhausted-looking woman gave her a hasty once-over. Pieces of her brunette hair had fallen out of its bun, and she tucked them behind her ears. "Can I help you?" She bounced a whelp on her hip, and judging by the boy's tearstained cheeks, he must have been the one she'd heard crying.

"You must be Aiden. Is Brantley home?"

"Who's asking?" The woman scowled at her.

"I'm Harlow... of Darium, the doormaker. Brantley and I were school chums at Rawkfist Academy."

Brantley's oversized grin appeared in the space above Aiden, his dark blond hair protruding wildly from the crown of his head.

"Did I hear that Hairy Harlow has graced our door with her presence?"

She offered him a familiar smile. "Brant the brat. How the hell are you?"

He allowed the whelp to grab his finger and tousled the babe's hair. "Pretty good, I'd say! Two strapping lads and a wonderful partner to help raise them." He gave the woman a passionless kiss on the side of the head. "Have you met Aiden?"

"No. But you told me about her last time we spoke at the pits. Haven't seen you there in a while."

He shrugged. "Been a bit busy."

Aiden blinked at her in such a way that Harlow wondered if she was sleeping with her eyes open. She adjusted the baby on her hip.

"Brant, is there somewhere we can talk privately? Just for a minute," Harlow asked.

He whispered something in Aiden's ear, and the woman drifted off toward the center of the house. He stepped outside and closed the door behind him. "Come round back."

She followed him to a set of simple wooden chairs propped in an overgrown garden and took a seat.

"I'd offer you a tribiscal wine, but I'm afraid we don't often splurge around here. Parenthood is expensive, and the quarry isn't paying what it used to."

"I've heard."

"It's the revolution. Now that markets are open, gold from Nochtbend is all the rage. People aren't spending as much on gemstones."

"It'll come back. The economy is just adjusting to the new world."

"Yeah."

She shifted in her chair. "Actually, money is why I'm here. I'm in a jam. I have an opportunity I think could help us both."

He tipped his head and gave her an exasperated frown. "I was serious about what I said before. What I did was a onetime thing. I can never do it again, and I can't go back there." He lowered his voice on the last part. She didn't blame him. If anyone else knew he'd conspired to throw a match so he could split the winnings of a friend's bet on his competitor, he'd be in a ton of trouble. Only Harlow, who knew Brantley's talent and fighting style so well, had seen through the ruse. She'd never divulged his secret to anyone.

She shook her head. "That's not why I'm here. I'd never ask you to do that."

"Oh." His guilty expression morphed into a shallow smile. "Sorry... It's just when you said this was about money... I assumed."

"I know you regret what you did."

"Enough that I can't face the other fighters again. Even Aiden doesn't know. She thinks I quit for family reasons. Nice story but not true. It was *all* shame." He sank into his chair. "My winnings did pay for my eldest's tuition at Rawkfist."

Rawkfist was the premier private school in Paragon. Harlow had attended because at the time her parents were wealthy nobles. Brantley had gotten in on a rare needs-based scholarship set up by Eleanor to win over commoner support for her reign. That's how it was then. The rich would do just enough to keep the poor complacent.

Back then, she hadn't thought about it much, but becoming poor herself had brought her a level of clarity on the topic she'd never expected. Brantley's father was a laborer who'd won the royal lottery, which meant Brantley became the token poor kid in an otherwise elitist academy. It was no secret who his parents were, or more importantly weren't, and the pressure to avoid him was high. But the moment he'd won his first school pit match, she'd been intrigued. Her love for the game had led to a fast friendship that had only deepened over the years, to her parents' dismay. They would have preferred her to keep her distance and spend more time with friends in her own social class.

Funny—now that she was poor, those so-called friends her parents loved wouldn't give her the time of day. But Brantley was still Brantley. Solid as always. Maybe that's why she refused to judge him for the choice he made to throw the match. In the same place, she wasn't sure she wouldn't do the same.

"This is nothing like that," she said. "I've been hired to coach someone."

"Coach them in what?"

"Pit fighting."

He gave a throaty laugh. "You're kidding."

She shook her head.

"Don't get me wrong, Harlow. You know more about pit fighting than anyone in Paragon aside from me. But you're a female."

"I've kicked your ass before."

"In the practice ring. It's different in the pits. Who exactly hired *you* as their coach?"

She paused, wondering if it was a good idea to share too much. But if she was going to convince him to be a sparring partner, he had to know whom he'd be fighting. "Marius."

His eyes narrowed in concentration, then widened as his eyebrows rose in shallow increments. "Royal, the-boy-who-might've-been-king Marius?"

She nodded. "He was raised from the dead. He has... physical challenges. He's trying to get back into it."

"And he hired you."

She sighed. "I was in the right place at the right time."

"What does this have to do with me?"

"I need a sparring partner for him. I can't coach him and be his partner. I'd pay you."

He stared at her for a beat. "You're serious."

She nodded.

"So, I spar with this guy a few days a week, and you would pay me. How much are you talking?"

Harlow did a quick calculation in her head. "Fifteen dragmars a day."

He scoffed. "Find someone else."

"Twenty!"

"Make it twenty-five and you have a deal."

Her stomach clenched and her lips barely moved as she said through her teeth, "Fine. Three days per week." She'd do exercises with him on the off days.

"It will have to be in the afternoons after my shift at the quarry. Aiden's going to hate it, but I'll convince her when she hears about the money."

"One weekend morning?" Harlow needed to test her champion at various times a day.

"Fair."

They both stared out across his property, at the back of the house behind him.

"I can't believe you scored this position. You're a phenom, Harlow. Fuck, if you ever get married, your husband is going to have his hands full."

A small part of her flinched at the thought. He made marriage sound like a cage. If she was forced to marry, would she end up like Aiden, looking like the walking dead with a whelp on her hip? It wasn't the whelp that scared her. She'd always thought she wanted children. She loved children. She just didn't understand why that meant she couldn't also pursue her interests. But she didn't want to rock the boat and risk Brant backing out, so she changed the subject.

"Can I ask you something about being married?"

"Sure." He shrugged.

"Did you ever tell Aiden about... you know?" Her eyes flicked to his, and she bobbed her brows.

He looked over both shoulders. "You mean about being bisexual?"

She nodded.

"We're married, not mated. She knows. So does everyone at the pits. It's not a secret. I have... partners. It's not about exclusivity for us."

Harlow nodded slowly. Their relationship wasn't anything she pictured for herself, but if it made him happy, who was she to say anything about it?

He studied her face. "Wait... Harlow, is that why you're not married yet? You're not holding out for *love*, are you?"

She balked. "Is it so wrong to want a mate?"

"No, but... You're almost five hundred years old. You know everyone in the kingdom. If your mate existed, you would have met them by now."

She sighed heavily. "I'm not so sure about that. Maybe my perfect partner is from another kingdom. Maybe I just need to give fate time to bring us together."

"You're a hopeless romantic."

"Maybe. I just don't see what's in it for me. I mean settling. If I take a husband just for the sake of having one, he'll expect me to cook and clean and have his babies. I'm much happier on my own."

"You don't feel like you're missing out on children?"

"Not at all. Dragons are immortal. I have plenty of time."

"But dragon females are rare. You must know that every year you wait, people are going to pressure you to take a partner."

"They already are." She looked down at her fingers. "Actually, that's why I'm doing this. I'm hoping to use the money I earn to rent my own place. My parents are starting to pressure me to marry. I figure if I move out and pay my own way, they'll have nothing to say about it."

He whistled through his teeth.

"Yeah. I know." It was unheard of for an unmarried

female to live alone. It wasn't illegal; it just never happened. "Don't worry about me. I have a plan. I'm going to be okay. And thanks to your help, my fighter is going to win."

He studied her for a moment. "Goddess, you're not just planning to train him. You're planning to bet on him in the pits."

She examined her nails. "Maybe, if he's any good. Honestly, I think he has the makings of a champion."

Brant rubbed his hands together. "I'm in, Harlow. I know that look on your face, and I can practically hear the coins clinking together inside your skull."

She stood and kissed him on the cheek. "Good. We start tomorrow."

CHAPTER SEVEN

Raven strode down the hall toward the dining room, a receipt from the court accountant in her hand. She smiled when she saw Gabriel and Charlie already at the table. They were laughing about something, Charlie's voice a tinkling bell. But it was the look on Gabriel's face that melted her heart. Her big, broody dragon husband was beaming as if his entire body were filled with light instead of fire. To see them like this, totally happy, was milk and honey to her soul.

"What did I miss?" she asked through her own smile. "You two look like you're having fun."

"Charlie was showing me her new trick," Gabriel said, raising an eyebrow.

"Another one?" As much as Raven enjoyed watching Charlie discover her powers, it was a little nerve-racking not to know when or where something new would appear. She tried to keep her expression positive and excited as she looked at her daughter and said, "Show me what you can do."

Charlie opened her hand, and Gabriel placed a small

round sapphire into it. Raven glanced skeptically at him, but he tipped his head toward Charlie. The little girl made a face like she was concentrating hard. The stone lifted off her palm and floated in the air.

Raven applauded. "Levitation! Good work, Charlie!"

The stone fell back into her hand, and she closed it into her fist.

"She's not done," Gabriel said around a tight smile.

Charlie looked up at her mother and opened her fist. A butterfly fluttered off her palm and danced between them, as bright blue as the gem she had transformed.

"Oh, Charlie, that's incredible! Transfiguration, too? Good girl!" Raven beamed at her daughter. The butterfly balled in on itself and turned again into a stone, dropping to the ground near her toes.

"It never lasts," Charlie said sadly.

"Don't you worry about that," Raven said. "It will last longer with practice." She kissed her daughter's cheek. "Such a smart girl we have."

"What's that?" Gabriel turned his attention to the paper in Raven's hand.

"It's a receipt from the royal accountant. Marius has withdrawn a large sum of money from his account to pay for pit training."

"So? Colin told me it's helping him recover physically from the trauma of his resurrection. He said Marius has recovered almost all the mobility in his leg since they've been working together, but he's too busy to train him anymore."

"Right." She tucked her hair behind her ear. "Did he happen to mention who Marius had hired to be his new trainer?"

His gaze settled on the firm line of her mouth. "No, but I'm beginning to fear his choice may be problematic."

"Normally it would be none of my business where Marius spends his money. It's his money. But when he mentioned what the money was for, the accountant thought I should know for reasons of palace security."

"Don't keep me in suspense."

"Harlow."

"Darium's daughter?"

"The one and only."

"You know, I believed we were doing the right thing letting Darium off the hook for his alleged support of Eleanor, Raven. After all, there was evidence he'd distanced himself from my mother in the months before the revolution. But I don't trust this family. He may not have been on the Highborn Council, but he was a nobleman, always on the fringes of political society. He benefited greatly from Eleanor's reign." Gabriel worked his jaw back and forth.

"We took away Darium's position. His business folded. Does he even have the resources to be considered a threat?"

"They have resources. Hundreds of years of amassed wealth and a network of influential friends. I'm sure Darium has already broken ground on a new venture. We took his business, but there's no law against him working. And now his daughter is training Marius in pit fighting?" Gabriel narrowed his eyes at the paper from Raven's hands and made a face at the amount. "For an impressive wage."

"Suspicious, right?"

Gabriel nodded.

Raven sighed. "We did invite her to the coronation for a reason. She isn't to blame for her father's actions."

"But you also don't completely trust her." Gabriel leaned against the table, looking equally concerned.

"No." Raven sighed. "It's just... Marius is vulnerable. He's never quite recovered from the trauma he endured in that in-between place Eleanor kept him. Someone like Harlow could prey on his insecurities."

"Does Marius know about Darium's punishment? Does he know that Harlow might be doing something... desperate to reclimb the social ladder?"

"I doubt it. He's barely left palace grounds the past year. And it's not something we ever talk about. He saw her at the coronation. I'm sure he assumes she's still part of high society."

"A socialite he thought would make a fine pit coach?" Gabriel squinted his eyes as if he just couldn't make sense of it.

Charlie picked the gem up off the floor and waved it around above her head as if she were making it fly. "It's because of his bad dreams," the little girl said absently.

Raven paused and squatted down in front of her daughter. "Is Marius having bad dreams, baby?"

"Really bad ones." Her mouth bent into a frown. "They scare me, Mommy. There are monsters and fire. Uncle stabbed a suit of armor because he thought it was a bad guy."

Raven felt her heart skip and took Charlie gently by the shoulders. "Is that what Uncle Marius told you?"

"No, that's what I saw in his dream." Her bottom lip quivered. "It made me very sad. It was dark and the monsters were scary."

"You... you saw Uncle Marius's dreams?" Raven's throat tightened and her voice heightened in pitch.

Charlie lowered her chin and looked at Raven through her lashes. "Don't be mad, Mommy."

"Oh, I'm not angry, sweetheart. But just like you

showed me about the rock, it's important Daddy and I know about this. How many times has this happened?"

"This many." Charlie held up four fingers. "And one time with Aunt Avery. But her dreams aren't scary. They're beautiful."

Raven studied her daughter. "Aunt Avery isn't fighting monsters in her dreams?"

"No. She's flying, and the light is so bright."

Raven glanced at Gabriel, but he just gave an almost imperceptible shake of his head. He didn't understand this magic either. Raven took a breath, smiled sweetly at her daughter, and forced the muscles in her face and shoulders to relax.

"Well, now that I know Uncle Marius is having nightmares, I will just have to find a way to help him sleep better. I'm sure we can scare those silly nightmares away."

"Oh, he already has. He doesn't have the bad dreams on days he fights."

"Fighting stops his nightmares?"

Charlie nodded.

"Has this happened with anyone else? Do you see Mommy's or Daddy's dreams? Or Uncle Colin's?"

Charlie shook her head.

"Thank you for telling me about this, Charlie." She kissed her daughter on the cheek and stood.

Charlie went back to playing with the gem in her hand.

"What do you think it means?" Gabriel asked.

"I thought she might be developing psychic abilities, but I don't think it's a coincidence that she's only seeing Avery's and Marius's dreams. I used her blood to bring them back from the dead."

"You brought me back from the dead with your blood. You don't see my dreams."

"We already had a bond. I had your tooth. We were already connected metaphysically, and I'd only recently absorbed your power. I might as well have been bringing you back with your own blood."

He rubbed his chin. "But Charlie wasn't connected to the others."

"No. She isn't like anyone, and her magic is something I've never seen before."

"So you think her blood has forged a psychic connection with her aunt and uncle."

"It seems possible."

Gabriel tapped the papers in her hand. "What should we do about Harlow?"

"In light of what we've just learned? Nothing. If Harlow is keeping Marius from experiencing these nightmares, we can't interrupt that until I figure out what's happening with Charlie and break the bond between them. I don't want her experiencing the darkness and monsters in his head."

Gabriel nodded. "We are in agreement on that."

Raven sighed. "I'll figure it out."

Gabriel kissed her lightly on the lips. "I know you will, little witch. You always do."

CHAPTER EIGHT

Marius tied his long pale hair back at the base of his neck. He'd received a falcon to meet Harlow at the practice arena that afternoon. Part of him couldn't wait. That part of him was in his pants. The rest of him desperately wanted out of this agreement.

He'd given his word that if she bested him in a match, he'd let her train him. He needed a coach, and she was undeniably talented and knowledgeable when it came to pit fighting. The problem was, she was also achingly beautiful, and he couldn't very well fight with a perpetual hard-on for her.

"Fuck it," he murmured, punching the wall of the locker room hard enough for it to hurt before striding out toward the arena. Harlow was already there. With another man. An attractive man with blond hair and eyes the color of new foliage. A man whose death and resurrection hadn't scarred him with symbols like some sort of weird zombie experiment. *Fucker*.

His inner dragon growled possessively. He squelched it by coughing into his hand. He had zero right to feel any sort of way toward Harlow. He hardly knew her. Still, the corners of his mouth felt heavy as he neared the other man. He was scowling. He tried to stop and failed.

"Who is this?" he barked.

Harlow beamed at him as if he were as cheery as a flower in the first rays of sunshine. "Marius, right on time! I'd like you to meet Brantley. Brant is a retired pit champion. He's generously agreed to be your sparring partner."

Brant waved. "Not that generously. She's paying me." He turned back to Harlow. "I expect to be paid, Hairy. Don't try to weasel out of it."

"Yes. Right. Of course." She smoothed the waist of her dress.

"Hairy?" Marius asked.

Harlow ignored his comment. "Marius, do you have my payment?"

Marius dug in his satchel and pulled out a pouch of thirty gold tallons—three thousand dragmars. He dropped the pouch into her hands. Her jaw popped open when she looked inside and counted it. "This is... more than we discussed."

"It's for the entire cycle," Marius said flatly. Never mind that he understood they would not train together every day. He'd decided to pay her as if they would. She must need it if she was willing to fight for it. "Easier for the accountant. Fewer transactions."

She didn't argue about the discrepancy. He watched her swallow hard and her eyes grow glossy. There was need in those eyes, like she was hungry and the purse in her hands meant a solid meal. It was a silly thought. Harlow had never wanted for anything. She was probably doing this out of boredom and a need for some spending money that was free from her father's control. Still, he watched her curiously as she counted out a portion for Brantley and then put the rest in her bag with trembling hands. Odd.

When she turned back to the arena, she composed herself. "Now that the formalities are out of the way, let's start with balance exercises."

"Balance exercises?" Marius grunted. In all his years of training as a youth, he'd never performed exercises strictly for balance. They were always incorporated into some other move. "We're not going to spar?"

"Not yet," she said. "You're still favoring your left leg. We need to balance you out or nothing else I teach you is going to be effective."

He grunted again. At least Brantley didn't look that thrilled with the idea either.

Harlow stepped down into the arena and lowered herself into a fighting stance. "Follow what I do."

Marius gave a low chuckle. "I can't even see what you're doing, *Hairy*. Your skirt's in the way."

She sighed and undid a button over her hip. His mouth went completely dry as she stepped out of the skirt and tossed it aside, leaving her in a set of formfitting breeches designed for a man. *Fuck*. And then to add insult to injury, she spread her wings. Goddess, he needed water.

Thank all that was holy, she wasn't watching him. She lowered herself into a low lunge, her fists up to defend her face. "Now do what I do." With all her weight on one leg, she squatted low and circled her other leg until her ankles crossed. Then she switched and circled her opposite leg. She continued the intricate steps, holding her wings steady while incorporating a series of fast, precise punches and sweeping blocks.

Marius tried to follow and soon discovered that Harlow had been right. He hadn't even been aware of it, but the exercises were far harder when his weight was on his left leg. Soon, he was panting hard and sweating profusely. The worst part was that Brantley made it look easy. His hair was still perfect. If anything, he looked bored.

Where the hell did she find this guy? Was he a lover? A friend? How did they know each other? When they'd spoken, they'd stood too close to each other to be just friends. Harlow was stunning; of course he was her lover or wanted to be. Perhaps he was the one who had taught her to fight. Someone must have, and it wasn't another woman.

The thought ate at him as he attempted to pivot and face the opposite direction. His shoulder slammed into the gravel. When had he lost his balance?

Harlow's face appeared above his, and she held out her hand to help him up.

He avoided it and scrambled to his feet.

"Get some water and we start again."

Dark clouds pressed in around him, and he shot Brantley a deadly look before walking to the water station to pour himself a glass. *Fucker.* If he was her lover, he hadn't done the honorable thing and married her. He was probably using her. His dragon chuffed and twisted. He couldn't wait to fight the bastard.

Marius chugged his water and returned to his spot, more determined than ever. He was going to get strong, and he was going to fight Brantley. And the first time he was good enough to pound the guy's head into the stones, he was going to enjoy it.

But after two more rounds of exercises, Harlow glanced at the clock and clapped her hands together. "That's all for today. We'll meet again tomorrow."

"YOU'RE PAYING ME A LOT JUST TO DANCE NEXT TO THIS guy," Brant murmured at the start of their third session. Harlow shot him a look out of the corner of her eye. She knew Marius was doing his best, but whatever damage his situation had caused was taking more time to heal than she'd expected.

For three training sessions, they'd practiced the same exercises. On off days, Marius was supposed to be doing the exercises Colin had given him. Marius was so close to mastering this routine. She could already see his left hip had loosened significantly since they started. Brantley's voiced impatience was echoed in Marius's angry glances. But she knew what she was doing. She had to wait until it was perfect. The groundwork for everything she would teach him lay in this footwork.

"He's close, Brantley. Stick with the program. The fundamentals are important."

"If you say so. Honestly, his balance might be better if he pulled the stick out of his ass."

"Brant," she hissed. "Stop it."

"He hasn't broken a smile in three sessions, Harlow. Goddess. I get why you find him attractive—"

"I don't—"

"He's a Greek god. A dark and brooding presence. Hell, he turns *me* on, but—"

"That's not what this is about—"

"He's a royal pain in the ass with that attitude. What did you sign us up for?"

She nudged him to shut him up when Marius returned from the water station. Brant was right. Marius's scowl was more pronounced than ever, and he was looking at Brant like he wanted to pull his spleen out through his nostril.

"One more time and we'll break for the day," Harlow said. "As we've practiced. I'm going to observe."

The two men fell into line and started the exercises. As he had day after day, Brantley performed the moves perfectly, effortlessly. But she had to smile when Marius did the same. His performance was not effortless. His muscles flexed and shook with his exertion. At the turning points when he had to switch his weight onto his weak leg, she wondered how he held it together. But he stayed on his toes, hips low, gritting his teeth and ending the routine in perfect position.

She clapped her hands and bounced on her toes. "Perfect, Marius! Excellent. You've officially graduated balance."

He rose from the crouch he was in, and for the first time that day, a smile flitted across his face. It didn't stay there for long.

Brantley slapped his shoulder. "Nice work, man."

The look Marius shot him could have soldered iron. She announced the end of class and that they'd start sparring the following session. Brantley abandoned the arena for the locker room.

"What is wrong with you?" She grabbed Marius's elbow before he could follow after him. "You've been rude to Brant from the moment you stepped into this arena."

He scowled. "We wouldn't want to be rude to *Brantley*. Might injure his fragile self-esteem."

"Seriously? Marius, what in Hades is your problem with Brant? You're acting like a child."

"You should have cleared a potential sparring partner with me," he said accusingly.

She scrunched her brows together. "What's wrong with Brant? He owed me a favor, and he's the best I could get on short notice. Do you two have some sort of history I don't know about?"

Marius glanced away from her. "No. It's not *my* history with him that bothers me." He mumbled the last part under a growl, and Harlow barely made out his words. Once she put it together, she started to laugh.

"Do I amuse you?" He wiped a towel across his sweat-stained forehead.

"Honestly, yes. You think I have a romantic history with Brant, and it makes you jealous." She raised her chin and preened. "It's very flattering."

"Hardly." He scoffed and rolled his eyes. "I'm paying you a small fortune. I don't want you to be distracted by your quivering loins."

"Did I seem distracted to you today?" She took a step closer to him, flashing him an insouciant grin.

"It was hard to see anything with him standing so close to you. He was practically wrapped around you at our last break."

"It was a break. Why would that bother you?"

"It's the principle, Harlow. For the love of the goddess, if you're going to be my trainer, I don't need to be distracted with personal displays of affection between you two. If this is going to work, you'll need to find someone else." He mopped his chest aggressively.

She stepped in closer and grabbed his towel in a firm grip. "What if I told you that Brantley is not and has never been my lover?"

He snorted. "Right." He tugged at the towel, but she pulled it closer.

"He's married with two whelps." She stepped in closer, their hands sandwiched between their bodies, still gripping the towel. Those strange silver eyes locked on to hers, and a flock of butterflies took off in her stomach. "We're old school chums. Have known each other since childhood. And between you and me, if he were going to pursue one of us, it would likely be you. You're more his type."

Marius's face softened, and he lowered his head toward hers. "He's not a past lover who taught you to fight?"

"No." She chuckled. "He did teach me to fight, but we were never lovers."

He leaned in. Was he going to kiss her? Her nipples tightened, her breasts straining against her dress. Her core clenched at the possibility. She wanted him. That hadn't changed, and having him near her, half naked and covered in sweat, certainly wasn't helping to inhibit her desire. Her fingers itched to stroke the velvet smoothness of his wings. His woodsy scent filled her nose.

"So you're not involved with anyone now?" he asked softly. His hand lifted as if he intended to cup her face.

She released the towel and swaggered back, smiling and shaking her head. Her gaze dropped to his erection. No one could miss it in his fighting breeches. An overwhelming desire to take that erection in her hand was almost her undoing, but she forced her spine straight and smoothed the front of her dress.

"The last thing I'd ever want to do is distract you, Marius."

"Harlow—"

Before she lost her resolve, she strode toward the exit and the carriage waiting to take her home.

CHAPTER NINE

Everything hurt. Marius strode through the palace, muscles aching from his physical training and his balls blue from unresolved sexual tension with Harlow. *Fuck.* Why had he tipped his hand? Now she knew without a doubt he wanted her. At least he'd discovered she was unencumbered. He sensed she wanted him too, even if she didn't act on it today. She was definitely flirting with him.

Who was he kidding? He looked like a ghost and had been dead for three hundred years. Not exactly the definition of what women wanted. And she was a socialite. Every polished young dragon male was likely sniffing at her doorstep. Those wings. Who could stop themselves from wanting her after seeing those delicate works of gold? His dick twitched just thinking about them.

"Oh my, what did the kitten do to make you want to kill it?" Raven appeared in front of him, dressed in a gown that made it impossible to forget she was the queen, although he'd started to think of her as a sister over these last months.

He forced a shallow smile. "Hmmm. No kitten

involved. You caught me coming from the training arena. I'm afraid this body isn't used to such hard work."

"Charlie says you haven't been sleeping well. You've been having nightmares."

"She told you about that, huh?"

"She did."

"Avery too. We compared notes, but my dreams and her dreams are as different as dreams can be."

"Charlie mentioned that too." Raven brushed her sleeve, as if any dust would dare cling to the perfectly pressed gown she was wearing. "I'd like to do some additional magical investigation on your condition—sketch the symbols on your torso. If I have a detailed drawing of each of the different symbols, I can research their historical magical usage and maybe determine what's causing your nightmares."

The fatigue he was feeling before seemed to double as he thought about his visions. "There are thirteen. Different symbols, I mean. They appear multiple times on my body. There are seventy-eight overall, but it's because the thirteen repeat."

"Fascinating. Can I send Alexander to you to draw them for me?"

He gave her a single nod. "There's something you should know. The nightmare Charlie saw—it doesn't only happen when I'm asleep."

Her hand went to her lips. "You have visions when you're awake?"

"Twice."

"We'll get to the bottom of it, Marius. I promise you."

"The training helps. I haven't had one since I started."

"Right. About that, I wonder if we might have a little talk." She raised a hand toward his shoulder. "Walk with me. I'm supposed to meet Queen Penelope for a late supper, but this can't wait."

Intrigued, he walked with her toward the dining room. "What concerns you about my training?" Marius wondered if Colin had gotten to her, filled her head with fears about him trying to compete.

"It's the coach you've chosen. Harlow."

He hadn't expected that. "What about Harlow?"

"It crossed my mind that in your absence and recovery, you might not be aware of the choices her family has made, or the consequences."

He frowned. "I'm aware that Darium was an aristocrat under my mother's rule and as close to Highborn as one could be without being a member, but my understanding is he pulled away from that relationship in the final years of her reign. After all, you invited Harlow to your coronation. I assumed that was a sign that all had been forgiven."

Raven stopped in the middle of the hall and cleared her throat. "Not exactly. Darium and Lemetria did distance themselves from Eleanor, but Gabriel and I have it on good authority that privately they supported her and benefited from her rule, right up until the end. However, we have no proof. Publicly, they denounced her."

"If you have it on good authority, why can't that authority give you evidence?" Marius wasn't surprised that Darium and Lemetria had done whatever they needed to do to maintain their social status, but it bothered him that gossip and conjecture might tarnish Harlow's reputation.

"According to palace records, Eleanor was paying Darium's business thousands of units a month—er, I mean a cycle—until she died."

"What does Darium say she was paying for?"

"Doors."

"Makes sense. He's a doormaker."

"We don't know what she was paying for, but this palace would be full to the rafters with doors if she'd been buying what he was selling. Some of the Council of Elders wanted to have him tried, but they settled on suspending his license to do business in Paragon."

Marius narrowed his eyes. "Are you saying that Darium and Lemetria no longer have an income?"

"Don't be too concerned. Considering what Eleanor paid them, their savings must be substantial. Darium is a skilled doormaker. If he wanted work, I'm sure he could get it. Still, they've lost social status and no doubt have had to tighten their belts. Last I heard, the family was living in the Swilton district."

A muscle in Marius's jaw tightened until it hurt. He squeezed his eyes closed. He'd never suspected that the reason Harlow might want to train him was that she actually needed the money. "If this is true, why did you invite Harlow to the coronation?"

"Because Harlow was never involved in her parents' affairs. She never shared their enthusiasm for Eleanor. Our sources say she's always been a rebel where her relationship with her parents is concerned, and honestly, once she's married or mated, she'll be a member of her own household. We want the support of that future household. Gabriel tells me she's of an age where that's imminent given our shortage of females."

He forced himself to nod even though the thought of Harlow marrying someone else made his stomach twist. He had no right to feel that way, no claim on her. Best to change the subject. "What is it exactly you wanted to tell me, Raven?"

She licked her lips. "I just want you to be careful. As

much as I believe that Harlow should not be punished for the sins of her parents, I can't imagine she feels warmly toward us after the change in her social circumstances." An expression that looked a lot like guilt tightened the queen's face. "The accountant mentioned to me what she's charging you. I'm just not sure there isn't more going on here than her desire to train you."

"You'd think an accountant would keep better confidence."

"He was concerned for security reasons."

"Why? Because Harlow might be taking advantage of me for a few extra coins?"

Raven sighed. "I don't know. I just think you should have all the information. Keep your guard up. Understand that she's in a place where her motivations might be beyond the obvious."

Dark thoughts filled his head. "You mean beyond needing money or a mate."

"Exactly. You are the ambassador to the Council of Elders. If her parents still carry any loyalty to the old guard, she could be getting close to you for more than a paycheck. She might seek status or information."

He must have flinched because Raven raised her hands. "I'm not saying she is, Marius. I liked Harlow when I met her, and as far as I'm concerned, it's possible for the apple to roll far, far away from the tree. I only wanted to make you aware out of an abundance of caution."

He grunted. "I get it. I'm not good with subtleties, Raven. You've known this since the afternoon you walked into my room in the Asfolk infirmary and I told you I had no desire to be king. Is this your way of telling me I should find another trainer?"

Raven took a deep breath, her arms dropping to her

sides. "No. If you trust her, we will trust her. My only request is that if something happens that changes that trust or introduces doubt, I want you to tell us. We're a new kingdom. We're vulnerable."

He raised his hand. "Enough said. I'm keeping her on for now. But my loyalty is to Paragon first."

Raven breathed a sigh of relief. Leaning forward, she kissed him on the cheek and squeezed his shoulder. "Thank you, Marius. I knew you'd understand."

She left him then, slipping into the dining room where Queen Penelope waited. The conversation settled into his soul like a fly into ointment. Everything made sense now. The chemistry he'd thought was between Harlow and him was invented, orchestrated. He didn't believe she was a political spy, but her motives were definitely financial. She was likely flirting with him out of a desire for a marriage that would save her from a life of poverty and social isolation.

He closed his eyes and gave his head a hard shake. Why hadn't he thought of that before? Of course she wasn't attracted to *him*. He was death itself. Someone like her, who carried the sun in her wings, wouldn't want someone like him. It made sense. She had flirted with him because she wanted something from him—a marital arrangement, the most likely suspect. His dragon coiled, and images of what she'd looked like above him with her wings spread filled his mind. Did it matter if her attraction to him was real?

No, he decided. It didn't. He wasn't above a transactional arrangement. Hell, what else could he expect now, like this? He wanted her, and he'd take whatever he could get.

CHAPTER TEN

Harlow paid the driver as she exited the carriage at her parents' home, feeling like she was walking on air. Marius had almost kissed her. Her heart thrummed with the possibilities. Twilight had turned the sky silver while she'd been traveling, and Ouros's two moons glazed the tightly spaced roofs of the Swilton district with silver light. Her breath caught. The color was exactly like Marius's eyes. She wondered if he was thinking about her at that moment, and the thought made her smile.

There was something between them, something more than simple chemistry. She wasn't going to rush it. Wasn't going to do anything to jeopardize his training or her job. His money was changing her life.

After their first session, she'd clutched her bag to her stomach all the way home. She hadn't been able to stop herself from counting it over and over. Never had she expected he'd pay her an entire cycle's fees at once. If she played her cards right and was lucky at the pits, she could put a deposit on a small house in a matter of weeks. If she didn't mess things up.

She wanted Marius, but she needed to be patient. The job came first. At least until she had her own place. Still, thoughts of him produced a dreamy, weightless feeling that propelled her through the front door. She crash-landed back to earth when she saw Adradys with her father at the dining table. She'd desperately wanted a few hours to relax, but now it appeared they were entertaining the most pretentious and excruciating snob she'd suffered in weeks.

"Finally! We were beginning to think we'd have to send out a search party," her father said. Was that a smile on his face? It had been so long since she'd seen one there, she almost couldn't believe he was the same man.

Her mother emerged from the kitchen, equally transformed. She was sober and wearing a new dress and an apron Harlow had never seen before. She placed a guiding hand on her shoulder. "You must be starving. Where've you been so late? Oh, never mind. It's all right. Have a seat."

"Yes, Harlow. Sit," Adradys said, pulling out the chair beside him.

She cleared her throat and forced a smile. Although the thought of spending an evening with Adradys didn't appeal to her, she was smart enough not to make a fuss. Had she misread her last interaction with him? Perhaps he'd taken their conversation to heart and had come to speak to her father about potential employment. Yes, that must be it. That would explain her parents' good moods.

She smiled sweetly. "I'm sorry I'm late. I was helping a friend."

"Just like Harlow to always lend a hand," Lemetria chimed in.

Harlow pointed vaguely in the direction of her room. She met Adradys's eyes and turned on the charm. "If you'll excuse me for a moment, I'll just go freshen up."

"Of course." His tone held all the pretentiousness of a man who truly believed that the woman sitting beside him should look her best. She dug her fingernails into her palm to keep from rolling her eyes.

"Do hurry, Harlow. We wouldn't want to keep our guest waiting." Lemetria spread her hands toward the set table. Didn't she look like the very picture of domesticity? What was happening? Had she passed through a portal to another dimension between the carriage and her home?

She laughed, high and light. "I'll be quick." She strode down the hall, into her room, and closed the door. Quickly she shed her dress and the fighting clothes underneath it. Oh, her father would have a fit if he'd known she was wearing breeches. She selected a dress they would approve of from her closet, a fitted purple number that contrasted with the gold in her eyes and hair. Looking every bit the socialite she once was, she slipped her feet into a pair of heels and strode back out to the table.

Maybe she'd overdone it. Adradys's eyes widened, and his grin turned wolfish. "Much better," he murmured as if his assessment was everything.

"Oh, Harlow, you truly are the loveliest of your age," her mother said.

Her father gave her an approving nod.

Adradys pulled out her chair, and she sat beside him, his scent a cloying stench in her nose. Had he smelled that bad before when she'd been close to him at the pits? She didn't think so. Maybe he had a new cologne. As she tucked in her chair, she made an effort to put a little more space between them.

"Yes, she is lovely," Adradys said. "I was just telling your father how I ran into you betting at the pits the other day. How unusual it was to see someone of your social standing involved in such a base activity."

"I enjoy the competition," she said lightly. "It can't be all bad. After all, you were there too."

"Well, yes, but I'm a dragon male. Women are far less frequent attendees, and never without a chaperone. To think you were there alone! Well, you were fortunate I came upon you when I did and not someone with less than honorable intentions."

She ground her teeth to keep from biting out that she'd fared quite well alone at the pits for centuries. He could shove his honorable intentions where the sun didn't shine. And oh, her bet had paid off, while his had not.

"You certainly were my good luck charm that afternoon," she said, smoothing her napkin. "My winnings were substantial."

The veiled blow must have landed because his smile faltered. "Well," he scoffed. "I suppose every dog has her day."

Dog! Who was he calling a dog? She plastered on a sweet smile and turned toward her mother. "What's for supper? It smells delicious."

"Elderbeast stew." She rushed to the kitchen and returned with a steaming metal cauldron filled with a delightful mix of meat and root vegetables.

Harlow rested her fingers against her mouth to keep from asking where her mother had bought the stew. She couldn't cook. Not even toast. She suspected she'd find packaging from the Silver Sunset somewhere in their garbage heap. Although she had to hand it to her mother, the presentation was fantastic. She'd managed a stunning table that would be fitting even in their Firedrake home.

Her mother gestured toward the ladle resting against

the side of the pot and looked at Adradys. "You're our guest. Please serve yourself first."

Adradys looked down his nose at her and chuckled. "Yes, I suppose you no longer have servants to handle such things. Understandable, considering the awful state you're in."

Awful state! It was all Harlow could do not to rip into the bastard. This was a table fit for a king, and that stew smelled like heaven in a pot. The fucker was just sitting there like he didn't know how to spoon stew into a bowl.

His soft, manicured fingers finally gripped the side of his bowl. But instead of serving himself, he handed the bowl to her! "Harlow, perhaps you could do the honors."

Her gaze locked on the bowl, and she had a miniature daydream of breaking it on the table and stabbing him in the neck with a shard of ceramic. But her father must have noticed her hesitation because he cleared his throat and gave her a pleading glare. Her father didn't plead. He needed this, and she'd play along for now.

"Of course," she said through a tight, reluctant throat, then added under her breath, "Wouldn't want you to stain that suit."

Adradys chuckled. "Oh, Harlow, kind of you to notice. It is the finest Paragon has to offer."

She turned her back to him and rolled her eyes as she obediently filled his bowl. Her mother met her gaze, and goddess bless her heart, seemed to be equally perturbed with their guest. She held Harlow's stare, darted her eyes in Adradys's direction, and flashed an obscene gesture in her lap where neither he nor her father could see it.

Harlow smiled before placing the dish in front of their guest and then filling her own bowl.

"Our situation is brutally disappointing," her mother

said suddenly, rising and reaching for her father's plate. "Harlow isn't cut out for this life. She is no servant and shouldn't be dishing anyone's food. I rather think she's a queen in commoner's clothing, don't you? Sit down, dear. I will serve the rest of the table."

Her father did a double take at Lemetria's words and sipped from the glass of dark purple liquor in front of him.

Harlow didn't turn her head, but she could feel Adradys's judgmental gaze raking over her, tallying all the ways she was definitely not a queen in commoner's clothing. He did not respond to her mother's comment.

"Adradys," she said sweetly, "I was recently telling my father about our conversation at the pits and how much you said you respected his craftsmanship."

Adradys waved a hand dismissively. "Everyone knows that Darium's doors were synonymous with prestige and quality. Why, the door to this house is an absolute work of art."

Now Harlow turned, watching him take a bite of stew. He nodded his approval to her mother. Maybe she'd misjudged the man. That sounded like a genuine compliment. Perhaps this dinner would pay off after all.

She attempted to close the deal. "You're in luck. He's a free agent now. You should snap him up before someone else does." Famished, Harlow took her own bite of stew. It *was* the Silver Sunset's recipe, but she didn't care. Delicious.

"I am open to new opportunities," Darium said humbly.

At that moment, Harlow was honored to be her father's daughter. His words warmed her heart. He wasn't haughty about the compliment, and his tone held a gentle question, a desire to work for this awful man who was once his closest competitor. It must have taken an act of superior will to cast aside his pride and make himself vulnerable.

But it would all pay off. This was it. She could see it on Adradys's face, the question poised on his lips. This was what they'd been waiting for. He was going to offer Darium a job.

Harlow gave Adradys a warm smile. "A wise businessman such as yourself must see what a valuable addition Darium would be to your team." Harlow layered on the charm and stared at him expectantly.

His answering smile was no less charming. "Unfortunately, as much as I respect the work you've done in the past, Darium, we receive many requests a day to replace your doors. I hate to be the bearer of such news, but no one wants to be associated with scandal. To hire you now, with your reputation as it is, wouldn't be good for the company."

Harlow's breath caught. Why in Hades had he come here if he had no intention of hiring her father? She pressed him again. "But surely you could give him a position behind the scenes. No one needs to know who is making the doors in your factory, and my father could teach your other craftsmen."

Adradys made a tsking sound. "I wish it were possible, but alas, you know how tongues wag. There are no secrets among the aristocracy."

Harlow's dragon wanted to tear out of her skin and claw at the man's face. His stupid, arrogant face. Her mother's cheeks were pink, and her father seemed suddenly obsessed with his stew. That was it. Her heart pounded in her ears as she turned toward him, ready to unleash her fury on the pitiful man.

He silenced her with a raised hand. "Please, let me

finish. I have a plan that I think will solve all your problems."

Harlow was struck speechless. She stared at him. "You do?"

"I planned to keep this for after dinner, but it seems the goddess has different plans." He pulled a small box from his pocket. "Marry me, Harlow. Become my wife, and together we will slowly rebuild your family's reputation, and in the meantime, not only will I make you comfortable but them as well. Marry me, and I will return you to the station to which you are accustomed." He popped open the box to reveal a sapphire ring, a smaller version of his own.

Open-mouthed, Harlow couldn't suppress the look of horror and disgust at the idea. She glanced between her mother and father, begging each with her eyes to help her out of this. She received no such help. Her mother gasped and raised her hands to her mouth, staring down at the ring as if it were the most beautiful thing she'd ever seen. Her father's eyebrows darted toward his hairline as if he'd just stumbled upon an abandoned pile of gold.

Engagement rings among dragons were not unheard of but also weren't common. All dragons had a magical ring that represented their heart in dragon form. Her amethyst ring could never be removed. This one was supposed to be worn on her opposite hand. It was a brand—a mark of ownership. She'd be literally wearing a replica of his heart on her ring finger.

And because of the size and the craftsmanship, anyone who saw it would know she belonged to someone wealthy and influential even if they didn't know it was Adradys. It would ensure that no male would dare come near her once they were wed, and anyone else who dealt with her would do so under the specter of his ownership. He would not be taking a replica of her ring, of course. That was unheard of in these relationships. After all, they weren't mates. He'd likely take a lover in a few years, as was common among the aristocracy, as soon as he grew bored with her body and their bed.

"No," she said with as much certainty as she could load into one word.

He tucked his chin in toward his chest. "Excuse me?"

Her mother leaped to her feet. "What she means is, that like any intelligent young woman, she would like to take some time to think about your proposal."

"I would be a terrible wife to you," Harlow blurted. "I like my freedom far too much."

He leaned forward and placed his hand lightly on top of hers. It reminded her of a snake's belly slithering over her skin. "I know what I'm getting myself into proposing to an older dragon." He gave her a condescending grin. "But I promise you, I run my household with a firm hand. I'll break you of your unfavorable habits in no time. Why, I will take pleasure in it."

"Any woman would be lucky to have you," her father interjected.

Harlow didn't know what to say. Everyone stared at her expectantly. She had no intention of accepting. Not while there was air in her lungs. But her skin crawled to end the tension in the room.

"As my mother suggested, it is customary for me to take time to think about my answer," she said stiffly.

He set the box beside her on the table. "Very well. Not too much time, Harlow. A man such as myself has many distractions." He smoothed the front of his suit, stood from the table, and gave a shallow bow before moving for the door. "Thank you for the stew, Lemetria. I do hope we can do this again"—he gestured vaguely around their cottage—"under more favorable circumstances."

CHAPTER ELEVEN

After a long night's rest blissfully free of nightmares, Marius met Harlow at the pit and was pleasantly surprised to find her alone. "Where's Brantley? I thought we were sparring today."

"Sick whelp. We'll work on conditioning." She raised an eyebrow. "We can make up the sparring session later this week."

A slow, wolfish smile spread across his face. He let his eyes gravitate to the breeches and tunic she wore, distracted by the way the curve of her calf sloped toward her inner thigh. "Unless you'd care to spar with me in his place?"

She snorted and gave her head a little shake. "Conditioning. Try to keep up." Without another word, she took off along the path toward Hobble Glen.

He snapped out of his enthrallment and jogged after her. *After* being the key word in that sentence. By the Mountain, she was fast. And although the view from behind her was pleasurable, he had his pride. Forcing his legs to move faster, he caught up to her before the guard tower and tried not to look like he was going to die as the guardsmen waved them through.

"Can I ask you something?" he huffed out. Honestly, as she picked up the pace, he wondered if he was physically capable of asking her anything around his pounding heart and labored breaths.

"You can ask. I'm not guaranteeing an answer." She shot him a sweaty smile.

"Did you take this job because of what happened to your family?"

Her smile faded. "Does it matter? I told you I wanted the money."

"You told me you *wanted* the money. You don't just want it, you *need* it. Your family is..."

"Struggling financially?" Her cheeks reddened and she cringed. "Yes, we are. I never said we weren't."

Was that true? He thought back, huffing harder. He couldn't remember speaking about it specifically. "Maybe it wasn't said, but at the coronation, you allowed me to believe you were still a member of the aristocracy."

She chewed her bottom lip, her pace slipping to his relief. Her voice was as thin as a spider's web when she finally spoke again. "Is that important to you? I can return your money if you want someone else. Well, not the amount I paid Brantley. I already gave him his money, and I'm sure he paid bills with it. He's in a bad way."

He grunted. "It's *only* important to me if there's something I should know. Some other motivation for you doing this."

"Other motivation beyond money?" She worked her jaw, her pace increasing again. "Like what?"

He gave her a loaded look.

"Are you worried I'm in it to try to snare you into

marriage?" The sharp edge of her voice cut deep, and she narrowed her eyes over a scowl. She mumbled something under her breath that sounded a lot like "Not you too."

Suddenly, his lungs were on fire, and Marius realized that in her mounting anger she'd again sped up to a pace he wasn't sure he could maintain. Hobble Glen was coming up fast. He hadn't run this distance this quickly since he'd come back from the dead. He'd offended her, and she was punishing him for it.

"You have to admit it wouldn't be... unexpected," he said between pants. "You've lost your social status." *Huff, huff.* "You live in the Swilton district."

She growled at him, bared her teeth, and ran faster. His thighs protested as he tried to keep up, and his breath sawed in and out of his lungs. He could no longer talk. He could no longer think. Only when she reached the far side of the city did she finally slow to a stop.

It was all he could do to keep himself from flopping onto his back on the grassy patch at the edge of the city. Instead, he leaned forward and caught himself on his knees, wheezing toward the packed-dirt trail that led toward the mountains.

"While you're remembering how to breathe, let me calm your fears," she said through her teeth. "I'm not looking for a husband, Marius. I'm not using you to improve my social status. I'm in this for two reasons: my love of pit fighting and the money."

He met her glare. Marius's nightmares featured hideous monsters and brutal landscapes, but the menace in her eyes was as unsettling as any of them. Still, her words didn't completely ring true to him. A muscle in his jaw twitched as he said, "The other day, you were going to—"

"What?"

"Kiss me. I thought you were going to kiss me." He hadn't invented that moment. There'd been something between them. He was sure of it.

She squeezed her lids closed and gave her head a little shake as if she was warring with herself. Her mouth opened, then closed again. When she opened her eyes, their usual spark was gone. "I won't deny it. But just because I wanted to kiss you doesn't mean I want to marry you—or anyone else, for that matter. It's not on my agenda right now, so you can pack those worries up for another time and another woman. It won't happen again." She folded her arms and looked away from him.

"But you wanted to..."

The look she gave him was laced with daggers.

"I've offended you," he said.

"Brilliant deduction."

"Why?"

She scoffed, jutting her chin. "Because you assumed that just because my family is currently down on its luck, I would intentionally try to seduce you into marriage for personal gain. That doesn't reflect well on what you think of my character."

Now she was just pissing him off. "Sorry, but were you not an aristocrat's daughter?"

"Of course I was. So?"

"I'd venture to say you might be the only one in all of history not interested in bettering their social position through marriage." He was right, and she knew it. It was no leap for him to assume this of her, not given the current social environment in Paragon.

She popped out her hip. "That's not— Okay, maybe there is some truth in that."

"That's settled, then. You're a unicorn. My mistake for

assuming you shared the predilections of the class in which you were raised." He gave her a shallow bow. "I'm sorry my inquiry offended you."

Silence unspooled between them. He could practically hear the gears of her mind grinding on whether she should let it go as she pondered the situation. *Hardheaded woman.*

"Fair enough," she finally said. "Forget about it." She wiped her hair out of her face. "How's the leg?"

He did a quick assessment. "Better." He glanced toward the palace and back at her. "I'm not sure if it was the distraction or something else, but this is the farthest I've run without resting, and we did it in half the time it usually takes me." He didn't admit that he'd almost collapsed from the effort.

"It's the balance exercises," she said with surety. "You're getting stronger. Before, you were overcompensating for your weaker left leg with your right and prematurely tiring yourself out."

He bent and straightened his left leg. It ached in an equal degree to his right, which was an improvement. "You know, I think you're right."

She gave him a halfhearted salute. "Glad I could help. I'll see you back in the pit tomorrow."

"You're not running back with me?" As soon as the words were out of his mouth, he realized how stupid they sounded. Why would she return to the palace with him only to have to take a carriage home?

"I think you can make it back yourself. If you need company, I'm sure with your high social standing, you could call for a servant to accompany you." She wrinkled her nose.

Ouch. Apparently Harlow wasn't quite as forgiving as she seemed. Marius searched for the right words to say to appease her, but then stopped himself. He wasn't wrong for asking her what he had. "I'll do just fine on my own," he growled.

She gave him a dismissive wave and took off toward Swilton.

MARIUS STARED AT THE FOREST BEYOND HIS BALCONY the next morning, mulling over his conversation with Harlow. The damned woman was a walking contradiction! She admitted she wanted to kiss him but then insisted she wasn't interested in marriage. At least it was clear she needed the money, but then why the almost-kiss? As he turned, he caught sight of himself in the wall mirror and frowned. He was a specter. A monster. He turned his face away from the white hair and pale eyes of his reflection. One thing was for sure, she hadn't wanted to kiss him for his looks. If it wasn't for his position, he still didn't understand her motivation.

"Marius." Alexander appeared in the hallway outside the open door of his room, sketchbook in hand. "Glad I caught you. Raven sent me to—"

"Sketch the symbols?" Marius said gruffly, tearing himself from his thoughts of Harlow. He'd been expecting this. "Right. Come in. Let's get this over with."

Grabbing the hem of the light tunic he was wearing, he pulled it over his head. The symbols seemed to taunt him in the light streaming in from his balcony.

Alexander whistled. "You are a work of art, my brother."

"Fuck you."

"No, I'm serious. In the human world where I spent the

past three hundred years, tattoos are quite popular. Let's just say yours would be appreciated by the ladies in that world. Plus, I was serious. They have artistic merit." He dragged a stool from the kitchenette out onto the balcony. "Sit here. I'll start with your back."

Marius sat facing the forest. "They make me feel like a freak," he admitted.

Alexander snorted. "Bro, we are all freaks. Our mother was a monster. Who murdered you. And then became a goddess. Whom we murdered. Our family history is nothing but bloodthirsty drama. I understand feeling like a freak. There was a time on Earth that the only thing I wanted in life was to end it all."

Marius shot him an incredulous look. "You? But you found your mate and your purpose. You have everything you ever wanted. Why would *you* want to kill yourself?"

"It's a long story. Suffice it to say that it wasn't always so. Maiara and I are the result of a lot of faith and a little magic."

"Nothing I can repeat, then."

Alexander frowned. "I'm sure it will happen for you someday if you stay open to it."

He looked over his shoulder at his brother, whose charcoal moved quickly over his pad of paper. "I doubt any female wakes up in the morning and thinks, 'You know what I need? A mate who was once dead.'"

Alexander laughed. "I don't see why not. Maiara was once dead."

Marius gave him an incredulous look. "What are you talking about?"

Without missing a stroke, Alexander broke into the story of how he met his mate. It was long but also incredible, and the hours flew by. He'd just explained her resurrection when he asked Marius to turn around.

And he almost fell off his stool. Behind Alexander, half his room had faded away into a red haze. Killian was there, mouthing something to him, his lips and hands working frantically. He thumped his chest while a weasel of a man sniveled at his side— Brynhoff! The image was clear now in his waking mind. They stood in a thick forest, balls of fire exploding in the sky behind them.

"Marius, are you okay, man?" Alexander glanced over his shoulder toward the spot where he was staring.

"Do you see them?" Pins of icy fear needled his skin. Rare for a dragon who had fire in his blood.

"See who?" Alexander glanced at the spot again and then back at him. He shuddered, stumbling from his stool and backing up a step. "Marius, look at the symbol near your rib."

Marius glanced down at himself. One of the symbols was moving, rippling under his skin as if it were alive. He slapped a hand over it as if it were a mouse or a bug. When he looked back up, the mist, Killian, and Brynhoff were gone.

Alexander was in front of him, hand on his shoulder. "Are you all right?"

He nodded. "Yeah. It stopped. Side effect of being dead." Although he chuckled at his own words, Alexander didn't. He pulled him into a tight embrace, thumping his back three times before releasing him.

"I have what Raven needs. She's going to figure this out. You know she will. There's a reason she's the queen. Just hang in there until she does." Alexander slapped him on the shoulder and glanced at the door. "I've got another project, but you're going to be okay, right?"

"A bastion of giddy bliss," he said flatly.

Alexander smiled softly. "Good enough for me."

THAT AFTERNOON, MARIUS HEADED FOR THE ARENA, thankful that there would be no balance exercises or conditioning today. He needed to hit something. He needed to fight. After what happened with Alexander that morning, it was clear the visions were back, and only exhausting himself physically would keep them at bay. Goddess, was he losing his mind?

He found Harlow waiting for him inside the ring and felt his dragon stir, stretching and sniffing in her direction. Her water-lily scent hit him like an avalanche, and his body kicked, coiled, and tensed. She had the audacity to smile at him. No, not just a smile, she beamed like he was the best part of her day. Fuck, he wanted her.

Everything they'd talked about and what Raven had told him came flooding back into his mind, and a frustrated growl rumbled in his chest. She didn't want marriage. Well, what did she want?

"What's your problem?" she asked. "You look like someone peed in your porridge."

He narrowed his eyes at her. "Why would anyone pee in another person's porridge? That's sick."

"Exactly. Who was the sicko? Who hurt you? I'll knock them into next week." She held up her fists and faked a jab toward his face.

He ran a hand over his face. "Where's *Brantley*?" he drawled. Goddess, it sounded childish even to his own ears.

"Running late. Whelp is still sick, but he's coming anyway. Crib cough. He sent a falcon. Will be here any minute." Her voice was soft, concerned. She strode toward him, and his breath caught. Her hand landed on his back.

"Come with me." She tenderly guided him toward the water station. "Let's have a drink." She filled a glass for him and handed it to him. He lifted it to his lips. "What's really going on? Are you nervous about fighting Brant today? You shouldn't be. You're a strong fighter, but if you want to work on balance another day, we can."

He rested a hand on the water station, his talons extending from his knuckles to graze the wood. "I want to fight. I need to fight."

Her brows squeezed together. "You're having a bad day and you need to work some things out? Don't worry—you'll have your chance." Her hand came to rest on his, the tips of her fingers absently stroking the length of his talons.

He scoffed. "You don't have to do that."

"Do what?" She removed her hand as if she thought her touch had hurt him. Damn, she was a fine actress. She looked legitimately confused.

He met her gaze. Marius had spent his life and death as a leader. He wasn't a child, and he didn't lean on formalities. He prided himself on being direct. Why waste words or energy? He wasn't bound by the expectations of the royal family anymore, and he had nothing to lose that wasn't already gone.

"We've already established you're not interested in marriage," he said brashly. "I've already paid you. You don't have to force yourself to touch me or pretend to be concerned about me. I know why you're here." He watched her squirm under the intensity of his gaze.

"I thought it was obvious I was here to train you," she snapped.

"Because you need the money." His jaw tensed.

"Exactly. Like I told you I did." She raised an eyebrow. "I train you. You pay me. That's how these things work."

"You're a fine trainer."

She balked and raised her chin. "Then what the fuck is the problem?"

"What type of lady uses that language?" he murmured.

"We just established I'm no longer a lady. I'm only trying to figure out what's going on here, Marius. And don't use words with me if you don't want me to spit them back at you." She placed her hands on her hips.

"Fuck," he muttered.

"Fuck," she returned, louder this time. "If you know my family's dirty history and you still want me as your trainer, then why are we even talking about this? My dad was an idiot. He tried to suck up to Eleanor, okay, because he thought she would win. I'm not him. I've already promised you I'm not trying to manipulate you into marriage."

"That's not what I have a problem with." He stepped closer to her, watching her. As she drew in his scent, her nostrils flared and her chest expanded. Above parted lips, her pupils widened and her body went soft, leaned in.

"What, then?" Her voice was as soft as a breath.

"This. The way you're looking at me like you want me. The way you touch me. The way you admitted you wanted to kiss me."

A blush rose in her cheeks. "You don't want me to touch you?"

"I don't want you to tease me."

"What makes you think I'm teasing?" Her throat bobbed on a swallow, and she inched closer to him.

He sneered and shook his head. "I've looked in a mirror, Harlow. I know what I am."

The words seemed to hit her like a slap. She took a step back and spread her hands. "And what exactly is that?"

"A monster, a ghost, a freak of nature." He said the words through his teeth. "A woman like you doesn't want a man like me... unless she needs something."

Her jaw dropped and she blinked slowly before leveling a heated glare on him. "Please, O knowledgeable one, tell me what it is I must need to dare act as if I'm attracted to you."

He didn't like her tone. She was mocking him, but it had to be a defensive tactic. "You're looking for an... arrangement. Not marriage but money. No matter how freakish I look, a relationship with me would offer you stability."

She inhaled sharply and gaped at him.

He shrugged. "We don't have to play this game where you pretend you want me. If you're looking for a sponsor, I'm interested. I'd be happy to pay you for sex if that's what you had in mind." There, he'd said it. He sipped his drink.

Her fist came out of nowhere, colliding with his jaw and knocking his water out of his hand. Stars exploded behind his eyes. He went down hard, his back slapping the gravel. Her face appeared within the circle of blinking lights dancing above his head. "Fuck you, Marius, and the mountain horse you rode in on."

She kicked him in the ribs.

"Sorry I'm late," Brantley strode into the arena and tossed his bag onto one of the observation benches. "Why is Marius on the ground?"

"Never mind," Harlow barked. "Assume fighting positions. Brantley, hold nothing back. Marius, let's go. Time to train."

CHAPTER TWELVE

Three training sessions later, Harlow was still taking immense satisfaction every time Marius's back hit the gravel, and it happened again and again. He was good, but Brant was better. After what Marius had suggested, she was happy to let her friend mop the floor with the royal. Accusing her of pretending to want him sexually for money, or worse, status! Goddess, she replayed punching his face again and again in her head. The bastard. If she didn't need the money from these sessions so badly, she would have walked out that very minute.

The sad part was that she *was* attracted to him. Even now, her mind wanted to go there, to the afternoon she'd pinned him between her legs and felt the massive length of him pressed up against her center. Those feelings had nothing to do with money. Her inner dragon thought he was a fine piece of male. She'd dreamed about those silver eyes more times than she could count. She found him undeniably sexy.

No, what bothered her the most was how he thought about himself. She'd known he was having a crisis of confidence when she'd offered to help him, but to describe himself as a monster? It almost made her feel sorry for him. Almost. Until she thought about him offering her money for sex. Then she wanted to knock his head off.

"Harlow?" Brantley was staring at her.

Marius was on the gravel, face bloody. He wasn't getting up.

"Congratulations, Brantley. Looks like you won again." She clapped her hands together. "That's all for today. Tomorrow is a rest day. Take it easy and allow your body to heal. We'll meet back here at the top of next week and keep going."

Brant reached a hand forward and helped Marius up.

Harlow grabbed her bag and headed for the exit. She'd decided to walk home today and save the money she'd been spending on carriage rides. Adradys would want his answer soon. She wanted to be prepared to move out of her parents' place before then. Both of her parents had suggested she save herself through marriage. She planned to prove she could save herself without it. That meant she needed every dragmar she had left in her mattress along with whatever she could win at the pits between now and then.

"Can I speak with you a moment?" Marius appeared in front of her, snapped his nose back into place, and wiped blood from his upper lip.

Brantley shot her a wide-eyed look and headed for the exit at abnormal speed. Coward.

"What's on your mind?"

"How long is this going to go on?"

She flipped over a hand. "You paid me for a month."

"You know what I'm talking about. This punishment for what I said."

"Punishment? The only punishment is watching your piss-poor performance in this arena."

"Ouch."

"Is that all?"

"No."

She waited.

"I'm sorry for what I said to you. I was wrong. It was a horrible thing to accuse you of, and my comments were hurtful. If I could take the words back, I would."

Harlow let out a deep breath, muscles in her shoulders relaxing. "Thank you for that. We can't take our words back, but it means a lot to me that you respect me enough to apologize."

"Of course I respect you. I never meant to imply that I thought less of you because of the change in your family's position."

She glanced down at her toes and kicked a few pebbles off them. "Well, you wouldn't be the first." Licking her lips, she released the anger she'd been holding. "I forgive you, and yes, the punishment will stop. Although I honestly think you almost held your own today. Either that or Brantley felt sorry for you."

"It's debatable."

"I have to go. It's a long walk home." She moved toward the exit.

"Where's your carriage?"

"Can't afford one anymore."

"I can lend you one." He pointed a thumb toward the palace.

She felt her cheeks warm and shook her head. As tempting as it was to take his handout, she had to learn to do things for herself, and walking home was something she could definitely handle.

"Oh, I can see why that might be awkward, given our previous conversation."

She turned again to leave. "It's all right. I know you didn't mean it that way."

"Will you allow me to walk with you?" he called, a hint of what she thought might be desperation in his tone. Interesting.

She turned back toward him. "You're covered in blood."

"Give me a few minutes, and I'll clean up."

She shrugged. "Okay." As she watched him jog toward the locker room, she tried not to think too much about the leap her heart gave at the thought of having a long stroll with the object of her hottest nighttime fantasies. Without the excuse of her anger, her inner dragon was all too happy to flirt with the idea of having him again. She sighed. A bad idea for a number of reasons. A long walk would give her time to get to know him. With any luck, he'd be a complete ass and nip her lusty feelings in the bud.

He met her at the door, and they strode down the path toward the main gate to the palace.

"Can I ask you something?" Her earlier thoughts were weighing heavily on her chest, and she needed to know the truth. When he looked at her expectantly, she barreled ahead. "Do you really believe all that about being undesirable?"

He looked away from her, toward the Dark Mountains of Darnuith. "I'm not a dragon prone to histrionics."

"You called yourself a monster, a freak. You can't believe that."

He glanced at her, his face impassive.

"Marius, it's not true. There is absolutely nothing off-putting about you. Quite the opposite." Embarrassed, she tried to hide behind a playful smile as she said, "On a purely objective basis, I find you... fetching compared to most dragons."

He scoffed and held his heart. "Hmmm. Fetching. You don't have to lie. I'm a full-grown dragon with a thick skin. I know what I am."

"I'm not lying! And it's not just me. The first time Brantley saw you, he called you a dark and brooding hunk of dragon male."

He chuckled softly. "I'll try to remember that next time he's smashing my face into the stones."

"There was nothing artificial about the way I looked at you before, Marius. At least believe me about that."

He stole a glance at her again, and she could tell this time he believed her. For a few moments, they walked in silence while he turned it over in his mind. "Have you considered that you knew me before and when you look at me now, you're seeing what I was and not what I am?"

They were drawing close to the guard tower, so she slowed to a stop to answer him where no one else could hear. "That's bullshit, Marius. I didn't know you before. I watched you fight from afar. I'd never even spoken to you until the coronation, and I didn't get to know you until we started working together. Frankly, if I had to compare, I'd say I like you better now than before. You seemed like kind of a dick when you thought you'd be king."

She turned and started walking again. They passed through the gate where Marius exchanged a nod with the soldier in the guardhouse.

When they were out of earshot, Marius said, "I *was* kind of a dick."

Refreshing, she thought, to meet a man who could admit it. She raised her eyebrows.

"Death is a humbling experience."

"Do you have memories of that time? Never mind. That's too personal." She chided herself for going there. Was there anything more off-limits than a person's murder and death?

She was surprised when he answered her.

"I have dreams... visions." He took a deep breath. "They're confusing."

"Confusing... Like you can't interpret what's happening in them through the lens of a living body?" Her voice had dropped two octaves and came out in a chilling whisper.

Marius looked at her and broke into unbridled laughter. Harlow folded her arms defensively.

When he finally settled down, he said, "No. Confusing because the images are terrifying, but I always seem to be in charge and have the same goal. I'm leading a group of people... souls... through a dangerous place to get to a temple. But I don't know why. The challenge changes, the topography changes, but the goal is always the same. And in my dreams, I never reach it."

"That sounds awful." How else could she respond to something like that? Three hundred years trying to accomplish an objective and failing.

"It is. Thankfully, the nightmares have almost completely stopped since I started training. I think you have a lot to do with it."

"Me?" She pressed a hand into her chest.

He smirked. "You keep my mind busy. You are one of the few things in this life that...challenges me."

His mind. Not just his body. Not just his libido. His mind. She loved that. "Hmm. You're welcome."

They walked on, discussing more common things. The weather, the unusual bounty of vaporfruit they were enjoying that season. Her love of the forest and the colors of twilight that time of year. Until they entered Hobble Glen and turned right, heading toward Swilton.

"Are you sure you want to come all the way to my place? This isn't the Firedrake district. It's no place for an heir."

"Former heir."

"Yes, Ambassador." She rolled her eyes at him. "People may recognize you. It won't be good for your reputation to be seen with me," she said honestly.

His mouth spread into a roguish grin. "Then I definitely want to do it. Let them talk." He reached out and threaded his fingers into hers.

"I knew there was a reason I liked you." Although she wasn't sure if he meant it as a joke, she didn't release his fingers. Touching him sent a delicious electric charge through her, coaxing that flock of butterflies in her stomach into an absolute tizzy. Her heart joined in the fun, dancing inside her chest at the unexpected contact.

Thankfully, his hand wasn't enough of a distraction to keep her from noticing a sign in a shop window: Room for Let. She took one look at the shoddy exterior of the little building and felt excited for an entirely different reason.

"I need to stop," she said to him. "There's something I want to see."

"Lead the way." He looked confused.

She led him to the store, only releasing his hand to push the heavy door open. It was a tailor's shop. Several dresses hung on mannequins and on a rack that was pushed against one wall. A portly woman at a worktable spoke around pins clenched between her teeth. "Can I help you?"

"The sign said you had a room?" Harlow pointed toward the window.

The woman's gaze raked over her dress. One of her

nicer ones that wasn't too frayed at the collar or the wrists. "It's nothing special."

"Neither am I."

She didn't miss the way Marius jerked at that admission, but he said nothing. The woman set down her work and pointed toward the back room. "Come with me, then."

A set of stairs led to a single room with a bed the size of a deep sofa and a bathroom small enough that she could touch both walls if she stuck her arms out.

"My mate died in the war," the woman said. "He was a soldier. Got caught in the chest by one of those Rogos grenades. Tears of the goddess."

"I'm so sorry."

"It was a horrible thing what Eleanor did to our kingdom."

They all exchanged sober nods.

"Anyway, we kept this room in case we ever had a whelp, but that's no longer in the cards for me." The pain in her voice almost broke Harlow's heart.

"How much are you asking?" she blurted.

"Forty-five dragmars a month."

What luck! Harlow bounced on her toes. The rent was incredibly low, lower than any she'd come across in the kingdom. She could afford it now! She didn't have to wait. "I'm interested."

"I'll need the first month's rent, and I have some paperwork."

"Can I come by tomorrow?" She hadn't brought any money with her, fearing if she had it, she'd cave and spend it on a carriage.

The woman looked between her and Marius, an appalled expression crossing her face. "Is this some kind of a joke? I didn't think you were looking for yourself. You can't both plan to fit in that bed even for an infrequent rendezvous! And if you don't mind my saying so, I know who he is, and he should provide better for you."

Harlow waved a hand in the air. "Oh! We're not together. He's just a friend. And it is for me. I need to move out of my parents' house."

The woman rubbed her chin and seemed to contemplate her options. "All right. Bring the money tomorrow, and we'll sign the paperwork."

Harlow clapped her hands and gave Marius an excited embrace. She had her own place! One more step toward her dream of independence.

CHAPTER THIRTEEN

Marius followed Harlow as she spilled out into the street. She was practically dancing. "You can't honestly intend to live there!"

"Why not?"

"Because you're a former aristocrat, and that apartment was barely large enough for a hound," Marius grumbled. The house didn't look safe to him. Would it fall down around her while she slept? Would she be robbed because the door didn't lock properly? Two women living alone in a place like that might as well paint a bull's-eye on their backs.

"It's what I can afford," she said cheerfully. "It's all I need. It's just me after all."

"It's a hovel."

She beamed back at him. "But it's going to be my hovel and mine alone."

Marius blinked at her and suddenly understood, or at least he thought he did. "You want to escape your parents' reputation."

She sighed. "That's part of it. Although honestly, that

reputation is undeserved. They're not bad people, and if it was only their reputations to be contended with, I wouldn't want to move."

"Then what is it?" He fell into step beside her and, before he could overthink it, slipped his hand back into hers.

"They're starting to pressure me to... move on to the next stage of life."

"To marry and bear whelps," Marius ground out. It wasn't an uncommon thing in their culture, but suddenly the idea left a bad taste in his mouth.

She gave him a knowing nod. "They have the best of intentions. Each of them framed it up as saving myself from a sinking ship. I understand they want better for me. But I'm not willing to marry to advance my position. I want to wait for love... for my true mate. I don't want to rush into a marriage just because I need the money or connections. I'd rather be alone and living independently in that apartment than carrying the weight of a contractual marriage on my shoulders. That's not a relationship. It's a cage."

Marius wrestled down an impulse to insist she absolutely *not* marry any other man. He had no business saying such a thing. He certainly was not marriageable material himself, no matter how much his inner dragon wanted to claim her as his own. Besides, to bring up such a thing at this moment, when she was opining her future independence, would likely put to rest any possibility of a future relationship.

His past self would have fallen into this trap, tried to force her compliance with his will. New Marius, with all his flaws and idiosyncrasies, understood he had no power and therefore nothing to wield over her. His only hope was to relate to her. And so that was what he tried.

"I understand what you're saying." His situation wasn't far off, was it? "When I was heir apparent, everything was decided for me. I had power and money but no freedom. Only now, when no one in the royal family could care any less about what I do with my time, do I realize how unhappy I was."

"You're happier now that you're free."

"Somewhat. The problem is that once you are free, you start over discovering who you are. I think that's part of the reason I wanted to fight again. It's the one part of my past that I enjoyed. I think it's part of who I am, even more than my royal title or my family."

She slowed to a stop and searched his face. "That's deep. But I can see where it would be true. For what it's worth, I like who you are now, just as you are."

He grinned until his cheeks hurt. "I like you as well, Harlow. Even when you're enjoying the sight of my face hitting the ground."

She giggled. "It'll be better next time. I promise."

His gaze caught on hers and held.

"I should go. My parents' place is around the corner. Don't take this the wrong way, but I don't think you should walk the rest of the way with me. They're in a vulnerable place, and seeing me with you, well, it would be too much of a temptation for them not to try to take advantage of our relationship. They don't know I'm training you. They're in a desperate position at the moment."

He nodded, wondering exactly how desperate Darium could be. Raven had made it sound like Harlow's family was comfortable, although they clearly did not enjoy the social standing they once did. Maybe she was worried her parents would try to use him to get to the queen. "I understand. If you think it's best, I'll head back to the palace from here."

"Thanks for walking me home." She hesitated for a moment, then lunged onto her toes and kissed him on the cheek.

Warmth traveled from that kiss straight to his cock. Fuck, he was in trouble. His dragon pressed against the inside of his skin, urging him to chase after her and throw her over his shoulder. Reluctantly, he watched her walk away.

"Harlow." His voice was a command.

She looked over her shoulder at him and raised an eyebrow.

"I could fit in that bed."

Her lips parted, and her cheeks turned a luscious shade of pink. Slanting her a wicked grin, he turned on his heel and started back toward the palace.

GODDESS HELP HER. EVERY CELL IN HER BODY KNEW beyond a shadow of a doubt that Marius would fit in that bed. He'd fit inside her as well, although based on the overall size of him, maybe not easily. Her body clenched at the thought. *He* wouldn't complain about the food, the lack of servants, or the size of the room. Not even the dirt under her fingernails.

When he'd said her name, it was as if her inner dragon had come to attention. Had he said "sit," she would have sat in the middle of the street. She'd halted immediately at the sound of his voice.

It wasn't a conscious thing.

He commanded something deep inside her. Part of her

she hadn't known existed. Her dragon *knew* him—his smell, his gritty timbre, the way he moved. *Fuck*, was this what it was like to have a crush on someone?

Drawing in a deep, cleansing breath, she turned and continued toward her parents' place. Would it be so wrong to take him as a lover? Once she had her own place, there would be no one to stop them, no reason not to give in to their desires. She had a couple of days before she'd see him again. Maybe she'd propose the idea.

She turned the corner, and her house came into view. Why was her father in the doorway? And who was that with him? Locked in a lively argument, the two men seemed to be barely containing their anger, and their raised voices had garnered attention. Neighbors hung their heads out their windows. The woman across the street leaned against her doorjamb, watching the exchange with a smile on her face as if it was more entertainment than she'd had all day.

"I'll get it to you. I said I'd get it to you." Her father's face was flame red as he spat out the words.

"I need it now, Darium. You've used up all your extensions."

"What's going on?" Harlow didn't like the way the stranger was looking down his nose at her father. Cold, beady eyes locked on her. His face was made of angles. Sharp, pointed nose, sunken cheeks, narrow chin.

"Mortgage is due, sweetheart. Your father is having trouble paying." His gaze skimmed over her. "I hate to throw a family such as yours into the street, but I'm not a charity, you understand."

She snorted. "There must be some mistake. We own this house. My father bought it outright when he sold our Firedrake residence."

Her father shot her an apologetic look and cleared his throat.

"Daddy?"

He hung his head as he said, "We took out a mortgage a few months ago. We needed the money for living expenses."

"What living expenses?" She flailed her arms. She hadn't bought anything for herself that she hadn't paid for with her own money in over a year. They had no servants, no luxuries. Hades, they rarely had anything in the pantry.

"This and that," he mumbled. "None of your concern."

"None of my—?" She glared at him in utter fury. Her father's inability to meet her gaze told her all she needed to know. She'd long suspected her mother's drinking habit and penchant for fine dresses was out of control. Her father's addiction to expensive tobacco and fine wine wasn't helping either. While she'd lived like a pauper, they'd squandered every dime they'd had left as well as what she'd earned them.

"How much do they owe?" she asked the stranger.

He told her a sum equal to almost all her savings. His mouth of narrow teeth bent in what was supposed to be an expression of pity but looked a little too much like a smile. No doubt if he repossessed the house, he'd probably profit heartily on its resale. "I'm afraid if the balance isn't paid in full today, I'll need to contact the authorities and initiate foreclosure."

Harlow's heart sank into her stomach. If she bailed them out, she'd barely have enough left for a single cycle's rent on the apartment. How would she feed herself? There wouldn't be enough left to gamble with either. And she'd already been paid for the work she was doing for Marius. There'd be no other money coming in until after the end of this cycle. She needed that nest egg to live off until she could establish herself in a career that was more stable than gambling on pit matches.

"Wait here," she commanded. No matter how crazy her parents made her, they were her parents. She wouldn't allow them to be thrown out into the street when she had the resources to keep that from happening. As hard as things had gotten these past months, she knew they'd do the same for her.

She strode through the house and into her bedroom, carefully closing the door behind her. She flipped up the mattress and wriggled her hand into the secret opening there. Her fingers closed around the bag of coins. She counted out what they owed and sighed angrily at the pittance that was left. She shoved it back into the mattress.

When she returned to the door, her father's eyes expanded into saucers at the sight of the gold tallons in her hand. "Here." She dropped the coins into the stranger's palm. "I'll need a receipt." There was no way she was going to risk this man pocketing the money and not crediting their account.

His sleazy grin widened, and he pulled a section of scroll from his bag, affixing a wax seal to the bottom. "Of course, my lady. Pleasure doing business with you."

CHAPTER FOURTEEN

"Where in Hades did you get that much money?"

Harlow ignored her father's gaping jaw and strode into the house, her chest heavy with the loss of the independent future she'd hoped for. It felt like a small death, and she grieved it. How she'd longed for that little room above the old woman's shop.

Her dad slammed the door behind them. "Harlow, answer me!"

"Don't you mean to say 'Thank you, Harlow, for saving me and your mother from certain homelessness'?" She leaned up against the table and crossed her legs at the ankle.

His lips pursed as if he'd tasted something sour. "Thank you, Harlow, but if you'd shared the money with us in the first place, Flavius wouldn't have called in our debt to begin with. Plus, we could have saved ourselves the embarrassing experience of being the neighbors' entertainment tonight."

"Are you sure? Because it seems like you've blown through every other amount I've given you since we moved here." She slammed her palms down on the table behind her, and it tipped on uneven legs.

He gasped, looking as offended as she'd ever seen him. Chin held high, he pointed a finger at the ceiling. "I don't think that's fair, Harlow. We've all suffered incredibly adjusting to our change in lifestyle."

Her mother came out of their bedroom then, looking haggard with a bag slung over her shoulder that rattled with her movements. "Is he gone?"

"He's gone," Harlow answered.

"Thank the goddess. I need a drink!" She smoothed the side of her elaborately coiffed hair.

"A drink is the last thing you need." Harlow strode toward her mother and unzipped the bag. It was filled with gold and jewelry. Thousands of dragmars' worth. "What in Hades? Why didn't you hock *this* to pay your bills?"

Lemetria's eyebrows shot up. "*Our* bills, Harlow. You live here too, and you're an adult. This is our insurance plan, only to be used in case of emergency."

Harlow gestured toward the door. "What exactly did you think that was?"

She tipped her head toward her shoulder. "We had one more warning. If he started foreclosure, we'd pay him then."

Harlow covered her face with her hands. "Fine, then sell it and pay me back for what I paid him."

"Two-thirds of it, you mean," her father said. "Again, it's the three of us here."

"Fine," she said through her teeth.

Her mother dropped the bag of jewelry on the table. "Ugh! This is all so stressful. Darium, do you have any more of that tribiscal wine?"

Harlow's hand came down on the table again with a slap. "No, Mother, you do not need a drink right now, or another dress! You don't need anything but to talk about what just happened and how to prevent it from ever happening again!"

"Honestly, Harlow, I think *you* need a drink. Relax. It's over. Let's all get on with our lives."

"Are you fucking kidding me?"

"Language!" Her father tossed a hand into the air in exasperation. "Your mother needs to slow her drinking. We get it. No need to swear."

"Hey!" Lemetria placed her hands on her hips. "I'm not the only one who spends money around here."

"Oh please. Oh please!" Harlow leveled a pointed stare on her father. "You don't get to point fingers. How much did you spend on elfish tobacco this month, Dad? And is that a new shirt? You *both* have to stop spending money. If you're going to survive here, you both need to make changes. Only eat what you cook for yourself. Drink water. Try to get work. Stop buying clothes."

"Don't you mean all three of us?" Darium said. "You've bought... things." He gestured vaguely around the room.

Her mother's heavy sigh interrupted any attempt at an answer. "We shouldn't be wasting energy fighting about this. Once you marry Adradys, our days of pinching pennies will be over! Thank the goddess he proposed to you. It's the answer to all our prayers."

Harlow closed her eyes and inhaled through her nose. So that was it. The truth ignited in her mind like dragon fire. Her parents weren't as worried about this as she was because they assumed that she'd be engaged to Adradys before Flavius had time to foreclose on the property. They wouldn't have to hock anything or tighten any belts. As far as they were concerned, all they had to do was delay total economic catastrophe for a few days.

Goddess, she had to end this. She had to end this now!

"I'm not marrying Adradys," she blurted. "I will never marry Adradys. The answer is no. Never. Not negotiable. I'm giving him back his ring as soon as possible."

Her parents gasped in unison. Lemetria held her hands out toward her, all color draining from her face. "Harlow, what are you saying? Have you lost your mind? Do you know what this marriage could do for us? Think about someone other than yourself!"

Her vision washed red, and her teeth clenched to the point of pain. She raised her chin into the air before answering in a low, steady voice. "The *only* person I should think about when considering a marriage proposal is me! I'm the one who'd have to sleep next to that rank and pompous slimeball every night. I'm the one who'd be expected to bear his children. 'Serve me, Harlow. I can't possibly fill my own bowl!'" she said in falsetto. "The man runs a doormaking company and doesn't have a single callus or splinter on his perfectly manicured fingers."

Her father grunted. "I have noticed that. What a poser."

"Exactly." She pointed at her dad. "He's a soft, spineless clown, and I will never marry him. You cannot force me. Under the new regime, it's against the law. If you try, I'll leave. I've already found a place. I will leave tomorrow if I have to." It was an empty threat. She didn't think she had the money to leave. Still, it needed to be said.

Her mother clutched the base of her throat. "You don't mean that! You've made plans to leave? Why? Where will you go?"

Harlow crossed her arms. The truth was like a river now whose dam she had destroyed. Words gushed out of her, pressurized from being held back for too long. "I'm tired of working my ass off to support you. You're both full-grown dragons. Dad, you started your company from nothing.

What's stopping you from doing it again? And Mom, if you got off your barstool long enough, maybe you could find a job at one of those dress stores you frequent. You've always had an eye for fashion, and you know everyone in the kingdom with money. Why not use that to your advantage? I've been the only one earning anything to support us this past year, and what do I get for it? You want to marry me off to a man you and Dad can't even stand."

"Oh, Lemetria, I knew this was a mistake. She doesn't like the man. Not even a little." Darium stuffed himself into his armchair and buried his face in his hand.

"How were we to know?" Lemetria groused. "When he sent the falcon to say he'd seen her at the pits and wanted to join us for dinner, I assumed the two had a connection! It said you sat with him, Harlow. You talked."

Harlow flung her hands down by her sides. "The only connection I had with that dragon was a few conversations where I suggested he'd be lucky to hire Dad for his second-rate door company. That's why I thought he'd come. And he had the audacity to give us that stupid excuse about his business's reputation." She made a gagging sound.

"He's absolutely wretched," Darium snarled.

"But very rich," Lemetria offered.

Harlow and her father stared her mother down.

"Fine, you won't be marrying the asshole." Lemetria sagged into the chair across from her father.

"Thank you," Harlow said.

"There's only one problem," Darium muttered, leaning back to stare at the ceiling.

Harlow laughed. "Only one?"

"A big one." Her father scrubbed his face with his hands. "What happened tonight is just the start. Without his money to bail us out, we're doomed."

"Exactly how bad is it?"

Her father frowned and glanced away. "Even if your mother sold every last piece of jewelry in that bag for top dollar, it wouldn't be enough to pay off what we owe."

Harlow's eyes widened. Her gaze darted between her parents, and panic gripped her shoulders. For a moment, she was tempted to flee the sinking ship. Their debt was not technically hers. She could leave, work hard, live simply. She could let them fail. But even as she considered it, she knew it was out of the question. As difficult as her parents could be, she loved them. Harlow was no whelp, but she'd lived under the shelter of their wealth for hundreds of years. Her father's prosperity had been her prosperity for most of her life, and he'd never begrudged her a single thing.

Never in all those years had her parents tried to force her to marry or to move out on her own despite her advanced age. Before they'd lost everything, her parents had never asked her to pay for anything, never expected her to contribute in any way. Even now, when they were desperate, they accepted her decision not to marry Adradys. There were no ultimatums. In fact, both of her parents looked at her with only love.

In her heart, she knew without a doubt that Lemetria and Darium were not lazy. Darium had started his door-making business from nothing, and Lemetria had helped him grow it. And they weren't cruel people. They never actually supported Eleanor's regime.

No, her parents were simply stuck. Their identity had been rooted to a reality that didn't exist anymore, and unlike her, they were struggling to adapt to their new circumstances.

"You're not doomed," Harlow said. "But if you continue to live like you have been, you will be." She thought of

Brantley. He and his family lived on a meager quarry income. Aiden didn't work, and they had two whelps. If he could make ends meet, surely they could with three adult dragons contributing.

"Oh, Harlow." Her mother sighed in exasperation. "Don't you think we know that we need to tighten our belts? We've tried!"

"No, Mom, actually, I don't think you have. What I know is that the reason you've stopped spending your days at the Silver Sunset is not because you have some newfound sense of responsibility but because Roosevelt cut you off. You haven't been paying your tab."

Her mother's face flushed red, and her gaze darted to the floor.

"And Dad, I know that wine you pulled out for Adradys was from the stash you keep for yourself. I've heard the rumors. Everyone in the marketplace knows your reputation, and I don't mean for doormaking. When we went together, there was a reason the vendors required dragmars instead of credit. You haven't been covering your debts, have you?"

"No credit." He massaged the bridge of his nose, looking positively ancient.

Silence stretched between them. At least her parents seemed genuinely contrite for their actions.

Neither one of them argued her point or would meet her gaze, until finally her mother crossed her arms and lifted her chin. "Well, Harlow, you seem to be the only one of us who has adapted to our new situation with any grace whatsoever. I'm ashamed to say, I don't know what to do. If I could marry Adradys, I would—"

"Excuse me?" her father protested.

"You know what I mean, Darium. At least Adradys

asked her. Harlow had an option. He didn't ask us. Any talk about hiring your father was completely dismissed."

Darium spread his hands, entirely humbled. "That is true. I would have taken the work. I would have swept the floor in his door factory if he'd have me."

"I know," Harlow said softly. "But we're out of options now. Each of us needs to find work. Anything we can get, and I mean anything."

Her parents stared at each other for a long time, communicating in that wordless way that dragon mates often did. Her father stood and faced her head on. For the first time since they'd lost everything, Harlow thought she saw a hint of who he once was in his eyes, which were powerful and determined.

"That's settled, then. Tomorrow, we find work."

CHAPTER FIFTEEN

Marius tried his best not to yawn as each member of the Council of Elders reported on their sector of the kingdom. It was all he could do to keep his head from bobbing. In fairness, the topics so far had been far from invigorating.

"Someone has stolen one of our mountain sheep from the herd," Elder Montdrake said, his eyes shifting to Varilus, the elder from a neighboring sector.

"Is that an accusation, Montdrake? For the goddess's sake, it's one sheep in thousands. Why would I risk your anger over a singular mountain sheep?"

Marius shook himself awake. "Probably a teenager," he muttered.

The queen glanced at him, raising an eyebrow.

He expounded. "They shift unexpectedly and have a hard time with impulse control. Always hungry. Mountain sheep are easy pickings." He focused in on Montdrake. "Anyone in your sector have an adolescent?"

His ears reddened. "Er, actually, my nephew."

"I'd check his treasure cave for bones. Varilus is right. If it was a common thief, you'd be missing more than one."

The two men nodded.

"Nochtbend is raising the price of gold again," Elder Shallice started in. His sector bordered the vampire kingdom and benefited greatly from the trade industry.

Queen Raven inclined her head. "I can speak with Master Demidicus, but Paragon's demand for gold is not based on need. Our citizens can survive quite well without it. If people are willing to pay the price, I'd say it must be worth the cost."

"But our economy depends on the trade!" Shallice blustered.

"If the decisions of Nochtbend will so strongly impact your sector, you need to consider how to diversify. We can't control the price they set, and I won't leverage what good-will we have built with the vampire kingdom over some-thing as trivial as gold. If people think it's too high, they should stop buying it. If they do, I think you'll see the price come down as quickly as it has gone up."

"Roosevelt, what's your update on Hobble Glen?" Marius asked, moving the conversation along.

"We've heard rumblings recently that an underground group of Eleanor's old supporters are organizing. I don't know how many there are or what they're planning."

Marius straightened in his chair. "Then how do you know they exist?"

"Someone left a flyer at the Silver Sunset. I brought it with me." Roosevelt rose from his chair and conveyed a piece of parchment to Marius.

He unrolled it and read the message.

Concerned that Queen Raven and King Gabriel are breaking the old law?
Want to see things return to how they were before the revolution?
Eleanor is gone, but supporters of the old ways are organizing. Discerning dragons will know us when they see us. You can't find us, but we'll find you.

He handed the scroll to Queen Raven. "Concerning, to say the least," he mumbled.

Raven glanced briefly at it, then returned it to Roosevelt almost violently, but when she spoke, she was as cool, calm, and collected as any queen could be. "Although it hurts me that any citizen of Paragon would feel that Eleanor's reign was superior to where our kingdom is now, there is nothing illegal about this scroll. Citizens of Paragon are allowed their own thoughts and opinions. Eleanor is dead. She will never sit on this throne again. Anyone who legitimately is calling for a return to the old law needs to look no further than Marius at my side. The old law would have him as king, and he has not only already refused that position but acknowledged my position here. Unless and until this group threatens to take the throne by force or undermines the kingdom through illegal means, all we can do is keep our eyes and ears open to their activities."

"I firmly agree," Marius added to back her up.

The council grumbled their agreement.

"Any other news to report?" Marius asked. When there was no response, he tapped his gavel and dismissed everyone. The elders stood and started speaking among themselves, but Raven turned immediately to him.

"May I speak with you privately?"

"Of course, my queen." He followed her from the room,

down the hall to her private chambers. Confused, he paused outside her door. "Gabriel will not like my scent being in your room."

"It's the only way to get to my ritual room," she said. "And my ritual room is the only place in the palace where I can guarantee our conversation will be private. Let me deal with Gabriel. Please." She gestured to a door at the back of the suite.

He growled, completely uncomfortable but unwilling to tell her no. If she required total privacy, this had to be a sensitive topic. Maybe something about his nightmares. Reluctantly, he followed her through the door she held open for him.

Inside, Raven's ritual room caught him by surprise. In a palace made of shiny black obsidian, somehow she'd created a room of sparkling white. The only color was the purple outline of a circular symbol on the floor and the bright green of the forest beyond the floor-to-ceiling windows on the far wall to his left.

"The white stone is marble," she said. "Gabriel and I procured it from Earth. It helps ground my magic to have something from home."

"Don't you worry about someone watching you?" He gestured toward the windows.

She smiled. "No. They're enchanted. That wall is made of stone. From the outside, all you see is the side of the palace. The enchantment is on the inside. It sees around the stone."

He blinked and walked closer to the window. A bird flitted by and landed on a tree. "This isn't real?"

"It absolutely is real!" Raven said like the thought offended her. "That bird is sitting in the tree on the other side of the wall."

"But it's not glass," Marius said.

"So? Do the materials matter if the view is the same?"

"I guess not." He turned back toward her. "What is it you wanted to talk to me about?"

"The scroll Roosevelt found at the Silver Sunset is more concerning to me than I could let on during the council meeting. What I said was true. Everyone does have a right to their opinion. What concerns me is that someone might act out violently against my sister Avery."

"Why Avery?" The queen's sister had always been kind to him and was the only one who wore one of the same symbols that was branded into his skin. He couldn't understand why anyone might want to hurt her.

"Because she's mortal," Raven said lightly. "Her innate power is to neutralize magic, therefore she can't take Xavier's tooth. She can't heal like you or I do either."

He frowned, remembering that was why she'd needed to be resurrected. "That does make her a target, but I was under the impression that her condition was a well-kept secret."

Raven rubbed her palms together and paced the room. "It was meant to be, but when we brought her back after killing Eleanor, we did so on the veranda. With dragon sight and hearing, I can't say for sure that no one else saw or heard what happened. If one of the soldiers was flying over or invisible—"

"You were out in the open. It's completely possible," Marius agreed. The queen was right to be worried. He hadn't thought about the specifics of that morning. He'd been catatonic at the time and had few memories of his own. But she was right. A dragon in the area could have easily made themselves invisible and escaped notice. They wouldn't have been scared off by the erupting volcano, and they wouldn't even have had to have been close to see what was happening. Dragons could see for miles and hear across great distances. Avery's secret was definitely not safe.

"What do you want me to do?"

She groaned. "It gives me no pleasure to ask this after our last conversation, but could you ask Harlow to keep her ear to the ground? Given her family's past relationships, it's possible someone will approach her or her parents. She might be the key to finding out who's behind this."

Marius raised a hand. "Let me get this straight. After warning me that Harlow might be a spy and that I should be exceptionally careful allowing her close to me, you are now asking me to *ask* her to be a spy for us?"

"I know it sounds ironic, but—"

Marius grumbled. "No."

"I wouldn't ask if it wasn't important. This could be a life-and-death situation. We're connected, you know. If someone kills Avery and she stays dead, Clarissa and I could lose our magic. We got lucky bringing her back when we did. Her soul was still with us. When Aborella unbound us before, we lost all our powers. A true death would likely mean the same fate."

He turned back toward the window that wasn't a window. Why couldn't anything be easy? "I'll consider it."

Raven dropped her chin once in silent agreement. "Now that that's settled, there's something else I need to talk to you about."

"Hmm." The bird in the tree outside the window had captured an insect in its beak. He watched the legs kick as it swallowed its meal down.

"I've studied the drawings Alexander did of the markings on your torso, and I have a theory about the symbols."

He turned back around and shot her an expectant glare.

"When Gabriel and I first met and he learned he could trust me, he explained that Paragon existed in a different *dimension* from Earth. At the time, I didn't have a good handle on what that meant. And when I asked him, he held up two napkins and explained that it was like two parallel worlds existing simultaneously, but that aside from the use of a portal, you could not reach one from the other."

She walked to the symbol at the center of her ritual room and passed her hand over it, muttering an incantation whose meaning Marius did not understand. A figure glowed to life. It looked like a stack of thirteen different pieces of white parchment separated by varying gaps that were filled by night sky and twinkling stars.

"Thirteen dimensions. But these aren't like Earth and Ouros. These aren't physical dimensions but spiritual ones."

Marius shook his head. "I'm not following."

"My first clue was when you said that the goddess was in the same place as you before we resurrected her. I understood the spell Eleanor used to kill her. Eleanor did not send Aitna to Earth or some other physical dimension. That doesn't work with spiritual entities. She sent her to the underworld."

"What does this have to do with the symbols?"

"I was examining Alexander's sketches, and I kept coming back to the spiraling symbol that you and Avery share. I could have sworn I'd seen it before. After extensive research, I realized I had... in an old grimoire. The symbol represents the afterlife. So I started thinking, what if the afterlife wasn't some abstract concept but a place? And what if it was layered?"

He squinted at the floating rectangles over the symbol.

"We have folklore in my world that hell has levels. Hell is how many humans think of Hades. Earth and Ouros have a shared history, so I started linking each of your symbols to a 'level' of Hades. Instead of researching in books on symbols, I read books on the underworld, and that's when I had a breakthrough."

Marius's head was spinning. He was trying to follow, but this idea of spiritual dimensions was not an easy one for his mind to wrap around.

"The easiest way for me to explain is to show you. I'm going to open a window to the first level, the one closest to us spiritually." She pointed at the first rectangle in the stack. "Tell me if you recognize what you see."

Her lips began to move, and so did her arms and hands. She drew intricate symbols and made large sweeping movements in the air as she circled and mumbled the words to some ancient spell. When she stopped moving, a blazing light appeared at the center of the symbol. With a grunt, Raven pulled her hands apart.

Marius stopped breathing. "I know this place." He stepped forward, reaching toward the warm yellow light and white tower beyond. His fingers bounced off an invisible barrier.

"It's a window, Marius. Not a portal." Sweat broke out on Raven's forehead.

"I've been there before. It's a good place. We tried to get back there as much as possible."

With a groan, Raven clapped her hands together, and the window closed.

"What does this mean?" he asked.

"It means that I think each of the symbols on your body represents a dimension that your soul traveled to while you were dead. The books I read on the subject suggested that normally when someone dies, their soul goes to one of these dimensions. It's a type of purgatory. The soul must pass a series of trials to move on. Eleanor's curse kept you from ever transitioning. She stopped you from truly dying."

"I was trapped." He studied the layers of his prison, memories flooding back to him.

"Your soul bounced from dimension to dimension over the three hundred years you were gone. You have a symbol for every bounce. Avery only has one because we pulled her back from that place."

He looked down at himself, at the symbols covering his torso. "I didn't bounce. I worked for every transcendence." Marius paced around the chamber. "When you're there, you're hungry. Not like a natural hunger, a soul-grating hunger that drives you. Not every place is as beautiful as the one you just showed me." He rubbed his temples. His head pounded, his mind filling with flashes, images.

"Maybe that's enough for today. You look like you're going to be sick." Raven strode to his side and placed a hand on his back. "I'm going to keep studying this, Marius, but I think we're close to solving the problem of your nightmares. If this theory is true, then perhaps your nightmares are just lingering memories from the thirteen dimensions. They should abate the longer you're among the living. Maybe they'll even eventually fade as you heal inside and out."

It made sense, and the more that Marius thought about it, the more a sense of peace settled over his heart. With one arm, he pulled her into an embrace. "Thank you, Raven. By the goddess, thank you."

CHAPTER SIXTEEN

By the time Harlow reached the practice arena the following day, she was mentally and physically exhausted. Not only had she had to forgo the apartment she desperately wanted the night before, she'd spent the entire morning applying for positions around Hobble Glen. With any luck, she'd be employed before sunset. Goddess, she needed a bit of luck.

She tossed her bag onto a bench, suddenly aware Adradys's ring lingered inside. She'd put off giving him her answer for far too long. As soon as practice was finished, she must return it and tell him the truth.

"How did the apartment work out?" Marius's grin held all the expectation it had two days ago. He was probably still thinking about fitting into that tiny bed with her. The sheer wanting almost made her cry. She'd loved that fantasy.

She rubbed her forehead and forced a smile. "Didn't work out. I'm going to stay with my parents a little longer."

He frowned. "But you were so excited about it. Did something happen?"

She slanted her head to the right. "Unforeseen expenses. I need more time to save. I'm working to find a second job."

"You don't make enough here?" He looked genuinely concerned.

"Not enough to pay off my parents' debts *and* move in to my own place," she said softly. It was too much. Unprofessional. It was one thing to get personal outside the ring. Another entirely when they were here to work.

"I can lend you money if you need it."

She shook her head once. "No. That's kind of you, but I'll handle it."

Thankfully, Brantley showed up then and interrupted any additional attempt Marius might have made to find out more about her situation. She clapped her hands together. "Okay, time to get serious. Take your places."

She stepped up on the platform and raised the flag. "Ready? Fight!" The flag dropped and Marius and Brantley collided, but unlike before, Harlow studied every nuance of the match. "Marius, pay attention to the placement of your wings." She stopped the match, jumped down, and adjusted them for him.

She was pretty sure he shivered when she touched the webbing. Her gaze met his and she smiled. "Try now."

Again, she watched carefully. After a week of letting him be Brantley's punching bag, she needed to make up for lost time. "Stop!" she yelled when it was clear Brant was one move away from slamming him to the stones. "Marius, you aren't low enough. He's going to knock you on your ass because your center of gravity is all wrong. Bend your knees."

To his credit, Marius took her advice without question.

By the end of their practice, he was holding his own. "Good work. I'll see you both tomorrow."

Brant gave her a wave and headed for the locker room.

Marius hung back. "Walk you home again today?"

She lifted her bag onto her shoulder, feeling the weight of the ring inside. "I'm sorry. Not today. There's something I have to do. Another time?"

He nodded but looked deeply disappointed. She didn't blame him. She felt the same way. A cloud passed behind his eyes. She knew that feeling too. Self-doubt. Self-loathing.

She grabbed his forearm before he could even think about leaving. "I enjoy spending time with you. I just have something... personal... I have to take care of. It's important and it can't wait."

His gaze traced up her arm and settled on her mouth, his lids heavy. "Another time, then."

She let him go and headed for the exit.

Twilight had fallen over Paragon by the time she arrived at Adradys's house in the Firedrake district. She straightened her best gown before knocking on the oversized and gaudily ornate door. A butler in the most pretentious uniform Harlow had ever seen answered. It was dark purple and trimmed with gold thread and buttons. Gold was exceptionally expensive these days. The uniform must be worth a fortune.

The man ushered her into a parlor that could have swallowed her entire house. "Tea?"

"No, thank you. Maybe some water."

He strode to a pitcher on a bar at the back of the room and poured her a glass. Bowing slightly at the waist, he handed her the crystal goblet. "The master will be with you in a moment."

"Thank you." She should have sent a falcon to let him know she was coming, but renting the bird was yet another expense she couldn't afford. She made herself comfortable and waited.

After several long minutes, she stood and paced the room. More time passed, and she examined the books on the shelves. She paced the room again. Poured herself another glass of water.

A full hour after she'd arrived, Adradys appeared in the doorway, not a hair out of place. While she was exhausted, in need of a meal and a bath, and utterly sick of waiting in that room, he looked like he had just climbed out of a hot bath to have his servant dress him and buff his nails. She'd never seen skin that smooth, not even on her own face.

"Harlow, I'm so glad you stopped by. What a pleasure." He held out his hand to her and kissed her fingers with weak, soft lips. His rank odor hit her square in the face. He really needed to sort that cologne. Ugh.

"Good to see you again," she forced out. "I've come to give you my answer." She reached into her bag and retrieved the box with the ring.

He scoffed. "Honestly, I'm surprised you're not wearing it. Do you desire me to place it on your finger?"

She held the box out to him. "I am flattered by your interest in me and know that you will make someone a wonderful husband or mate someday, but my answer is no."

He chuckled and stared down at the ring. His eyes flicked up to hers and then back down at the ring as if he were waiting for her to say something else.

"You must be joking," he finally said, his smile fading into a scowl.

"No. I'm sorry." She jerked her head to the left once. "The truth is we'd be miserable together. I have too many habits that you wouldn't appreciate in a wife, plus there's your reputation to consider. If you can't hire my father for fear of his past ruining your company, I'd say you'd be taking far too much risk to marry his daughter." She pressed the ring into his hands, then turned around to reach for her bag.

His hands were on her in the blink of an eye, his fingers digging into her shoulders. "Don't you turn your back on me, wench. If I say you're mine, you're mine." The words hissed through his teeth with such aggression that Harlow froze. He turned her around in his arms, crushed her in a bear hug, and smashed his lips into hers with such force their teeth clacked.

It took much too long for Harlow to overcome the utter shock and confusion of the moment to react. His lips were cool and entirely too soft, as was the rest of his narrow body aside from the very short length of maleness pressed into her hip. Once her brain regained its footing, she found her balance, jerked her head back, and headbutted him as hard as she could.

"Oww!" His hand rose to the red mark on his forehead just as she stomped on his foot and kneed him in the balls. He collapsed in a heap of angry male dragon.

"I am not and will never be your wench, Adradys. And as of now, don't even call me your friend. Stay away from me." She swept her purse from the couch and strode toward the door.

A deafening crash came from the foyer before she got there, and Harlow heard the butler scream. A purple-and-gold blur raced for the kitchen. Harlow tentatively peeked around the corner to see what had spooked him. The door had been kicked in and hung off its hinges. Marius loomed in its place like Hades himself come for a soul. In the moonlight, his pale hair and eyes glowed like silver flames, truly terrifying. His chest rose and fell in huffs, and his wings seemed to take up every inch of the front room.

Harlow stepped into the foyer. "What are you doing here?"

Marius frowned. "I saw through the window. He put his hands on you. Do you need... assistance?" The words came awkwardly, as if he'd acted before he'd thought it through. A low growl rumbled in his chest.

She tilted her head. She'd been in here over an hour. "Did you... follow me here?"

"I wanted to make sure you made it home safely." His gaze sliced to the side.

She couldn't keep the corner of her mouth from twitching. "You've come to save me."

Marius glanced away and grunted noncommittally.

They were interrupted when Adradys appeared in the door to the salon, red-faced and hunched as if he was still in pain. He sneered at Marius. "What are you doing here?"

Marius sneered right back. "As it turns out, nothing."

Harlow looped her arm into Marius's. "Come on. Let's get out of here."

As they turned to leave, Adradys snapped, "You'll rue the day you rejected me, Harlow."

"I find that highly unlikely."

He roared after them. "Things are changing. Mark my words, there will come a time when you'll be begging for the opportunity to shine my shoes."

She shrugged. "Just as long as I don't have to kiss you again."

At that, Marius gave a low chuckle and withdrew a fistful of dragmars from his belt. He tossed them at Adradys's feet. "For the door."

Side by side, they exited the house, turned themselves invisible, and took to the skies. She soared after Marius, a deep heaviness forming in her chest. Adradys was powerful. He was wealthy. Only a fool would underestimate his ability to make her life miserable. He was a devil, and they'd just invited all his demons to come out and play.

CHAPTER SEVENTEEN

Marius followed Harlow's scent to the top of Passage Hill at the far side of Hobble Glen. The suns had set, and Ouros's two moons drenched the forest around them in silver light. She landed among the trees and dropped her invisibility.

"What an asshole," he said, his feet touching down beside her.

She whirled and faced him. The smile she'd given him in Adradys's place had been replaced by a reproachful expression he didn't fully understand. She marched toward him and shoved him in the chest, hard. "What gives you the right to follow me without my permission?"

He folded his arms. "I didn't think I needed permission to make sure you got home safely."

She scoffed. "Well, you do. Where I was going tonight was none of your business. I told you I had something to take care of."

"You did."

"I told you I couldn't walk home with you tonight."

"You did."

"Ugh, Marius, do you not understand that you following me was an invasion of my privacy?"

He rubbed his chin and narrowed his eyes. "My intention was only to follow you to the guardhouse. Then I couldn't help myself."

"It was none of your business where I was going."

"No. But after we'd spoken last, I knew you were in dire financial straits. I was afraid you'd do something... desperate."

She spread her hands in the universal sign for *are you kidding me* and gaped at him. "And how is that your concern?"

He grunted. The dragon in him wanted to growl that he wouldn't apologize for protecting her, but he'd spent enough time with her to know she'd roll her eyes and head for home the moment it was out of his mouth. Instead, he reined in his baser instincts and gritted out, "You're right. Despite my good intentions, it was an invasion of your privacy... I apologize."

Her eyes wrinkled at the corners. "That was difficult for you, wasn't it?"

"The fucking worst."

A laugh escaped her, and her expression softened. "Apology accepted." She looked out over the city, her hands resting easily on her bodice. "It was sweet, although misguided."

"I was going for sweet." He watched her carefully. "Will you tell me what you were doing there? At first, I thought maybe you two were..."

"A couple?"

"Yeah. Well, until you kneed him in the balls."

"Hmm. Right." She studied the ground in front of her toes. "The truth is he asked me to marry him."

Marius could not stop a wave of possessiveness from plowing through him. He took a step toward her before he had a second to think, then pulled up short. He had no reason to be jealous with Harlow. She wasn't his, no matter how interested his dragon was in her. "I take it your answer was no."

She smiled at him then. "I couldn't. It was tempting, mind you. It would have been the easy way out—a way to solve our financial troubles—but the man is a pompous ass. I just couldn't do it. I went there to return the ring he gave me and tell him unequivocally no. I think I bruised his ego."

A small part of him jumped up and cheered. "Bruised more than that by the looks of things."

The corner of her mouth twitched. "He needed a reminder that whom I marry is my choice."

Marius concealed a growl behind a cough. She shouldn't have to remind anyone of that. What little respect he'd held for Adradys dissolved under a newfound desire to bloody his nose. "My offer still stands. I can help you... financially."

She frowned and shook her head. "It's generous of you, but I can't accept. It wouldn't help. Anything you'd give us... my parents would likely spend it. We need to get ourselves out of this mess. I think it's important that my mother and father work to feel in control of their circumstances. They're both wallowing in self-pity. It's like they've never accepted the reality we're living. We'll figure it out on our own." She looked back out over Hobble Glen. "Or we won't, and we'll face the consequences, but we'll know we brought about our own destiny. You probably think I'm foolish, but it's the way it has to be."

Marius studied her for a moment. "I don't think you're

foolish. I think you love your parents. They're lucky to have you."

"They're not the terrible people others make them out to be."

Just like Harlow to see the best in everyone. "I get it," he said. "Believe it or not, my mother wasn't always awful."

Harlow shot him a skeptical look. He supposed to those outside the royal family, she had always come across as hard and tyrannical, and he wondered how much he should share about their personal life. But Harlow of all people understood the complexities of family. He decided to trust her.

"Growing up in the palace, I had very few moments to bond with my parents. Ruling a kingdom takes time and focus. Pit training started early. As soon as I could walk—I couldn't say how old I was. I was not the best fighter. Not at first. When I would win, my trainer would call Killian, and I'd enjoy several hours of my father's undivided attention. We all loved my father, so those times were cherished."

Harlow winced. "Only if you won? Your father's presence was offered as a reward for winning?"

Marius stared at the moon and continued. "As princes, my brothers and I often sparred with one another, and in private, as whelps, there were no unwritten rules against my siblings beating me as there came to be when we competed publicly. So it wasn't just that the winner was rewarded with Killian's presence but that the rest of us would watch our father leave with the victor, knowing that our brother would be treated with sweets and affection while we would spend the rest of the afternoon with our studies."

"That's awful!" Harlow shook her head. "To treat children like that—"

"It made us tough. It made us warriors." He raised a brow. "It made us talented pit fighters."

Harlow's fallen expression radiated sympathy. "I'm sorry, Marius, but I feel withholding affection from children to make them fight harder against one another is abusive. All those years I watched your matches, I had no idea..."

"You'd never treat children that way, would you?" He could picture it. Harlow would be the type to dote on her children. "You'd make a wonderful mother."

A blush warmed her cheeks, and she glanced away. "You were saying... about Eleanor."

"Right. One afternoon, I lost to Xavier. I lost a lot to Xavier in the beginning." He slanted a smile in her direction, thinking of his most stubborn brother. "I became furious. I wanted time with Killian. I wanted my father to be proud of me. I had tried my best and I was the oldest. In my young mind, I deserved to win every time. So I ran to my mother and interrupted the meeting she was in. Now, looking back, she was likely convening with foreign dignitaries. She could have had a guard carry me out and dealt with me later, but she didn't. Eleanor excused herself without hesitation, took me by the hand, and led me to the kitchen."

"Really? Eleanor?"

"Really. She ordered tea, and we sat at the servants' table. For half an hour, she listened to me rant and wail about how unfair the matches were and how especially unfair it was I didn't get time with Killian every day. It seemed easy for Xavier. I wanted it to be easy for me."

Harlow's eyes were saucers. "In the servants' dining room? Eleanor? Honestly?"

He nodded. "I ranted until I simply ran out of words. And when I was done, she gestured around us. She asked me, 'What do you see?' I looked around and answered, 'Servants.' Our kitchen staff was well paid, but they worked for it. They looked worn and tired. Their clothing was not what mine was. She said, 'What makes you better than them?' I remember feeling so confused. I blurted, 'I'm a prince!' She grabbed my hands in hers and said, 'Exactly. If you want a servant's life, give up your throne and work here. Here, you need not follow any of the rules for princes, and you can see Killian any time you are granted a break from your work.' 'But I do not want to be a servant!' I wailed. She smiled. 'You are worth more than *easy*, Marius. You were born the son of a queen, but it takes training to be a prince. You can choose not to rise to the challenges before you, but you should know that if you don't, someone else will." Marius scraped his nail against the side of his thumb. "Believe it or not, I thought of that day when I decided to abdicate the throne and give it to Gabriel. She was right. I am worth more than easy, and the person willing to rise to the challenge should get the crown. Stepping aside was hard but absolutely the right thing to do."

Harlow laughed. "I don't think that's what your mother meant. She was trying to toughen you up. She never actually thought you'd choose a servant's life."

"Whether she meant it or not, she taught me both sides of that lesson."

Harlow moved closer to him, and her water-lily scent surrounded him. Goddess, she was stunning in the moonlight. "Do you regret stepping down?" she asked him softly.

He scoffed and shook his head. "Never." He brushed a hair back from her face, his fingers lingering near her ear. "Adradys would have been an easy solution, but you're worth more than easy too, Harlow. You made the right choice tonight."

"You really think so?"

For the first time, he thought he understood her. She wanted to be her own champion, just like he did. Having things fixed for you, whether in the pit or at the bank, lost its appeal quickly. "If there's one thing I've learned about you, it's that you do what you set your mind to. I never thought a slip of a woman like you would best me in pit fighting, but you did. And you have one hell of a right hook. I don't plan to experience that one again." He rubbed his jaw. "If you say you're going to get yourself out of this, I believe you."

Her lips parted as she met his gaze. The moonlight reflected off a silver line along her lower lid as if she was holding back a tear. "Thank you. It means a lot to me to have someone who believes in me."

He inclined his head and slanted her a supportive smile.

"What are you doing right now?" She arched a brow. "I have an idea." She unbuttoned the neck of her dress, and he went completely still. Almost. A certain part of his anatomy kicked in his breeches.

"Color me intrigued."

"Let's shift. It's a beautiful night. Are you up for releasing your inner dragon?" Her amber eyes flashed.

Oh, was he. He pulled his shirt over his head, smiling at the way her eyes traced his torso. She'd seen him before at practice, but this was different. When her gaze settled on his tattoos, there was nothing but appreciation in her eyes. Appreciation and... *hunger.* His inner dragon sent scales rippling over his skin. Shifting together, flying side by side, it was an intimate thing. This was an invitation to get closer to her. There was no way he'd refuse. "After you."

She backed behind a bush, and soon her dress flew at him over the greenery. He swallowed hard and folded it neatly beside his shirt. He barely got his pants off in time to shift. As his silver paws landed on the moss between them, he gave himself over to the beast within.

A moment later, a caramel-colored dragon stepped into the clearing, her gold wings warring with the dual moons behind her for the title of most beautiful. In dragon form, their thoughts were far less refined than in their soma form, but it felt right when she nuzzled his snout, then took to the night sky with a wild gleam in her eyes. He followed after her, his beast's mind clearing of all thoughts. Only feelings remained. He soared above Paragon, Harlow's water-lily scent alive in his nose, perfectly content just to be with her.

CHAPTER EIGHTEEN

As weeks passed, Marius enjoyed more walks with Harlow and more late-night flights. They'd become friends. Close friends. He desperately wanted more. She was a heaven he would gladly die to enter. Thoughts of her invaded his dreams. More than once, he'd awoken hard and ready for her with no choice but to reach between his legs and find his own release. Flying solo. Pathetic.

Sadly, the closer they'd grown, the harder it was for him to act on his desires. She'd always said his appearance didn't bother her, but he knew in his heart that couldn't be true. At times, he'd noticed her watching him with lust in her eyes. He'd thought she'd wanted him in the same way he'd wanted her. But afterward, he'd remind himself that she was kind. Unwaveringly kind. Her warm heart refused to allow her to see him for what he was.

But Adradys was right. He was a freak. And when it came to a romantic relationship, a deep, unreachable part of him thought Harlow deserved better even if she refused to admit it to herself. In the beginning, he'd thought there was a chance with her, but she'd been distracted these last weeks. More than likely, she'd come to her senses and realized he was friend material and nothing more.

The problem was, Marius thought she was mate material. His dragon pined for her. He thought he might even love her if he allowed himself to go there. He wouldn't, of course. Admitting he loved her would be painting a bull's-eye for a heartbreak arrow.

If his unrequited love for Harlow had any benefit at all, it was that Marius poured all his frustration into his fighting. The past two classes, he could tell that Brantley had to work his hardest to beat him. And today... He felt good about today.

"Take your places." Harlow held up the flag. "Ready, and fight!"

Even before the flag hit the gravel, Marius had Brantley's wings hooked into his own. As Harlow had taught him, he stayed on the balls of his feet, allowing the weight of his wings to draw him back, draw his opponent to him. He sliced an uppercut between their bodies and into Brantley's ribs, then blocked the dragon's blow with his elbow. His knee drove into Brant's inner thigh.

Brant tried a hook to his temple. Wasn't happening. He swept his leg, sending him off-balance. The hook glided in front of Marius's face and connected with nothing but air. Marius cupped behind his elbow, unhooked his wings, and kicked his sweeping leg up. Brantley went flying, his feet kicking over his head. He landed flat on his back in the pebbles.

Out of the corner of his eye, he saw Harlow take a tiny step closer to the edge of her platform. *Yeah, baby, I'm not done.* Marius stood back, waiting for Brant to get up. The other dragon exploded from the ground, going from horizontal to his feet in a heartbeat. It was a common tactic. Any fighter who countered too slowly would have their teeth kicked in.

Marius was ready. A leg was longer than an arm. A body was longer than a leg. Before the man could come within striking distance, Marius faked like he was falling backward, flapped his wings, and drove both feet into Brantley's chest. He hit him like a low airborne missile before bouncing back and skidding on his knees.

Brantley flew out of the ring and crashed down in the stones. He did not get back up.

"Three... two... one!" Harlow was beside him, a beaming smile spread across her face. "Marius, you've just won your first match." She grabbed his hand and lifted it above their heads. "Goddess, you did it! You did it!"

With a groan, Brantley slowly climbed to his feet. "Fucking Hades." He rubbed the back of his head. "I think you've created a monster. My work here is done."

"You're not quitting on me yet, Brant. You're paid up for two more lessons," Harlow said.

"Can we go back to balance work?" He hobbled over to them.

Harlow checked the back of his head. "Already healed."

Brant thumped Marius on the back. "I think this is cause for celebration. Wife's probably going to kill me for coming home late, but how about a pint at the Silver Sunset?"

Harlow's smile faded, and her eyes shifted. Money was clearly still a concern for her. Marius stopped himself from offering to pay. She probably wouldn't accept, and he didn't want to damage her pride. She'd turned down every offer of financial support he'd ever made.

Brant rolled his eyes. "I'm buying, Harlow."

The smile returned with a clap of her hands. "Then I'm happy to participate. Marius, are you in?"

Fucker! "Wouldn't miss my own celebration, although I'm sensing if I don't come, you will go on celebrating without me." He fought back a wave of jealousy as he glanced between Harlow and Brantley, although he'd never witnessed anything but friendship between them. His dragon became anxious and moody that Brantley would get to pay for her drinks.

Her eyebrow inched up. "Stop. It wouldn't be much of a party without our champion."

Champion. He liked the sound of that. He wasn't sure yet if he had what it took to win in the public pits, but he knew for sure that Brantley hadn't gone easy on him today. And for that, he deserved a drink with the woman of his dreams.

"Give me a second to get cleaned up." Marius headed for the locker room, then made a trip to the office to give the attendant there a command. Twenty minutes later, a royal carriage pulled around to pick them all up.

Brant whistled through his teeth. "Going in style!"

"You know this isn't necessary," Harlow said. "I don't mind walking or flying."

"It's free, Harlow. Get the fuck in the carriage." Marius opened the door for her.

"Language!" she said through a smile that wasn't the least bit offended. She climbed in and took a seat across from Brant. The carriage lurched into motion en route to Hobble Glen.

"Now that I have you captive," Marius began, "are you going to tell us what's been up your ass the past week or so? You've been in a mood for days."

He'd asked her before, but she'd evaded the question.

Well, she couldn't avoid it this time. What was she going to do, dive out the door?

She leaned back against the velvet seat and stared at the ceiling. "Personal stuff. It's depressing, honestly. You don't want to know."

"Try me." Of course he wanted to know.

Brantley nodded, backing him up. "Try *us*. I've been worried about you for weeks."

She groaned. "You know how my parents and I have been trying to find work?"

They both nodded.

"We've applied everywhere. Everywhere. Even the quarry. No one will hire us."

Marius narrowed his eyes. He'd wondered why she hadn't snared another job yet, but he'd assumed she was finishing the work he'd paid her for before starting another position. Never had he suspected that no one would hire her.

"That's impossible," Brant said. "They take everyone down at the quarry. They'd allow whelps to work if it was legal."

"Not us." Harlow sighed. "They said they were fully staffed."

"That's narwit fodder. They've been trying to hire anything that walks for months."

Harlow's gold eyes turned stormy, and her previously jovial mood became pronounced with frustration. "I think we're blacklisted. Every day for the past two weeks, I've applied at business after business in Paragon. No one will even talk to me, let alone hire me. I know my dad supported Eleanor, and some of it is deserved, but we're one bad bet away from not being able to feed ourselves."

Marius's eyes narrowed. "That wasn't part of the deal."

"Huh?" Harlow tucked her hair behind her ear.

"Darium's punishment for supporting Eleanor was losing his license to sell doors. There's nothing in the sentence that doesn't allow him to work or sell something else. Other business owners were never encouraged by the crown not to hire him. And you, Harlow, you were found innocent, as was your mother. Why would you be blacklisted by anyone?"

"I don't know. All I know is I've been busting my ass to find work. So have my parents. No one will hire us. Not even for the jobs no one else wants."

Marius frowned at the glint of tears in her eyes. He'd known she was struggling, but she'd hidden her frustration well these past weeks. Seeing her like this made him want to shove every business owner who had ever rejected her up against a wall and show them personally what a need for mercy felt like.

"Sorry, Hairy," Brant said. "That's a tough deal."

She rubbed a hand over her face. Suddenly she looked thinner to Marius, more fragile. He watched her pull herself together and force a smile. "The good news is, I'm just as much an ace at the pits as always. And once Marius is back in the ring, I'm sure to make a mint betting on his fights."

Marius snorted. "Will you be betting for me or against me?"

"Depends on your competitor." She laughed.

"Ouch."

The carriage halted, and they all piled into the Silver Sunset and got a table near the back. Marius pointed toward the bar where Roosevelt was busy stocking shelves. "I'll get the first round."

Brant and Harlow were all too eager to agree. He understood. Money was tight for both of them. He was a royal ambassador, but he wasn't so removed to not understand what it was like not to have anything.

Roosevelt wasn't just a friend. He'd been a member of the resistance, working with Sylas and Colin to build up the Defenders of the Goddess in Paragon. The man had his ear to the ground. Nothing happened in Hobble Glen without his knowing.

Marius approached and tossed a handful of dragmars on the bar. "Two pints and a tribiscal. And some of those elderbeast sliders for me and my friends."

"Anything for a Treasure of Paragon," he said with a wink. "If you don't mind my saying so, it's good to see your face in here. I started to worry you'd never come out of the palace."

He shrugged. "Some things take time to heal."

"That's the truth." Roosevelt started preparing the drinks and called their food order back to the kitchen.

"Can I ask you something?" Marius leaned across the bar. "You see and hear everything in this town, right?"

He scoffed. "Not everything, but more than I want to know."

"Why can't my friend Harlow find work?"

Roosevelt frowned. "You say she's your friend?"

"Close friend."

"Do you know who Adradys is?"

"Yeah, I know him." A muscle in Marius's jaw twitched, and he balled his hand into a fist at his side.

"Was her father's biggest competitor. Took all the business when he folded. A couple of weeks ago, his people came in here and asked that we not hire her or her family. Said they were thieves who'd stolen from him when he tried to give them a chance. He warned everyone about them."

"And you believed him?"

Roosevelt planted his palms on the bar and leaned closer. "To be honest, if she weren't with you, I'd have found an excuse to throw her out. Her mother ran up a tab here to the point I had to cut her off. It's overdue, and I haven't seen a single payment. Her father was a known supporter of Eleanor. I have no reason to believe Adradys, but I also have no reason to doubt him, and given her family's track record, what sort of business owner would take the risk? They're former aristocrats. You know people like that can't do a thing for themselves."

Marius ground his teeth. He hated hearing Roosevelt talk about Harlow like that. "I can tell you without a doubt that Harlow is not a thief. She's been working for me up at the palace for the past month. She's a good friend and a hard worker. Tougher than she looks."

"Yeah?"

"How much is her mother's tab?"

"Four hundred dragmars."

Marius reached for his purse and placed the exact amount on the bar.

"Are you really paying her entire tab?"

"Only if you give Harlow a chance. She needs a job. Offer her anything. Have her wash dishes, sweep the floor—"

"You think a former doormaker's daughter is going to be happy sweeping the floor?"

"I think she'll surprise you."

"You do realize that the amount you are paying for her mother's tab is equal to a month's wages if I hire her. You could just give her the money."

"She needs the work, Roosevelt. Do we have a deal or no?"

"Deal. Do you want me to go over there now?"

"No. Send her a falcon tomorrow. Don't mention we had this conversation, and please don't tell her about the tab."

"Goddess, you have it bad for her, don't you?"

Marius glanced toward the table and the back of Harlow's caramel-colored head. "The worst."

CHAPTER NINETEEN

Why had she drunk that fifth glass of tribiscal wine? Harlow sipped the water she'd switched to and laughed at one of Brantley's stupid jokes. The thing was, in her current condition, she actually thought it was funny. That was all the indication she needed to know she was likely intoxicated.

"So, Harlow, what happens in two days?" Marius asked. How was he not drunk? He had rows of empty glasses in front of him. The man could hold his liquor, that was certain. "Are we on for another month?"

Her head throbbed. She should say yes. It was good money. Money that she desperately needed. But while Marius was at the bar, Brantley had told her he was out. He couldn't take time away from his family anymore or Aiden was going to divorce him.

"You don't need it," she blurted before she lost her nerve. "You're ready to compete. You should sign up for trials at the pits." Trials were how they vetted competitors and determined fighting class. After trials, a fighter might rank beginner, intermediate, remarkable, advanced, or champion level. Only champion-level fighters competed for the championship. Harlow was convinced that Marius would be ranked either advanced or champion level. Brantley was champion level, and he'd confided in her that he'd never faced an opponent as skilled as Marius in all his years as a fighter.

"Even pit fighters need coaches."

She grinned at him. "You want to hire me as a coach? You do know you'd be the only fighter with a female in that particular role."

"I don't even think it's allowed," Brantley chimed in. "Too dangerous."

"It's allowed. Queen Raven and King Gabriel removed all gender restrictions on the games recently. It may not have happened yet, but it isn't illegal anymore." Marius shook his head. "Besides, why would it be dangerous?"

Brantley snorted. "Have you forgotten that there're three males to every female in this kingdom?" The ale in his mug splashed across his fingers as he lifted the glass and pointed at Marius. "Can you imagine the sort of sexual frenzy she'd cause, showing up, looking like she does, among a group of males itching for a fight? One glimpse of her wings, and they'd all but kill one another for a chance with her. Might even try to force themselves on her if they had the opportunity."

The growl that ripped through Marius's throat made Harlow sit up straighter. He'd leaped to his feet and was baring his teeth at Brantley like he might rip his throat out. The bar sank into silence. All the other patrons turned to stare at them.

It took her a minute to understand what was going on. Gently, she placed her hand on Marius's arm. "He was just telling you the truth. He's not threatening me."

His gaze locked with hers, silver and intense and filled with that protective and possessive glint she'd only ever seen among mated pairs. Warmth spread from the center of her chest to the tips of her wings, tucked away inside her. *Whoa.*

She'd been attracted to Marius from the start, but was this something more? Even the possibility both scared her and invigorated her. She wanted him physically, but a dragon male's affections could be a dangerous thing. She brushed aside the thought. It was far too presumptuous to call this affection. More likely, it was the product of drinking and fighting and the natural urges of males and females.

Brantley lowered his drink to the table and took on an air of contriteness. "Sorry, bro. I think the ale's gone to my head." He stood. "I'd better call it a night. Aiden will hand me my ass if I'm out too late again. Congratulations, Marius. Best of luck to you if you decide to give the pits another go." He bowed.

Harlow gave him a hug and said her goodbyes and then watched him leave. Thankfully, she'd sobered up enough to walk home. It was probably best if she did. Things were getting... weird. She turned back to Marius. There was one thing she needed to say before they parted ways.

"I should go too. But I wanted to tell you thank you for taking a chance on me and letting me train you. The money kept my family going, and it's an experience I'll always cherish." Her eyes started to burn, and she focused on a spot on the floor. "Not many dragons would have suffered being coached by a female. You've always treated me with respect, and I appreciate that."

He stood, the weight of his stare penetrating her skin. "I'll see you home."

"You don't have to. It's close."

"My driver is waiting. It's late. You've been drinking." His expression left no room for argument. That inner part of herself keyed into his voice would have done anything he said anyway. Her gaze locked with his, and the flock of butterflies was back, tumbling through her lower abdomen and leaving her feeling restless and wanting.

"Okay," she said softly. It was out of her mouth before she consciously decided to say it. Weirdly, all her muscles seemed to have gone slack too, as if the most they could be asked to do was hold her up.

He stepped forward and pressed his hand into the small of her back, guiding her toward the door. She noticed halfway there that she was the only female left in the bar, and every male had turned to watch her. Marius's left wing rose to arch above her head. Those masculine gazes snapped back to their drinks at the sight. It was a powerful, possessive message, and no one was going to challenge a dragon of Marius's size and position.

A deep part of herself stretched and preened at Marius's attention. She valued her independence, but unlike Adradys who'd wanted a slave, Marius's presence felt more like a partner's. After weeks of working together, she knew for sure that he respected her as an equal. If he didn't, he would have never allowed her to coach him.

He opened the door for her and ushered her through. The scent of deep woods and dark spice filled her. Mountain, he smelled good. Her inner dragon coiled and flipped, chuffing for a lick. Heat blossomed between her legs.

The door to the carriage appeared in front of her, and he lifted her inside. So close. So warm. She slid onto the bench and was both pleased and surprised when he sat, not across from her but beside her.

"Oh..." Desire thrummed within her. Brazenly, she splayed her fingers over the hard expanse of his thigh. The door closed, plunging them into darkness.

Dragons could see in the dark, but there was a sense of intimacy to it, as if the darkness had wrapped them both in velvet. It softly teased her skin, urging her closer to him. Goddess, he seemed to fill the carriage. Was there any air left? Her next breath trembled, heavy with promise as it brushed over her tongue. His silver eyes never wavered from her face.

"Where?" he asked. In no way did she think he was asking where she lived. He knew where she lived. This was a question within a question. An invitation. A proposal. In one word, he'd handed her the reins. She could state her address and he would most certainly take her home, or she could make a counterproposal. He was waiting for her signal.

She licked her lips. "I can't invite you to my place. My parents are there, and the walls are thin."

A low rumble filled the carriage and his eyes flashed. He thumped the roof with his fist to get the driver's attention. "The palace."

The carriage lurched into motion. There were so many things about this situation that should have bothered Harlow. She was vulnerable, both financially and physically, and he knew it. She'd be at his mercy in the palace. Anyone who saw her enter would be on his side and tell only his story. If he wanted to, he could ruin her reputation and make life in Paragon even harder for her and her family.

Only, she didn't care. The effects of the wine had worn off, and the realization that she was two sessions away from never having an excuse to see him again settled in. Soon, she would no longer be in his employ. They were friends. Close friends. But they didn't run in the same social circles anymore. She had no employment, no means, no station. If he had any sense whatsoever, he'd spend his time on a woman who was his equal, someone wealthy and beautiful who fit in at the palace.

Someone unlike her.

The reality was that this might be her last chance to be with him. And she wanted him desperately.

She'd take what she could get.

He was staring at her. Through her. Studying her. So close. Close enough to kiss. Why didn't he kiss her? They were heading to the palace. She'd decided to come with him. Why not make his move?

A wolfish smile turned his lips, and Harlow had the strangest feeling he could read her mind. He spread his arms over the back of the bench, one hand sliding behind her shoulders. His long legs stretched across the carriage. "I know better," he mumbled.

"You know better?" Her brow furrowed. "About what?"

Only his eyes moved in her direction. "I know better than to make the first move. I like my balls attached to my body."

A nervous laugh bubbled from her throat. Was he seriously expecting her to come on to him? She checked herself. Why did it bother her so much if he was? The smile faded from her face as the truth barged into her mind like a mountain bear after his next meal. Part of her had wanted him to push her. She'd wanted the excuse of feeling pressured. It would make things so much easier if she regretted this tomorrow. She could blame him, the alcohol, anything but herself.

And he was calling her bluff. He was a man of honor.

He didn't take his women or pressure them into sex. And wasn't that the sexiest thing she'd ever encountered?

He was studying her again, frowning. "I can tell the driver to turn around."

She licked her lips. "That would be a tragedy." She turned in her seat and slid her hand across his chest and under the collar of his shirt. She heard his breath hitch and preened at the thought of taking him apart and putting him back together. "I think a man who waits for me to take the lead is very sexy."

Hiking her skirt, she lifted her leg and placed it over his, giving him an unobstructed view of her thigh. He made an inarguably male sound deep in his throat and slowly moved his hand to the space above her bare knee. She brushed his hand away, then pivoted in front of him, settling to her knees on the floor of the carriage, between his legs. She pressed both hands against his deliciously hard stomach. He didn't say a word, but his eyes widened and his breath quickened.

Not so cool and collected now, are you? She was going to enjoy this.

Her hand slid lower to the sizable bulge inside his breeches. "Is this for me?" She cupped him, digging her fingers under his balls and gently dragging her palm toward the head of his hard length. Goddess, it just kept going. She swallowed down some trepidation at the size and stroked him again. He tried to lean forward to catch her mouth with his own, and she arched out of his reach. His lips twitched and he leaned back against the seat.

She licked her lips and stroked him again, then reached for his fly.

CHAPTER TWENTY

Marius was the luckiest dragon in Paragon, and if he wasn't careful, his cock was going to explode the moment Harlow touched him. Mountain, she was beautiful. Never in his wildest dreams had he thought she'd agree to come home with him. This wasn't how he'd expected the night to go. But when Brantley had mentioned another man attempting to be with her, his dragon had leaped up and screamed *mine* inside his head. After that, he had no choice but to try.

He'd decided to leave it up to her.

He'd thought she'd say no.

She didn't.

And wasn't that even more surprising than being raised from the dead? Harlow could have anyone. Any dragon she chose. Why would she want him, with his strange scars and stranger history? Why would she risk giving herself to him?

She'd untied his fly, and her long, slender fingers closed around his shaft. *Fuuuuck.* He moaned and closed his eyes. The head of his cock pulsed with need. Goddess, he was close. Although dragons could perform multiple times for their females, coming all over her the first time she touched him was definitely not how he wanted to start this night off.

Stroking down to the base, she trailed her nails over his balls, then moved her grip up, twisting over the head. How did she know that was just the way he liked it? The pressure, the slow, languid strokes. It was like she was stoking his fire. In fact, he was putting off enough heat to steam the windows.

He reached for her again, wanting to touch her, wanting to make her feel like she was making him feel. But her golden gaze pinned him in place. If she didn't want him to move, he wouldn't move. If she wanted him to crawl across broken glass, he'd happily comply.

She held his gaze and gave him a slow, wicked grin. Then she lowered her head. Goddess, she wasn't thinking of—

All conscious thought left him as she drew him into her mouth and slid her lips to the place where her hand still squeezed the base of his cock. His breath came in ragged pants. She swirled her tongue and sucked hard, slowly rising to the tip.

"Harlow... *Fuck...*" If she heard him, her only acknowledgment was the hot gold of her heavy-lidded stare as her head sank again, drawing him to the back of her throat. Her tongue stroked and swirled, and then that slow, steady suction caused his heart to pound against his ribs. His hips thrust forward of their own accord, and he forced them down into the seat. He didn't want to hurt her. Didn't want to fuck her mouth before he'd even made love to her.

But she grabbed his hips and buried her face in his groin. He was so close to coming he could feel his bones throb with need. He watched her work between his legs, unable to look away as her head bobbed faster and the pleasure became a burning ache. Her velvet mouth drew him closer, his balls tightening.

And then she spread her wings.

One look at the smooth golden flesh and he was reduced to nothing but throbbing desire. He pitched over the edge, his orgasm powering through him. She sucked him in deeper as he came, her throat convulsing as she swallowed what he gave her. A growl tore from his chest along with a deep rattle that could only be his mating trill. He wondered if she heard it as she licked the last bit of come from the tip of his cock and smiled up at him with a look that was pure Harlow and could only be interpreted as *I own you*.

She prowled up his body and kissed him on the lips. "Okay, now you can turn the carriage around and take me home."

His mouth dropped open. "You want to go home? Now?" The words sounded gritty, and he hated every syllable. The carriage rolled to a stop. She placed her hands on either side of his face and kissed him again.

"Hades no." She laughed. "Not even a little bit." Her eyes flashed the same color as her wings in the dark interior, and Marius was hard again in an instant. A thump indicated the driver had jumped down. He lifted her off him and set her down in the seat before fixing his fly and positioning himself across from her a fraction of a second before the door opened.

"We've arrived, sir." The driver stood at attention. Marius had to hand it to Harlow; she looked positively innocent as she smiled sweetly and stepped down onto the drive. No one would have ever guessed his cock was in her mouth just moments ago. And he was harder than obsidian just thinking about it.

He held his jacket in front of his waist, took her hand, and practically ran for the door.

She giggled beside him as he whisked her through the dark halls and into his chambers, closing and locking the door behind him. He did not need Charlie or anyone else wandering in tonight.

Harlow's laugh filled the room as she took a few running steps inside, but ended abruptly with a sharp intake of breath. He watched her step out onto the balcony and stare, open-mouthed, at Ouros's two moons—almost full tonight—surrounded by thousands of twinkling stars.

"The stars..." She shook her head, eyes brimming. "I'd forgotten how bright they are on the mountain. Is it always open like this? What do you do when it rains?"

"It's spelled to keep out the elements." He placed his hands on her waist and tucked himself between her wings to nuzzle her neck. A deep sigh left her lips, and she softened against him, but her eyes stayed locked on the sky.

"In the Swilton district, the streetlights never go out and the homes are built so close together, at most you see a sliver of the sky. I used to spend hours staring at the sky when we lived in Firedrake. I'm not sure when it happened, but after we moved, at some point I just stopped looking up."

Every muscle in Marius's body tightened. He hated the thought of Harlow living where she did. Hated the idea that her soul had been slowly crushed by her circumstances. Life wasn't fair. He knew that better than anyone. Only, Harlow deserved better. He wanted to give her everything.

He released her and strode into his chambers, finding the oversized settee he liked to lounge on in his salon. He picked up one end of it and started dragging it toward the balcony.

"What are you doing?" she asked as the scrape of the legs on the stone reverberated through the room.

He positioned the settee where she'd have the best view of the stars. "Sit."

The smile she rewarded him with was pure gold.

"Tea?"

"Love some."

He poured two cups of boiling water from the special tap in his kitchenette that drew the liquid from deep within the hot belly of the volcano and added the best tea blend he owned. It was a special brew, a gift from Rogos. The finest in Ouros, or so he was told. He'd never had occasion to use it before. He put it all on a tray with some cream and sugar and carried it out to her.

She'd curled one leg and leaned back against the armrest. Just as he'd hoped. Now she wouldn't have to strain her neck.

He slid the tray beside her and took a seat on the other side of it.

Her gaze flicked down to his. "You're unexpectedly sweet."

He grunted. The next look he gave her was anything but sweet. Her cheeks reddened.

"Okay. Maybe not sweet. Maybe... patient."

He winked at her.

She fixed her tea and then, to his surprise, fixed his for him just the way he liked it. "I watched you do this once, when I was a girl at a society event. Two sugars and a splash of cream. Did I get it right, or have your tastes changed over the years?"

"It's right." His heart swelled at the gesture. It meant she'd seen him. Noticed him. Remembered him. He lifted the cup and took a sip, never taking his eyes off her. The tea was good, but he was far more interested in continuing where they'd left off. He returned the cup to the tray and watched as she drained most of her cup.

She tipped her head back again to stare at the sky. "I'd never tire of this view. I'd move the bed out here if I were you."

"Good idea. Do you want me to move it now?"

She grinned wickedly. "No. This is fine... for now."

Funny, he wasn't remotely fine, but he was about to be. Rising, he stalked around the edge of the tray until he was standing before her, knee to knee. His gaze locked on her full, rose-colored lips, warm and plump from the tea. He pictured how those lips had looked stretched around his cock. Leaning over her, he caught himself on the settee, arms braced on either side of her head. The cup in her hands rattled against the saucer. The stars above reflected in her gold eyes as she carefully set what remained of the tea on the tray.

Unable to wait a moment more, he captured her mouth with his. There was no resistance this time. No game of control. Her lips were nothing but soft acceptance and welcome heat. She opened for him, and he tasted her, his tongue stroking, exploring. He was hard again. Ready. Aching.

He started gathering the fabric of her skirt, working his hand beneath the hem until his fingers met the firm silk of her inner knee. He stroked toward her center. Warm, wet heat waited for him at the apex of her thighs. Her undergarments were soaked. He slipped his fingers under them and delighted at the gasp she gave when he found what pleased her.

His mating trill rumbled in his chest again, too loud to miss. Too intense to hide.

He drew back to look at her. He had to know if this was okay. Flirting with a mating bond was dangerous. They had to both understand what they were getting into.

She placed her hand on the center of his chest and surely felt the rumble there. Her lids lowered. "I'm sorry, but this is never going to work."

CHAPTER TWENTY-ONE

Marius's pained reaction made Harlow regret her choice of words immediately. He pulled away as if she'd punched him. Smiling, she caught his face in her hands. "What I mean is, it's never going to work around this dress. It's too bulky, and you feel way too good to have it between us." Quickly, she stood and reached for the neckline.

She unbuttoned her top slowly, then unfastened the clasp holding her skirt. The fabric pooled around her ankles. Females of her species traditionally wore a one-piece undergarment under their dresses. She slid the straps off her shoulders and peeled the fitted fabric from her body. Totally naked now, she locked eyes with him as she kicked the pile aside, almost tripping over the garment. He didn't seem daunted by the ungraceful display.

Marius's hungry gaze raked over her, his mating trill a deafening hum in her ears. Pure male need turned the corners of his mouth, and he stalked toward her again like the predator he was. When he kissed her this time, it wasn't gentle. He grabbed her waist and crushed her to him, claiming her mouth in a way that stole her breath.

He kissed her like the king he almost was and the man who was so much better. He kissed her with all the heat of Hades and the power of heaven. This kiss was honey-coated promises and silken daggers. She absorbed it all, all the passion and the fear. She needed him closer. Every inch of him.

Desperately, she tore at his shirt, only satisfied when he shrugged it off and the tips of her breasts finally skimmed his bare, tattooed chest. While her mouth worked, she grazed his wings with her nails, stroked the mounded muscles of his shoulders, and traced the deep groove of his collarbone. And when she worked his breeches over his hips and he was finally naked in her arms, her exploration of his physique could only come to one conclusion: the man was a god.

A high-pitched warble started in her own chest. It was a sound she'd never heard before, and it startled her. Was that her mating trill? It was different from his. Lighter. Silvery.

He broke from the kiss and looked at her like she was the reason the moons hung in the sky. There was no hiding the sound, and they both knew what it meant. For a moment, he lowered his chin and closed his eyes, just listening. When he opened them again, the smile on his face was equal parts wicked and possessive.

With one powerful beat of his wings, she was back on the settee. The tray clattered to the stone floor, and he stretched her out on the blue velvet, stroked her hair back as he gave her one long, unhurried kiss. He tilted her chin up. "Watch the stars."

She obeyed, losing herself in the purple velvet night and the smattering of light above her. The diversion of her gaze only served to make her skin hypersensitive, her body wishing to feel what she couldn't see. Hot breath traveled along her neck, between her collarbones. A kiss landed between her breasts, then on her navel. *Fuck*, she was a raw tangle of nerves. Her core throbbed as he kissed his way closer to her center. She glanced down, and he stopped abruptly and pointed at the stars. She snapped her gaze back to the heavens.

And his tongue lapped up her folds.

The feeling was so intense she nearly came. Electric sparks ignited in her blood. His tongue dipped into her and flicked over her most sensitive flesh, the vibration from his trill buzzing against her, drawing her out. The stars grew brighter. Her hands clawed into the velvet chaise as his mouth swirled and sucked. All at once, the stars seemed to rain down around her. A howl escaped her throat as she pitched over the edge. For a moment, she was soaring, glowing brighter than the moons. Her back arched off the settee as pleasure rolled through her body, sending her inner dragon into a frenzy.

She'd just started her descent when he entered her. Her body convulsed around the invasion. He was thick, massive. In one perfectly slick thrust, he buried himself in her, stretching her to the limit. All the air left her lungs. The sheer intensity threatened to throw her over the edge again.

Slowly, steadily, he began to move, the even rhythm teasing her higher until her need to come made even the feel of her hair against the velvet sweet torture. She tried to speed the pace, but he grabbed her hips and ground into her.

"More." She wrapped her legs around his hips and dug her fingers into his ass. "*Mine!*"

His fingers tangled in her hair, supporting his weight on

his elbows as their gazes locked. The full weight of what she'd said settled between them. She hadn't planned to do it. But here, under him, she couldn't fight nature. Her dragon wanted him. Wanted him desperately with a wanton hunger she couldn't control. She'd claimed him as her mate. As foolish and crazy as it was.

"*Mine!*" The growl of possession that ripped from his throat left no room for misunderstanding. It was done.

He quickened his pace, sweat gathering at the base of his neck. She licked her way to his ear and bit gently. That earned her a barrage of quick, hard thrusts. The legs on the chaise gave out, and they crashed to the floor. He didn't quit. His wings hooked into hers, just as they had that first day she'd fought him in the pits. The tug against her wings ignited the same inner violence. The same luscious edge. A hair split between pleasure and pain. He thrust harder, faster.

She cried out and soared into the stars again. He followed her into oblivion, his body shuddering over her. She couldn't get enough. She pulled him closer, deeper. Her body milked his, her desire demanding, squeezing every ounce of pleasure from the moment. Time became meaningless. There was only this tangle of limbs, this endless indulgence.

A long while later, she lay tucked into his chest, under the shelter of his wing. Her thighs were coated with him. The air was thick with their mingled smoky scents. By the Mountain, she'd never experienced anything like that before. She wasn't a virgin before tonight, but she might as well have been. Nothing in the world could compare to this.

Their gazes locked.

"I think we broke your sofa," she whispered.

He chuckled. "More where this one came from."

She stroked her nails gently over his ear. In the shelter of her arms, he closed those haunting silver eyes and slept.

HARLOW WOKE FROM A DEEP SLEEP, UNABLE TO breathe. Someone was choking her. She opened her eyes but couldn't understand what she was seeing. Marius was over her, his hands wrapped around her throat. She grabbed his wrists and dug her nails into his skin. Spots swam in her vision. He was strangling her! Hurting her! Why was he doing this?

His eyes were open, but it was like he couldn't see her. Was he... doing this in his sleep? She tried to make sense of it while pain needled her throat and lack of oxygen addled her brain. A symbol on his chest blinked and rippled in the dim room. Or was that her mind playing tricks on her?

Survival instinct finally kicked in just as darkness nipped at the corners of her vision. She threaded her arms between his and punched him in the throat with everything she had, while at the same time digging the talon of her wing into his shoulder.

She gasped as his grip loosened. Above her, he blinked with such confusion on his face she'd feel sorry for him if she weren't so busy trying to fill her lungs with air. He staggered off her, onto his feet, tearing his shoulder free of her talon. Blood sprayed across her chest, her face. She blinked against it, her breath whistling.

"Harlow!" He choked back sobs. "Oh my goddess, what have I done?" He held up both hands, palms toward her.

She tried to answer him but couldn't form words. Her throat would produce nothing but a raspy squeak. He raced from the room and screamed at someone in the hall.

Pounding feet retreated into the distance. The sound seemed far away. And then everything went dark.

HARLOW WASN'T SURE HOW LONG SHE WAS unconscious, but she woke to the concerned face of a woman with dark skin and soulful eyes leaning over her. The woman had unusual features, similar to an elf's but with rounded ears. A long black braid dangled over one of her shoulders.

Behind the woman, a bright light glared in Harlow's eyes. Where was she? Where was Marius? She squinted against the blinding brightness. The dark-haired woman removed a cold towel from Harlow's neck and adjusted a sheet that was covering her body. "Can you speak?"

"Who are you?" Harlow rasped.

"Praise the Mountain," she heard Marius say.

Harlow searched the room for him, but he must have been standing out of her line of sight.

The dark woman squeezed her hand. "I am Maiara, palace healer. You are in the infirmary. There's been an... accident. Do you remember?"

She nodded, her eyes roving again to try to find Marius. She could feel him there. A dark stain of pain and regret hovered somewhere near the right corner of the room.

"Marius—"

"He's here. You are safe now." The one called Maiara gently patted her shoulder. Did she mean to comfort her with his presence or from it?

"I want to see him. Please," she said firmly.

Maiara frowned and glanced toward the corner. "Perhaps it would be best if you rest."

Harlow tipped her head back and twisted, looking for him. Her neck muscles were still tight, and the position was terribly uncomfortable. "Marius, come here—now!" she commanded.

Footsteps neared her bed. The man who came into view was Marius but wasn't. His eyes were red and bloodshot like he'd been weeping, and his complexion was as pale as she'd ever seen it. He was shirtless but wearing a loose-fitting pair of athletic breeches. His white hair was a mess, and his expression... He looked like a dragon on his way to a guillotine.

Harlow made eye contact with Maiara. "Can we have the room, please? I'd like to speak with my mate. Alone."

Maiara's eyes widened, then darted to Marius. With a curt nod, she rose and left the infirmary.

She held out her hand to him. "What happened?"

He snorted and shook his head in disgust. "I tried to kill you in my sleep. You should go, Harlow. I'm dangerous. I could hurt you."

She took his hand and pulled him closer. "I'm fine, and I'm not going anywhere. Have you forgotten already what happened in that room last night?"

A tortured expression compressed his features. "I'll never forget. It was the single best day of my existence."

She swallowed the lump that formed in her throat. "We're mated. It's not what I expected, but it happened, and I'm not going anywhere until we figure this out." When he looked away, she tugged on his hand. "You aren't responsible for what you did in your sleep. Has this happened before? You looked terrified."

He swallowed. "Not in weeks, but yes." His eyes shifted as if he couldn't bear to look directly at her. "They stopped when I started training with you. I don't know what triggered this one."

She perused his face. "From the first day I talked to you at the coronation, I sensed you carried ghosts of the past. You've been dead, for Mountain's sake. The tattoos themselves are a mystery. I knew they signified something dark. And you mentioned the nightmares that first night you walked me home. I knew you had secrets... I just didn't think those secrets would lead to you trying to choke me in my sleep." She chuckled softly, trying her best to quell the torture he was clearly in.

Instead of being comforted, he looked as if she'd kicked him in the gut. "I'm so sorry, Harlow. I never thought this would be an issue. I haven't experienced a nightmare in weeks. And the queen is close to a solution. She thinks she can cure me."

"Cure you of the nightmares?"

He nodded. "And... seeing the dead."

She raised an eyebrow, a chill climbing her spine. "You see the dead too?"

His silver gaze dropped to the floor. "Sometimes."

"What were you dreaming about... when you choked me?"

He tipped his head and cracked his neck. The place she'd stabbed him with her talon was healed but still scarred pink. She must have driven it deep.

He stared, unfocused, at the wall as he spoke. "There's this place I remember from before where creatures chased us. Hunters. They're monsters—all bones and sinew, teeth and talons. I can't shift in that place, and in that world, it's always dark and the creatures never sleep. In my dreams, we have to make it to the temple. The temple is the only way out. So we run and we fight. I... I thought you were one of them."

She studied him and was surprised to find emotions radiating down their bond. She'd never known this connection with another dragon. Everything he felt, she was experiencing it with him. "This was more than a dream. It was a memory. You go back there in your mind, don't you?"

He nodded.

"Mountain, I'm lucky you didn't take my head off."

He slumped in on himself, and Harlow thought she'd never seen a dragon look so distraught. This had destroyed him. It was a gaping wound he'd never intended to let her see, let alone experience. Harlow refused to lose him to shame or anything else. But somehow they needed to fix this.

"When you were choking me, this symbol on your chest was moving." She pressed her fingers to a U-shaped symbol bisected by a squiggle. "What does it mean?"

He sighed heavily and brought her hand to his lips. "I don't know for sure, but Raven believes each of these symbols represents a level of the underworld."

Her breath hitched. "Each one is a place you've been?"

He nodded. She clutched his hand, and silence stretched between them. Finally, when she couldn't bear the tension in the room a moment longer, she asked, "Where does that leave us? How do we get beyond this?"

Pain clouded his eyes as he said, "Until I figure this out, you need to sleep away from me. If I hurt you again, it would destroy me, Harlow. Do you understand?"

She nodded. "You need time."

He squeezed her hand and kissed her on the forehead. "I need time."

CHAPTER TWENTY-TWO

"Try to relax, Marius," Queen Raven said. "Your energy is throwing me off."

Marius sank back in his chair and crossed his arms. No one disrespected the queen, but fuck if it was possible for him to relax. It just wasn't going to happen. "I could have killed her, Raven."

The dark-haired witch paced around the symbol at the center of her white ritual room, analyzing the thirteen dimensions of the underworld floating before her. "But you didn't," she said absently. "And frankly, I doubt Harlow would have let you. She's not exactly a fragile flower. Maiara told me the wound she inflicted on your shoulder went clear to the bone."

He grunted. He'd never expected to take Harlow as his mate. Finding a mate was the last thing on his to-do list. What had happened between them was all instinct. It was dragon nature. He couldn't have stopped it if he tried, and now he'd have to live with the consequences. "How do we stop the nightmares from happening again?"

Raven paused before one of the levels in her multidimensional model of Hades. "This is the dimension that correlates to the symbol Harlow said lit up on your chest when you were choking her. I'm going to open a window to it, but I won't be able to hold it for long. This dimension is the furthest from us."

He nodded. If it was the place he'd seen in his dreams, he'd know.

She moved her arms as she had before, whispered the incantation, and pulled her fingers apart. His nightmare opened before him. Dark jungle. Clawed beasts. Sky raining fire. She released, and the window closed with a snap.

"That was it." He nodded.

"Are you sure?"

He shot her a look. "You don't forget a place like that."

Raven paced the length of the room, rubbing her palms together in slow circles. "The thirteen symbols on your torso represent the thirteen dimensions of the underworld. We know that for sure. We even know which symbol represents which dimension."

He grunted. A lot of good that did him. What did the dimension matter when he was at risk of strangling his new mate?

The queen flung her arms down at her sides. "We know what, but we don't know why. I think the why of it is the key to making it stop."

"Seems reasonable." He rubbed his forehead. It was midmorning, and he already needed a drink or a fight. "Any idea how we figure that one out?"

"Tell me again about what happens in these dreams." She took a seat in a white leather chair beside him. He knew she had more important things to do. She was the queen after all. But as long as she was here, he was going to accept her help. He needed it.

"It's always the same." He rubbed his palms on his thighs. He hated words. How could he accurately describe what he was experiencing? Words didn't do it justice. "We have to get to the temple, and I have to lead them. And those things, the hunters, they're trying to kill us."

"What happens if they kill you?"

He didn't know, did he? He concentrated. Closed his eyes and tried to put himself back there. The sizzle of fire scorching earth. The roar of the beasts in the dark jungle. If they were caught... If they were killed... His stomach twisted, and he ran a hand over the symbols. There were thirteen and they repeated but some more frequently than others. The U-shaped symbol repeated the least.

His eyes popped open, and he focused on her. "If you get killed, you have to start back at the beginning."

Raven went absolutely still. "Goddess, that's it!" She stood and paced around the symbol again. "That devious bitch!"

"Who are we talking about?"

"Eleanor! Your wicked mother." Raven turned the emerald ring on her finger. "When I brought Gabriel back from the dead, he hadn't been gone long. He described the place where he was and that he had a strong feeling that had he wanted to, he could have moved on for good. Our bond is what held him to that place, and when I brought him back, I did it using his own magic. I'd had his tooth, and I'd absorbed dragon magic right before he died. It was my blood that brought him back."

"Do you think that's why he doesn't have a symbol in his skin?"

She nodded. "I think there's more to it than that." She

pointed at the first dimension in the stack. "When Avery died, she saw the same thing that Gabriel did. Bright, warm light. It's the hallmark of the dimension represented by the spiral, the symbol tattooed on her arm. I used Charlie's blood to bring her back. The same blood I used on you."

"So it is Charlie's blood that causes the symbols?"

Raven shook her head. "No. Not directly. Marius, we've established your skin is a stamped passport. Those symbols designate every time you passed from one dimension to the next. I think Gabriel doesn't have one because the stubborn bastard never actually moved on. Our bond was so strong, so magically tight, his soul never passed into that next dimension. And we were on Earth when he died, so our position with the underworld was different." She sighed. "But you and Avery both died here. She can't take Xavier's tooth, so while they are mated, she doesn't have the same magical link to him as I have to Gabriel. Her soul passed into this first dimension. We pulled her back."

"The spiral." Marius's eyes narrowed. They were on the edge of something. He could see Raven working it out in her head. "If she'd moved on to the next dimension, she'd have had two symbols when you pulled her back."

Raven shook her head. "I don't think so."

"Hmm?"

"I think normally a soul sees one dimension. Which of the thirteen you visit likely depends on the circumstances of your death. Normally that first stop is a place for the soul to find its peace before it passes, permanently, into the beyond —that place we all go when we die. Under normal circum- stances, a soul would never see a second dimension."

"But I didn't move on."

"You couldn't. Eleanor bound your soul to your physical heart, and she kept control of it. Your soul kept trying to move on. That's why you needed to find the temple. I think it was a metaphor for transcending. Don't you see, Marius? You were trying to free yourself from purgatory by finding the temple and moving on, but because of Eleanor's spell, you couldn't. For three hundred years, you fought your way through dimension after dimension, trying to get out, and there was nowhere to go but to start over."

A chill ran the length of his spine. He knew she was right. It made sense now. He ran a hand down his chest. "Why won't they leave me alone?"

Raven's lips pressed together, and she stared at him, concentrating. "When you told me about trying to reach the temple, you said you had to lead *them*. Who is them?"

He was sure he'd told Raven this before. Then again, maybe not the specifics. "Killian and Brynhoff. I never knew if it was them or just a mental construct of them, but Killian has appeared to me— Why are you looking at me like that?"

Raven had paled. She looked like she'd seen a ghost. "They're still trapped."

"Hmm?"

"Eleanor did the same thing to Killian and Brynhoff as she did to you."

"But she's dead. The spell should be broken. Wouldn't they have moved on by now?"

Raven shook her head. "A dragon's heart is a self-contained power. I pulled the golden grimoire out of Tavyss's heart long after his death and the death of the witch, Medea, who put it there. Marius, I think the reason for your nightmares is that your father and your uncle are still trapped within these dimensions and they're using their connection to you to ask for your help."

"How? Why?"

"You said you were their leader. Now you're gone. They still need you. You must have formed a bond over your time together."

"Where are their hearts? Can you bring them back as you did me?"

Raven frowned and shook her head. "Resurrection after being dead so long is not a good idea. That type of blood magic has a price. You must understand that what happened with you was a side effect of us using your heart to resurrect the goddess. We never intended to bring you back as well. We never knew we could."

He buried his face in his hands. Resurrection had a price. His was an accident, but he was pretty sure he was paying the dues anyway.

"That doesn't mean there's nothing we can do. If I can find their hearts, I can break the spells on them and allow their souls to move on. That should break the connection between you and them and end your nightmares."

"What do you mean, *if?*"

"Eleanor's ritual room was destroyed when the volcano erupted during the revolution. We rebuilt the palace on top of it. As far as I know, Brynhoff's and Killian's hearts are buried under tons of rock and debris, somewhere inside the mountain."

He stared at her, disbelieving what he was hearing. His eyes stung, and frustration caused his talons to sprout from his knuckles. "How?"

"How do we get to them? I'm not sure," Raven said softly, her gaze falling on the sharp points in his partially shifted hands. "I need to talk with Nathaniel. But I will find a way, Marius," she added sincerely. "I'm not going to let you suffer. If we have to tear out the walls, we'll do it."

He released a blustery sigh. Not ideal. It would take more time. But it was more than he'd hoped for.

CHAPTER TWENTY-THREE

"Thank the goddess! Where have you been? Your father and I were worried sick!" Lemetria charged toward Harlow the moment she walked through the door and pulled her into her arms.

"Out, Mom. I'm sorry I didn't send a falcon. The night... got away from me." Harlow slumped into the kitchen chair. She needed a bath and some time to think.

"We feared something horrible had happened to you. Between what happened with Adradys and our debts—" Lemetria sniffed the air, her brows knitting together. "What is that... scent? You smell like..." She cocked her head to the side, her mouth dropping open by degrees. "Is that your mating scent?"

"And his."

"Not Adradys?" she asked incredulously. Of course she'd assume that. She wasn't aware Harlow had any other suitors.

"Never."

"Then who?"

Harlow coupled her hands under her chin. "You can't tell anyone. Not anyone."

"Why not? If you're mated, why wouldn't we be screaming it from the rooftops?" Her face fell. "He's not already married, is he? Not... Brantley!"

"No and no."

"Then who?" She slid into the chair across the rickety table from her.

"Where's Dad? If I tell one of you, I should tell both of you."

"The pits, trying to win us money enough for dinner. He won't be home for hours. You'll have to settle for telling me." Lemetria held perfectly still and stared intently at her. She loved that her mother was excited for her but wondered if she was repeating *Please let him be rich* over and over again in her head.

Harlow sighed through a smile. In truth, she could hardly keep it to herself. She loved him, truly loved him. He'd said he needed time. All they had was time. A mating bond was eternal. She was sure down to her bones that he'd fix this and they'd be together eventually. If she didn't tell someone, she was going to pop. "Marius."

Her mother's grin faded, and her nose wrinkled. "Which Marius?"

Harlow pointed in the general direction of the palace. "*The* Marius, Mom. Former heir apparent."

"Oh my goddess. Oh my goddess!" Her mother's hands flew to her mouth. "How? When did you even meet?"

Fuck. She'd never told her mother about what happened with Marius. Harlow gave her a sheepish smile. "I've been coaching him in pit fighting for the past cycle. He's where I got the money from to help with the bills. Most of it anyway. Some I won in the pits."

Her mother reached across the table and squeezed her shoulders. "And to think we thought you'd settle on Adradys. You're going to be a royal! A princess!"

"He's not exactly a prince anymore, Mom. When he stepped aside to make room for Gabriel to become king, he renounced the title. He's an ambassador."

She waved a hand through the air. "Pish... Same difference." She clapped her hands together. "When can we meet him? Have you started thinking about the wedding?"

She shook her head. "Let's take it slow. This isn't something either of us expected."

"What do you mean?"

"I mean it snuck up on us, that's all. We were friends first. Let's just get our bearings before we start planning the royal event of the season." Harlow said it sarcastically, but the look on her mother's face suggested she'd already picked out a wedding dress in her head and was picturing Harlow striding along an imaginary runner toward the altar.

"But I don't understand. If you're mated, why wouldn't he want you there now? Mated couples never want to spend time apart."

By the Mountain, Lemetria was a dog with a bone.

"Marius has some things he needs to take care of. We're going to give it time."

Now her mother's face grew worried. "That dragon always did seem a little strange."

"He's not strange. He's perfect. I'm perfect. We're perfect. And you just have to keep your mouth shut about it until we can adjust to this. It was very unexpected."

Her mom shrugged. "Fine. Although it's going to kill me, you know that."

"I'm going to go take a bath." Harlow stood.

"Oh, I suppose you'll want to turn down the offer from the Silver Sunset, then."

"What offer?"

Her mother stood and retrieved a small roll of parchment from the kitchen. "This came for you by falcon last night."

Harlow unrolled the tiny scroll. *The Silver Sunset thanks you for your application and would like to offer you the job of server. Please stop in for your schedule and to discuss pay.*

"Great news! I'll stop over there as soon as I'm bathed and dressed."

"But—" Her mother gaped as if she wasn't sure what to say. "Surely you're not going to work as a server when you're mated to Marius."

"Yes. Yes, I am. Until something else comes along, I need the job, and until Marius marries me, we need the money. I'm not going to use our mating as my own personal piggy bank. I'm going to work."

"But—"

"Mom, it's going to be okay. Besides, this is the first offer any of us has gotten. I have to take it. After someone blacklisted us, showing people we're good employees is the only way to rebuild trust in the community."

Her mom draped an arm over the back of her chair. "You know, there is one thing I can say about you, my girl."

"What's that?"

"You never take the easy way out."

"Never."

Hours later, Harlow found herself at the Silver Sunset with an apron tied around her waist, trying her best to keep up with the dinner crowd. She'd come in as directed. Not only was she hired on the spot, but she was given an immediate shift. Thankfully, she was a fast learner. And her natural hustle had paid off. Her pockets were full of tips. Her being female and cute might have had something to do with it. In any case, she'd have plenty of money to keep her parents afloat while she worked out what was going on with Marius.

Once the dinner rush had cleared out, Roosevelt asked her to wipe down the tables in the mostly empty bar. It was while she was doing so that she came across a flyer.

Tired of laws that benefit every kingdom but Paragon? Want things to return to the way they were before the revolution? The New Order is working for you. If you're an interested party, make it known. History is on our side. We'll find you.

Roosevelt came up behind her and tore it from her hands. "Another one! Mountain help us, these assholes just won't quit."

She shook her head. "Who would want to return to how it was under Eleanor?"

He looked at her strangely. "Honey, until you started working here, I assumed your parents were behind this."

"What? We would never!"

"Oh, I believe you. No one of your previous station would work as hard as you if they thought they could go back to how it used to be. But your mom, she was always in here..."

"My mom doesn't want this either. Believe me. It's not her. She's not smart enough." It was out of her mouth before she could think to correct herself. Her mother was smart, but not in the organized, devious way it would take to run something like this.

Roosevelt laughed. "Maybe."

"What do you want me to do with it?"

"Toss it out. Whoever is doing this doesn't know who they're dealing with. The good witch who sits on that throne is more powerful than she lets on, and the dragon who sits beside her is no fool. They've won the hearts of the majority. Whoever is behind this would be wise to simmer down before they boil over and fizzle out." He raised his brows and turned to stroll back to the bar.

Harlow glanced down at the paper. Frowning, she looked over both shoulders, folded the flyer, and put it in her pocket. She wanted to talk to her father about whether he knew anything about it and then share what she'd learned with Marius. He needed to know there was a group gunning for the throne.

Once the tables were cleaned and the last patron walked out the door, she said her goodbyes to Roosevelt and started for home. Night had fallen over Paragon. She smiled at the memory of watching the stars while Marius sent her soaring into them. Goddess, she couldn't wait until he was over this bump. It was all she could do not to run toward the palace and beg to be in his arms again.

"There's a lesson in the past. What's happened before can happen again." A stranger stepped from the shadows and waited in a patch of moonlight. The deep hood the person wore hid their face, but the voice was undeniably male. Not one she recognized. The hood inclined toward her pocket.

Eyes narrowing, Harlow remembered the flyer. *We'll find you*, it had said.

"History is on our side," the man beneath the hood said.

"Who are you?" Her voice held an edge that she hadn't meant it to. She saw the moment the man went on the defensive. He backed up a step. "Wait!" She reached for him, her fingers digging into the cloak. "When are you meeting next? Where?"

He yanked his arm away from her. And then he was gone.

CHAPTER TWENTY-FOUR

Raven wasn't above asking for help, and when it came to obscure magic, the smartest wizard she knew was Nathaniel. The dragon had studied both human and dragon magic for longer than she'd been alive, and his mate was her sister, a powerful witch herself. Although Clarissa was finishing a project in Everfield, Nathaniel, thankfully, was able to give the problem his full attention.

With Charlie by her side, Raven showed him her model of the thirteen dimensions and explained about Brynhoff and Killian. "We think they're stuck in a perpetual loop, fighting their way through dimension after dimension."

Nathaniel gestured at the model. "Imprisoned in the underworld."

Raven nodded. "Exactly. These levels are not where souls go to rest. Eleanor locked them into a purgatory meant to be temporary."

"Mother kept them from moving on. It's brilliant magic and also incredibly cruel. Her trademark. I presume you want to free them so they can rest."

"The problem is that Brynhoff's and Killian's souls are bound to their hearts by magic. Those hearts were buried with Eleanor's ritual room. Do you have a spell capable of retrieving them without bringing down the castle?"

Raven was distracted by Charlie hopping by her, pretending to be a rabbit. She usually didn't allow her daughter in here, but the girl had been clingy today. For some reason, even Gabriel wasn't enough to placate her. She didn't feel well and wanted her mother. Raven didn't have the heart to send her away. Besides, in the past when Charlie'd felt this way, she'd either experienced a growth spurt or some new magical ability. It was best to keep her close.

Nathaniel stared at her model of the thirteen underworld dimensions. He brought his pipe to his lips and lit up. The magic smoke circled his head, bending and twisting with his concentration. "I suppose you've tried a simple retrieval spell?"

"Multiple times. Multiple ways. The problem is a dragon's heart is a jewel, and this mountain is full of jewels, each with a similar magical signature. Yes, these two have souls, but the mountain itself has a similar magical signature because of the presence of the goddess. It's like trying to find two grains of rice buried somewhere on a beach full of sand."

The palace magician straightened the lapels of his suit and took another puff on his pipe. Raven found it charming that Gabriel's younger brother had returned to wearing human apparel. Once he'd retrieved his oreads from Mistwood Manor, he'd gone back to formal suits and ties. Although the look wasn't popular in Paragon, it went with his personality. Besides, what court magician dressed like everyone else?

He blew out another puff of smoke, the tendrils bending in on themselves and flipping over in the air in front of him. With delight, Raven realized he was using the smoke to analyze the problem. The beauty of the twining tendrils made her smile. Charlie was enjoying it too, staring at the show as if he were bending balloon animals for her amusement.

"Together, we might be able to pinpoint the souls," he said. "With enough power and the right symbols. The problem I see is retrieving them. It's one thing to float a couple of objects across the room. An entirely different one to pull them through tons of solid rock."

"Exactly." Raven tugged at her long black braid. "We could locate them and then use a different spell to blast through the stone to physically get to them."

He sighed. "Thought of that. If we do it, we'll have to evacuate the palace. There's the risk that we could cause a collapse or a landslide."

She ran a hand through her hair. "Not a good time for that, Nathaniel."

"There's never a good time for this type of spell. But it may be the only way to get them back."

"No. You don't understand. The palace is warded against malevolence. It's safe here, for all of us." She glanced down at Charlie but thought of her sister Avery. The wards on the palace were keeping all of them safe.

"Surely we could find another, temporary location—"

"There's a group called the New Order that has become a growing threat. We've received malicious messages at the gate. Enchanted messages that appear from thin air."

"They have a witch working with them?"

"It appears so. And they've painted a bull's-eye on all of us." She stared out the windows to the forest beyond and folded her arms. The last one had threatened her personally, although her own health and safety were the least of her worries.

"Have you talked to Queen Penelope about this?"

"I have. She's not involved. She allowed me access to her mind to prove it. We've become friends, Nathaniel. I know it's not her." Raven prided herself on the positive relationship she'd built with Darnuith and wasn't above asking Penelope for help if she needed it.

"Hmm. It's a problem and a risk." His smoke tangled into a knot and sank back into his pipe.

"I keep kicking myself," Raven said. "If only I'd thought to take the other hearts when I took Marius's, while Eleanor's ritual room was still standing." Charlie tugged at her skirt, and Raven pulled her into her arms.

Nathaniel snorted. "Even the most powerful witch can't go back in time, Raven. You can't beat yourself up."

She shook her head. "You didn't see Marius's face. He almost strangled his mate, Nathaniel. Think about if something like this were keeping you from Clarissa. He's tortured. I've never seen such pain. He's vowed to stay away from her until we fix this."

Charlie squirmed in Raven's arms, and she let her down again. The girl couldn't stop fidgeting. Raven needed to get her outside. Maybe she needed exercise.

Nathaniel scoffed. "How can he tolerate it? Once I was mated to Clarissa, I couldn't stand to be apart from her."

Raven pressed a hand over her stomach, remembering what it was like to try to stay apart from Gabriel when she thought she might drain him to death. "You'd find a way if you thought your presence might hurt her."

"True."

"Mommy?" Charlie tugged on her skirt again.

"Just a minute, honey. Uncle Nathaniel and I are almost done talking. Then we'll go play."

Nathaniel sighed. "I still think the best course of action is to evacuate the palace and muscle through it. If your relationship with Queen Penelope is strong, perhaps she can allow safe harbor in Darnuith. She could protect our families while we do what we have to do. It shouldn't take us more than a day or two."

"Mommy, look what I can do." Charlie wriggled at her side.

"Just a minute, honey." Raven reached for her but addressed Nathaniel. "Let me talk to Gabriel about it."

"As you wish." Nathaniel tucked his pipe inside his pocket.

"Mommy!"

"Yes, Charlie!" Raven turned to her daughter, completely exasperated. Charlie was standing at the edge of the symbol, staring at Raven's map of the thirteen dimensions. The spell would keep her out. Only Raven could manipulate the representations inside. Still, she didn't like the way the stars reflected in her daughter's eyes. She looked ready to dive in. "Stay away from there. That's not for you."

Charlie's smile lit up the room. She brushed her platinum curls aside. "But I can do it!"

"Do what, sweetheart?" Nathaniel asked.

Charlie spread her hands, and a window to a fourteenth dimension opened. Time seemed to slow as Raven recognized the scene inside it. It was Eleanor's ritual room. She saw herself with baby Charlie in her arms. Eleanor had Marius's heart in her hand.

"No," Raven said, shaking her head. This shouldn't be possible. She was looking at a scene from the past.

"I'll get the hearts, Mommy!"

"Charlie, noooo!" Raven lunged for her daughter. But she was too late. With a flap of her feathery wings, Charlie was gone.

CHAPTER TWENTY-FIVE

After a night without his mate, Marius wanted to kill someone. Yet another reason he couldn't be with her right now. He was too afraid the next person he'd kill might be her if he wasn't careful. He didn't trust himself. Not until Raven figured out a way to stop his visions and nightmares of the underworld.

Staying away threatened to rip his heart out, though. He'd received a falcon from her that morning with a note that read, *I'll wait as long as it takes or not at all. I'm not afraid of you.*

He'd sent one back that read, *I've waited for you too long to risk losing you.*

He'd never had a way with words. It wasn't enough, but it would have to do. Raven had promised him she'd figure it out. She was meeting with Nathaniel that very moment to search for a way to retrieve Killian's and Brynhoff's hearts and set their souls free. Once the nightmares stopped, he could truly be a mate to Harlow. Not before.

Which left him with an ax to grind and only one place in Paragon to grind it.

"Help you?" the man behind the desk said without looking up.

"I'm here to complete the trials and be ranked for competition." Marius stared down at the top of the dragon's head. It tipped up slowly, and the guy gave him a slow once-over. He leaned back and crossed his arms.

"You sure you want to do that?"

"I said I do."

"No one's going to let you win this time, Marius. In fact, there are plenty of fighters who remember you and would love to see you hurt or dead."

"I'll take my chances."

The man scribbled some notes and handed him the slip of parchment. "Fill this out. What level do you want to try for first?"

"Champion."

The man's brows stretched toward his hairline. "There's a difference between being confident and having a death wish, Marius. Are you sure you don't want to fight a season in advanced? Different rules in that league."

"Champion."

"All right. It's your head. Try to keep it attached to your body."

Marius frowned. Had things changed so much since he'd competed before? "It's illegal to try to sever an opponent's head."

The guy shrugged and narrowed his eyes. "Accidents happen. In the champion league, we let them."

Marius completed the form and handed the parchment back to the man. "Champion."

"Arena B." He pointed vaguely to the left and handed him another parchment with a number on it.

Marius followed the scent of sweat and the sound of

grunts through the underground tunnels to a small, sparsely populated arena.

A stern dragon held out his hand without looking up from his clipboard. "Number."

Marius handed him the parchment.

"We allow observers in champion trials. People like to get a take on the competition before they place bets on future matches. Try not to get blood on anyone in the stands."

Marius grunted.

"Take your place."

His heart beat faster as he entered the ring and scanned the stands. He wanted to see her. Harlow spent time at the pits, had made a living for a year gambling here. She wasn't there. Of course she wasn't. Why would she be? It was the middle of the afternoon. Roosevelt had sent word that he'd hired her at the Silver Sunset. She was probably working.

The thought of her serving other males suddenly made his blood boil. As soon as it was safe, he was going to marry her, and then she would only do the work she *wanted* to do, preferably somewhere like the palace, or really anywhere not frequented by men... ever. Still grumbling, he stepped up to the line.

His competitor strode in from the opposite side of the ring. Fuck, the guy was a chunk of mountain. He stopped at the opposing line. Marius, who was no small male himself, looked up, up, and up to meet his stare.

"Dax," Marius said by way of greeting.

"Marius," the mountain sneered. "They said it was you, but I didn't believe it." He cracked his knuckles.

Marius swallowed. "How many times have you been champion now?"

"Since you died and I didn't have to pretend to lose to

you anymore? Over a hundred. Went pro decades ago. I do this all day, every day." Dax's eyes were cold pits of steel that glowed with the presence of his inner dragon. This guy was a beast.

Marius snorted. "Seems odd they'd require me to beat *you* just to fight in the same league as you, considering your rank."

He smiled with a mouthful of chipped teeth. "I don't often trial new competitors, but when I heard it was you, I just couldn't help myself."

The matchkeeper raised the flag. "On the ready!"

Marius lowered himself into a fighting stance. It was too late to change his mind now. Across from him, Dax lowered himself too, his dark copper wings hulking over his shoulders. His talons were as big as Marius's head.

The flag dropped. "Fight!"

Before Marius could throw his first punch, Dax dropped, grabbed his ankle, and flung him over his head like a rag doll, slamming him into the pebble floor. The crowd went wild. Were they setting off fireworks in Dax's honor? No... No... Those were stars. Marius shook his head.

"Seven... six... five..."

He leaped to his feet, this time keeping some space between them as he healed and tried to think of what to do. Dax laughed. "Come here, little Marius. Let me give you a hug." The dragon opened his arms as the observers laughed. A hug from Dax would mean two broken wings for sure.

What would Harlow do? Dax was bigger, but then, he'd been bigger than Harlow when she'd beaten him. Size wasn't everything.

Mind your balance. Stay on your toes. Use your wings. Stay low. Her voice echoed in his head.

Dax's fist shot out and Marius bent back, slipped to the outside, and yanked the guy's wrist. Dax went rolling out of the ring. A few people clapped. The oversized brute bounded to his feet and crossed back into the ring before the matchkeeper could even start counting.

Marius circled. That's when he noticed the bastard. Adradys sat in the stands in that ridiculous suit of his, next to a man who must be his assistant because he was writing down everything Adradys said. Visions of the doormaker forcing a kiss on Harlow filled his head. Marius narrowed his eyes as fury coursed through his veins.

Dax's fist soared toward his temple. Marius dodged, but the blow nipped his jaw. Sparks exploded behind his eyes. The pain did nothing to distract from the rage welling in Marius. When his mate had rejected that bastard, Adradys had retaliated. He remembered the threats thrown at them as he left with her. And now Adradys smiled as if watching Marius get creamed by Dax would be the best thing to happen to him today. Well, Marius had other plans.

He rushed Dax, fists flying as fast as he could move. Dax blocked every blow, but Marius landed a knee in his side. Hooking the talons of his wings into Dax's, he planted a foot in his opponent's groin and used his wings for leverage. Like a slingshot, he drew back, coupled his two fists between them, and plowed up and under the guy's face. Blood sprayed. Dax tumbled. Pain exploded in his fists.

He unhooked his wings and delivered a kick to Dax's shin before dancing out of reach, shaking out his hands. Nothing broken. They were already healing.

Wiping blood from his face, Dax rebounded, but he was far less steady on his feet. A section of his jaw puckered. Marius realized his blow had broken the bone. That would heal, but it would take time. Which meant he had a window of opportunity to leverage the injury to his advantage.

Dax was fast, even with his above-average size. There was a reason he was ranked as high as he was. What Marius needed was to tempt him to attack before he was ready.

He crouched into a fighting stance, then intentionally shifted his weight ever so slightly to the left. It was easy enough to imitate the limp that had plagued him up until his training with Harlow. *Take the bait.* He willed the other man to attack.

Marius had to suppress a grin as Dax charged. With a flap of his wings, he shot straight up and delivered a kick that focused every ounce of his weight directly on the man's jaw. A sickening crack sounded as his toes jabbed through bone and into soft tissue. Dax went down, cradling the pieces of his face together, and taking Marius's foot with him.

Ooomph. Marius landed flat on his back, all the air exiting his lungs in a rush. *Fuck.* He had to stand for the count. Scrambling to his feet, he balanced as his head swam and pain throbbed in his torso.

"Three, two, one!" The buzzer sounded. The match-keeper, a squat dragon with orange wings, stepped off the platform and attempted to raise Marius's hand, which ended up around the height of his shoulder given the man's lesser stature. "Winner," he declared. He slapped a piece of parchment against his chest. "Congratulations, Marius! You qualify for the champion league!"

Beaming, he'd started to leave the arena when he glanced in Adradys's direction. The man was frowning like someone had pissed in his porridge. More than just disappointment in a pit match dwelt in those eyes. Adradys looked like a man playing chess who'd just realized there was an extra piece on the board he hadn't accounted for. Marius flashed him a shallow but smug smile and bowed contemptuously.

"Get over it, fucker. There's a new player in town, and he's already captured your queen."

CHAPTER TWENTY-SIX

As thankful as Harlow was for the work, time seemed to stop when the Silver Sunset was slow. She leaned against the bar and thought about Marius. How close was he to a solution to his violent nightmares? She wasn't sure she could go another day without seeing him, but she hadn't received a message from him since that morning. She'd thought she could give him time, but her body disagreed. All night she'd tossed and turned, resorting to pleasuring herself to try to find some relief. It only made her want him more.

And when she'd finally drifted into slumber, her dreams were full of him. His crooked smile, the twinkle in his silver eyes, the way his wings flexed when he came. She wanted him on his back. She wanted him chained to the bed. Chains. He couldn't hurt her if he was in them. Maybe if she proposed the idea...

The door opened and there he was. She blinked twice. Was he a daydream? No, still there. She pushed off the bar, her smile widening until her cheeks hurt. And then she was in the air, her legs wrapped around his hips and her arms clinging to his neck. Had she moved to him or the other way around? Oh, what did it matter? He was here and they were kissing. Goddess, she'd missed this.

"Hey!" Roosevelt bellowed from behind the bar. "By the Mountain. This is a public place!"

Marius looked around her shoulder at her boss. "Can I borrow your office? We need to talk."

Roosevelt rubbed the back of his neck. "Talk. Right. You're killing me, Marius! Fine. Go. She's got a fifteen-minute break, but I swear if you break anything, you're paying double."

Marius gave him a nod and a wink and started walking toward the back room. She remained clinging to him like a breastplate.

"You know, you could use your own two feet."

"What fun would that be?" She pressed her forehead to his.

He carried her through the door to the office, his hands gripping her ass, and pressed her back against the wall. Fuck, he was hard. Now that he had leverage, she could feel every inch of him. She squeezed her legs and ground against him.

"Fifteen minutes isn't going to be long enough unless you get in me right now." She nibbled on his mouth. "Is that blood?" She spotted a drop of red on the neck of his tunic.

"It's not mine."

"Oh? Whose is it?"

"I have something to show you."

Reluctantly she slid off him onto her own two feet. He reached inside his jacket. She cursed the space between them but smiled curiously as he handed her a bit of parchment. She unfolded it.

"You made champion level?" She squealed.

He stroked a hand down his chest. "Faced off against Dax."

"Dax? Your trial was against Dax? Mountain, you're lucky to be alive."

He frowned.

"No! Not like that. I have faith in your abilities, but he's a slab of stone, Marius."

That quirky smile flashed again. "And now he's cut down to size."

She grabbed him and kissed him firmly. "I'm so proud of you. You're going to win, you know. I'm going to be mated to the next champion."

"Let's not get ahead of ourselves."

She reached for his breeches and started unfastening the ties. "You're right. Let's celebrate the old-fashioned way." She worked her hands inside his pants and fisted his cock. Velvet over steel. She stroked down to his balls.

His mouth met hers, and he started pulling up her skirt. She almost cried when three firm knocks came on the door, interrupting them.

Marius growled.

"Marius, we've received a falcon from the queen." Roosevelt's voice held a note of panic as it came through the door. "She says it's an emergency. She must see you right away."

"Tell her I'm on my way." He dropped her skirt and started adjusting his breeches.

"She wants you to bring Harlow. Normally I'd make her finish her shift, but it says it's urgent. Royal business..."

Marius straightened his tunic and slanted a serious look in her direction.

"Of course I'll come. Do you think she's found a way to help us?"

He flipped a hand toward the door and gestured with his chin. "Let's hope."

PARAGON'S TWO SUNS WERE BRIGHT RED ON THE horizon and had painted the sky violet and azure behind the sacred mountain when they arrived at the palace. The Master of the Guard himself, Colin, met them at the door, looking shaken as he grasped Marius's shoulder. "You both need to come with me right away."

Harlow tensed. Colin had led the resistance. He'd seen death and destruction and endured having the flesh of his arm burned away when he grabbed an enchanted orb from the bottom of a pool of the goddess's tears. *Nothing* shook this man. Her hopes that they'd been called here on good news melted away.

Briefly her mind went to the flyer she'd taken from the Silver Sunset and the strange man she'd encountered. Was this about her? Did they think she was part of the New Order? No, if that were the case, she'd probably be in cuffs right now. This was something else. Something worse.

They were led into the king and queen's quarters, foreboding prickling her skin as they navigated to a room in the back. The door opened, and they were surrounded by white marble and shelves of magical accoutrements. At the center of the round room was a symbol, above which floated a model of the universe sliced into fourteen sections. The queen was on her knees in front of the symbol, eyes red and her face carved with tears. The king crouched beside her, a hand on her shoulder.

The palace magician, Nathaniel, turned when they entered the room. He was dressed in an unusual costume with a pipe smoldering in one hand. Harlow had a bad feeling about this. "Thank the Mountain. They're here."

The queen looked up. "Marius, something terrible has happened. It's Charlie."

At her side, Harlow felt Marius stiffen, and his grip on her hand tightened with his anxiety. "What happened?"

"Nathaniel and I were here with her, researching how to retrieve Killian's and Brynhoff's hearts. We wanted to set their souls free and end their hold on you. Charlie heard us and decided she wanted to help."

"What are you talking about, Raven? How could Charlie possibly help with my situation?"

Raven pointed to the first of fourteen slices. "She opened a new portal. Even if I wanted to, I couldn't repeat this magic. Charlie went back in time to the last moment we saw the hearts."

Harlow turned her head to stare at Marius, but the look on his face told her that his niece leaping through time was as surprising to him as it was to her.

Marius seemed incapable of speech, but Harlow had to know what was going on. "I'm sorry, but did you just say your daughter traveled back in *time*? Are you sure?"

Raven wiped under her eyes. "We watched her. Nathaniel was able to hold open the window long enough for us to see her get the hearts."

"Wait, are you saying it worked? She has them?" Marius's excitement was contagious, but if it had worked, why was Raven so upset?

Nathaniel puffed on his pipe. "It seems that Charlie has the power to move through time and between dimensions. The problem is, she has not been able to get back to us." Nathaniel reached into the model and turned the slices so that Harlow could see a window into a dark place where a child with angel wings carried a satchel Harlow assumed contained the dragon hearts. It looked like the Charlie she'd met at the coronation but older.

"Is that Charlie?" Marius asked.

Gabriel answered, voice strained. "Yes, our daughter appears to have aged with her travels. We estimate three human years."

Harlow covered her mouth with a hand. What did you say to parents who'd lost their child in time?

"Raven devised a way to see into these dimensions," Nathaniel explained. "What she didn't understand is that time isn't consistent within them. Each dimension is a separate river, and when we leap from one to the next, we aren't traveling linearly. Where we land depends on the magic, will, and intent of the traveler.

"We watched Charlie enter Eleanor's ritual room. She knew where to go because she'd been there. She'd seen the hearts as a baby. She pulled them from a pile of collapsed shelving while our mother was distracted with killing the goddess. When Eleanor destroyed the room, Charlie tried to leap back to us, but she was sucked into the underworld with Aitna by Eleanor's spell. Charlie leaped forward, back into our time, but she landed in the dimension Aitna had landed in back then. The one we resurrected you from."

"Fire planet," Marius said.

Harlow's stomach filled with shards of ice. "The one with the hunters? The place you thought you were when you were strangling me?"

Marius nodded, and she thought she might be sick. That was no place for a child.

Raven wept openly, and her voice came out high-pitched as she said, "We don't think she knows the way out. We can see her, but she can't see us. She can't hear us. She's scared, Marius. She isn't spirit. She's there bodily somehow. She can be hurt and killed."

"She has to make it to the temple." Marius's voice was more dragon than man. "What do you want me to do?"

The queen stood and walked to him, took his hand. "I want you to go in and show her the way out."

"There is no way he's going back in there!" Harlow's voice felt high and tight. Part of her understood she should not be speaking to the queen like this, but the idea of sending Marius back to the place he'd been trapped for three hundred years was too cruel to be a valid consideration. She bared her teeth.

Gabriel growled a note of warning, but Raven held up a hand. "I understand it's too much to ask, but I don't think there's another way."

Marius pulled Harlow's back against his chest and wrapped his arms around her. "Easy," he whispered in her ear.

Her heart pounded but she remained silent, allowed him to handle it. "I don't know how to get back inside."

Good. He had no intention of going. Harlow wanted to get the girl back, but...

"You can't go inside your body," Nathaniel said. "Charlie is the only creature to ever walk into the spiritual realms body and all as far as we know."

"Then how do you expect me to help her?" Marius asked.

"Remember how we talked about the levels of Hades and the idea that if you could navigate to the last temple, you could escape, but that Eleanor had cursed you to repeat the levels over and over again?"

Marius's expression grew darker. "In theory."

Raven glanced at Nathaniel. "We think..."

"We want to... suspend your life for a few hours so that we can put your soul into the same dimension we took you out of. Enough time for you to find Charlie and guide her out. Then once your soul is free, we'll put it back into your body."

Oh hell no. Harlow glared. "You must fucking be kidding! You want to kill him?"

"Only temporarily," Nathaniel said.

"My ass!" Harlow tossed her hands in the air, breaking from Marius's hold. Her gaze darted between Raven and Marius, whose expression was far too complacent. "He was trapped in there for three hundred years. What makes you so sure he'd even be able to find his way out this time?"

"Because he's done it before, Harlow," Raven said. "He would have been freed many times over if not for Eleanor's spell. Dragons don't belong in purgatory forever. Even dead dragons."

A growl worthy of a dragon twice her size ripped from Harlow's throat, and her eyes stung. "Over three hundred years! I won't let you condemn him to that again. No! Marius, tell them no."

"He'll come back," Nathaniel said softly. "He'll know the way this time because he's... He's..."

"Tethered to you," Marius finished, his gaze locking on Harlow. "That's why Harlow needed to come and why she has to be here. We're mated, so I can follow the bond between us, at least in theory."

"In theory," Harlow growled.

The sound of a child's scream came from the symbol. Raven whirled and clawed open another window. "She can't make it to the temple without you."

"Fuck! What are those things?" Harlow stared in horror as the little girl dodged fireballs and was chased by a monster whose entire face consisted of rows and rows of eyes and razor-sharp teeth. Charlie ran back into a small dark cave.

"Fire planet," Marius murmured. "She'll never survive."

Harlow's mouth dropped open. Was her soul being torn in two? She couldn't imagine her mate not going to rescue the girl. It was who he was. In her heart, she understood it, but the thought of him dying in front of her... *Intentionally* dying. She wanted to scream.

Marius tried to take her hand, but she yanked it away. She couldn't breathe as he said, "I have to do this."

Pain swallowed her. Inside, she beat the walls of her mind with her fists. She lay on the floor, kicking and screaming. Outwardly, she went as still as the statues in the garden. Hot tears carved paths along her cheeks. If he didn't go, he'd never forgive himself. She felt it down the bond. She'd known he'd struggled with his self-esteem these past weeks. Going into the underworld might kill him, but staying behind when he knew he was the only one who could save Charlie would kill him in an entirely different way. The second was a slow, painful death. He'd never feel worthy of love or anything else if he didn't do this.

She had to force her throat to work. "It's your decision."

"I have to. She'll never survive without me."

Eyes cloudy with tears, she mumbled, "I'll be here when you're ready to find your way home." How had she found the strength to voice those words when what she really wanted to say was *find another way, you're not going anywhere?*

Marius turned back toward Nathaniel and the queen. "Where do we begin?"

CHAPTER TWENTY-SEVEN

In all the time since Marius had returned from the dead, he'd never thought he would voluntarily allow himself to be sent back to the underworld. He was a grown dragon and a fighter, but his nightmares frightened him deeply, all the way down to the part of him that remembered what it was to be a child, to be absolutely helpless.

Once he was separated from this body, he would not be able to shift into his dragon form, and his wings were only marginally useful in the fire-raining skies of the dimension where they planned to send him. Was there any guarantee he'd ever get out again? No. In theory, if he reached the temple with Charlie, he should be free, and Raven and Nathaniel should be able to pull him and Charlie back here. But reaching the temple was no easy task. If he died trying, his spirit would endure and be forced to start over, but what would happen to Charlie? She was there body and soul. Could she die there?

And then there was Harlow. His mate. If he died for real or was trapped on the other side, it would destroy her. Mating among dragons was their most sacred bond. He'd never understood before why dragons who lost their mates often begged for death. Now it made sense. He'd liked Harlow from the moment she'd approached him at the coronation. He'd grown to love her over the weeks they'd spent working together. But the night their dragons had chosen each other, their souls had adhered. Could they even be separated without cleaving one or the other in two?

But then, that's what Nathaniel and Raven were counting on. His and Harlow's relationship was an unbreakable tether that might anchor him to this world and guide him home from the temple.

While Nathaniel drew a symbol beside and tangential to the one with Raven's model of the underworld, Gabriel stared at Marius, face etched with pain. His brother understood, perhaps better than anyone, what Marius was about to do. Without saying a word, his expression conveyed everything. *Thank you for sacrificing yourself again, my brother, not for me but for her.*

He thought of Charlie. He loved his niece. Everyone did. What kind of dragon would he be if he left her in that nightmare all alone? He gave his brother a nod of acceptance.

"Marius, it's time," Nathaniel said.

Harlow's arms were suddenly around him, her eyes bright with panic. She pulled him to her and kissed him in a desperate, frantic way. "Come back to me. Do what you have to do, and then come home."

Home. She was his home now, wasn't she?

She licked her lips, and all at once her eyes filled with heat, as if she'd flipped off the part of her inching toward hysteria and forced an air of calm about herself. He realized instantly she was doing it for him. The corner of her mouth trembled as she said, "We have unfinished business."

He forced a smile, thought back to the office in the Silver Sunset. "Yes, we do."

"Marius..." Raven's voice cracked with emotion. "Please. There's no time."

Harlow kissed him again and then shoved him toward the symbol. Fuck, she was strong. As he lowered himself to the floor, he thought she must be made of steel.

Nathaniel rested his fingers on Marius's temples and stared down into his face. "Raven is going to knock your soul out of your body and toward Charlie. I will keep you in suspended animation until you return to it. Try not to linger, brother."

He narrowed his eyes. "I'll keep that in mind."

Raven's face appeared over his, the pain in her eyes almost unbearable. "I'm sorry," she whispered just to him. Then she drew a symbol in the air with her hands, crossing and uncrossing her forearms before forming her fingers into claws and shoving one hand into his chest.

Now he understood why she'd apologized in advance. Pain sliced through him, and magic torqued his body off the floor. When he finally dropped, so did his spirit. The pain ended, then ignited again when he smacked hard and fast into stone.

Darkness. Was he unconscious or gone? With effort, he moved his hand, found his hip, and then felt along his torso. He was back in his leather armor again, as if he'd never left this dimension. He blinked. He must be back in the cave. He waited for his dragon sight to adjust to the total darkness.

An aura of golden light entered the corner of his vision. It grew brighter and brighter until a pale face with platinum curls appeared where Raven's face had been.

"Uncle Marius?"

"Charlie?" He stared at her in total awe. The girl was putting off her own light, as if she'd swallowed a star.

She sniffed, and a tear rolled down her face. He wiped it with his thumb, and his hand glowed until the wetness dried. "I think I did something bad."

CHAPTER TWENTY-EIGHT

Marius sat up and took Charlie by the shoulders, forcing himself to give her a gentle smile. "Well, life wouldn't be very interesting if we didn't get into trouble now and then, would it?"

"This isn't interesting. It's scary."

He shuffled to his feet and noticed the satchel on her hip. "Is that...?"

She opened the flap. "I got the hearts Mommy wanted."

Marius looked down at the two giant gems, lit from within by the souls of his father and uncle. "Good girl."

"I can hear Mommy cry, but I can't get back to her." Charlie sniffed.

"But now I'm here, and I'm going to help you get home." He reached out his hand, and she slipped her fingers into his. She was taller than when he'd last seen her, but slight, waifish. He wondered at her fast rate of growth. When would it stop? Was she mortal as her mother or immortal as her father? If she was mortal, would her life be abnormally short? He set the line of thought aside. None of it would matter if he didn't get her out of here.

A hunter's scream came from outside the cave, sending the girl clinging to his waist.

"The hunters are scary. It was smart of you to come here to hide."

"I leaped here from the last place," she said in a shaky, high-pitched voice. "I tried to leave, but it was too dangerous."

"Hmm. Well, the good news is I know the way home, but we need to leave this cave to get there. In order for us to get out of here, we need to make it to the labyrinth and then the temple. The temple is the doorway home."

Her lower lip trembled. "How do we get to the labyrinth?"

"We leave the cave and cross through the forest. Then we'll walk through a tunnel and wade through a lake. The door to the labyrinth lies beyond the lake."

Her big blue eyes shifted fearfully toward the exit.

"Now tell Uncle Marius, have you seen weapons in this cave? A spear with carvings on it? A sword?"

She pointed toward the bend that led to the opening to the cave. He patted her back and took her hand again. He'd never seen the cave in the light before, but it might as well be high noon the way Charlie was glowing. The floor was littered with bones. Animal and human. It stank of sulfur and death. He found a sword and scabbard right where he remembered the weapons being on his last journey here and fastened it around his hips. The spear beside it was one Killian once used. He examined the carvings. Greek symbols in bone. It killed the hunters, he remembered. That's all he cared about.

He balanced it in his hands, got the feel for it again. "Perfect. Charlie, the hunters are attracted to light. Can you dim yourself? You don't glow this brightly at home, do you?"

"No, but it's so dark and scary." Her bottom lip trembled again.

"I know, darling. But for us to make it, we need to be very fast and brave. We have to hide. And that means being as dark as the night. Do you trust me?"

In the blink of an eye, the cave went perfectly dark again. She clung to his side. "I'll need to put you on my back so I can use my spear. If you fall off, stay close to me at all times and do as I tell you. Promise me."

"I promise." The words cracked in her throat.

"Good girl." He edged to the doorway. A fireball soared through the sky and collided with the ground just beyond the cave, illuminating her terrified face. He comforted her with a squeeze of her hand. Thank the Mountain she was fireproof. Still, one of those could injure or kill her if it knocked her out of the sky, which was why they needed to do this on foot. He scanned the forest beyond. No signs of hunters.

Shifting her satchel around, he pulled her onto him, piggyback style. "Hold on tight, kid."

Her cheek brushed his ear as she nodded. He tightened his grip on the spear, felt the comforting weight of the sword at his side. With one last thought of Harlow, he sprang from the cave and ran.

Weaving in and out of the trees, Marius drove forward with a single-minded purpose. He could see the white dome of the temple in the distance, beyond the dark and twisting labyrinth. If he could just make it to the tunnels.

The hunter came out of nowhere, dropping from the trees and landing on top of them. Marius fell backward. Crying out, Charlie slipped from his back before he hit the ground. Somehow he managed to angle his spear up in time.

It pierced the thing's chest, but the creature drove forward anyway. He wedged a foot between him and it.

Foul breath roared into his face, rows of teeth circling his head, snapping mere inches from his nose. Fingers bloodless with his grip on the spear, he watched the light slowly drain from its many eyes until finally it hung lifeless above him. Rolling, he thrust its body off him and yanked his spear from its flesh.

He circled the clearing, searching for Charlie in the darkness, tempted to call out for her but knowing to do so would be a death sentence for them both. A hunter's screech came from behind him. He whirled. Charlie stared into the face of another hunter. Marius hoisted his spear onto his shoulder and threw it like a javelin. It pierced the monster's heart.

The hunter froze, then fell over twitching. Marius swept Charlie into his arms, abandoning the spear and racing for the tunnel. He wasn't going to risk checking to see if the creature was actually dead.

"It's okay. I've got you." He helped her to his back.

"I couldn't move. I was too scared."

"It's okay. We're almost there."

He could see the tunnel ahead. It was made from the hollowed-out trunk of a massive fallen tree. Once they were inside, they'd be safe from the hunters who couldn't fit through the opening. The trees above them rustled. "Charlie, now would be a great time to use that zappy zap you showed me in the palace. Do you think you can do it?"

"Mommy says not to."

"Mommy would agree it's okay to use against monsters."

The screech of a hunter came close above their heads. Her hands lifted from his neck, and the forest lit up with her magic. The hunter backed off in a flap of wings. But then another screech pierced the night, and then another. More flapping wings. *Fuck*, she'd scared away one, but the light and the sound were attracting every hunter in the forest.

Branches snapped, and the sound of flapping closed in. No spear this time. He poured on the speed, his breath coming in pants. How was it possible to be breathless and have his heart in his throat when he didn't technically have a body?

Charlie screamed as he dove into the tunnels. She tumbled over his head into the darkness. Talons snatched at his feet through the opening. He crab-walked deeper inside, out of the reach of slashing teeth and claws. When he reached Charlie, he pulled her into his arms.

"You okay, kid?"

She wept softly against his chest. He stood, bonking his head on the top of the tunnel, then slumped slightly so he could tread forward, deeper into the safety of the passage.

"Charlie? Give me some light so I can see you're okay."

Her glow started, soft as a lit match, and then increased to the radiance of a candle in his arms. He ran a hand along her limbs. No blood. No injuries.

"Scared?"

She nodded and wiped under her eyes.

"We're safe in here. Until we reach the other side at least." He set her down and took her hand.

They started to walk.

"Can I leave my light on?"

He looked down at the slip of a girl. She wiped under her nose.

"I think that would be okay. Just until the water."

Their footsteps thumped against wood as they followed the tunnel. In the light, he could confirm it was a hollow log.

Strange insects fed on the wood inside. It was they, he realized, that had hollowed it out, not some lost soul fighting for its freedom. He wasn't sure how that made him feel. Was it better to know that some force in the universe had provided the tunnel through luck or providence? Or that another soul or souls, through sacrifice and hard work, had made the escape route?

Maybe it didn't matter. There was only so much credit a higher life-form could take for their existence and survival. He was thankful for the tunnel, no matter who or what was responsible.

"I see the water, Uncle Marius. It looks cold." Charlie's voice was laced with worry.

"It is cold."

"Can we fly over?"

"Too dangerous. The vines that hang over the top are deadly, and the fireballs could knock us out of the sky anyway." One splashed down in the lake outside the tunnel and sent up a pillar of steam. "It's best to wade through the water. Trust me on this one." He glanced down at her.

She was making that face again, the one that tore him up inside. Helpless. Dependent on him. He was a terrible hero.

He exited the tunnel and eyed the crisscrossing vines above the water. His hand drifted to the sword at his hip, his only remaining weapon. "Here's what we're going to do. You'll stand on my shoulders. You won't even get wet."

"But won't you be cold?"

He would be. A deep aching cold that even his dragon flesh was not immune to. "I have my armor."

That seemed to appease her, because she held up her hands to him with total trust in her eyes. With his help, she climbed up his back and squatted on his shoulders. Careful to keep her under the vines, he sank into the dark, murky water. Instantly, ice filled his veins and his teeth chattered. He began the slow trudge forward.

He was halfway across when his eyes started to close. It would be so easy to fall asleep here. The needles poking into his skin would stop. He'd grow warm again. He knew because he'd died here before. He'd sleep and wake up in the cave, ready to face another day.

"Don't stop, Uncle. We're almost there." Charlie grabbed his ears and pinched.

He startled awake. They were not almost there. In fact, the opposite bank seemed like it was getting farther away. Cold. So cold. But if he just closed his eyes...

"Jump, Charlie. Soar to the opposite bank, low to the water. You can make it if you don't flap your wings. The labyrinth is at the end of the path. The temple at the center will take you home."

She pinched his ears harder. "You have to show me, Uncle," she cried.

He took another step. No farther. He wasn't going to make it. "You can do it by yourself. Use your zappy fingers."

"Keep going! We're almost there!" she screamed.

"Do as I say, kid." His lids drooped, and the words came out slurred. With his last scrap of strength, he reached up, grabbed her hips, and tossed her toward the shore. Her wings caught the air, and she landed gently on the opposite bank. He hated the look in her eyes when he gave up. Disappointed. Horrified. Mercifully, he didn't have to suffer her expression for long. He sank into the water, his eyes closing. He waited for death.

Strange—his body seemed to be rising rather than sinking. He cracked his lids as he rose out of the water, facedown and dripping over the surface. He glanced toward

Charlie. She was glowing again, her hands outstretched, sweat beading on her contorted face. As soon as his head was over the dirt, he dropped like a rock, legs still dangling in the water. She was on him immediately, digging her fingers into his collar and pulling with all her might.

"Get up! Get up now, Uncle! You're being bad." She yanked hard and then slapped him in the side of the head.

"Ow."

"Now!" she screeched, and Marius could not help but to hear her mother's voice in her mouth. He army-crawled forward, pulling one leg, then the other, from the icy water. He rolled over onto his back, staring up at the trees that sheltered the path.

"Charlie," he said, mostly so that she wouldn't slap him again while he regained his strength. "Did you levitate me out of the water?"

She squatted down beside him. "I had to. You fell asleep."

"When did you learn to do that?"

"A few days ago." She frowned. "I don't think I could do it if you were in your body. You'd be too heavy."

He nodded. "Makes sense." No, it didn't make any sense. That wasn't a dragon power, and a witch needed training to manipulate the elements like that. Not to mention, she'd seemed to tug at his very soul, like she'd not just lifted him but commanded him to come to her.

He sat up, feeling wet, exhausted, and aching from the effects of the cold. "Thanks for saving me."

She tossed her arms around him and hugged. The gesture had an oddly invigorating effect. Slowly he climbed to his feet. "All right, then. Let's get on with it. The labyrinth isn't going to solve itself."

"What do you mean, *solve* itself?"

"It's a puzzle." He decided it was best not to say more. Didn't want to scare her. "Are you up for a game?"

The corners of her mouth pulled back. "I don't think I like this world's games."

He took her hand, and they started along the path. "Well, there's only one way out, and that's to win. So if you have any other hidden talents, kid, don't hesitate to use them."

CHAPTER TWENTY-NINE

"His hands are ice cold. He's been gone too long. We should try to bring him back." Harlow sandwiched Marius's hand between her own, cradling it in her lap. His fingers felt colder than a corpse's, like his body had frozen on the side of the Dark Mountains. She rubbed his hand between her own, trying her best to warm him, but the cold must have come from within. He looked dead, his diamond heart silent in his chest.

"We can't bring him back yet," Queen Raven said. "He must come back on his own. I can't reinsert a soul that isn't here into this body."

Harlow pulled her knees into her chest, never letting go of Marius's hand. "It's been hours. How long can this go on?"

Nathaniel, whose fingers still pressed into Marius's temples, glanced at her in annoyance. The position he was in couldn't be comfortable, but aside from mumbling an incantation every half hour, he hadn't moved. He stretched out one leg now and cracked his neck. "It will go on as long as it takes. Pray not longer than the queen and I can stay awake."

"What happens if you fall asleep?" Harlow glanced back and forth between the two.

Behind Raven, Gabriel started to pace. The king embodied dark menace. People in Hobble Glen often whispered fearfully of the queen. Dragons had been conditioned to fear witches after all. But it was the king Harlow thought they should be afraid of. Between the two of them, he looked more deadly and less forgiving.

"We won't fall asleep," the queen stated firmly, giving Nathaniel a stern look. "And Marius will make it back soon with Charlie. We have to believe that."

Harlow gave her a nod. She hoped what she said was true, but if there was one thing she'd learned this year, it was that the rug could be pulled out from under her at any time. As much as she hoped for a happy ending, she held back a piece of herself from believing in it, preparing for the worst. She wasn't sure how she'd survive it, but she refused to give herself over entirely to optimism. Too dangerous.

"Harlow, you can sleep. We'll wake you when we need you." Raven gestured toward the floor as if to say she could stretch out next to Marius.

"I'm fine." She stroked Marius's arm. If they could stay up, so could she.

Time uncurled and stretched lazily between them. It had to be the middle of the night. The forest beyond the windows in the white room was completely dark aside from the silver light from the two waning moons.

"I owe you an apology, Harlow." Raven shifted her legs to the other side of her body.

"He's my mate and my love. I know he wouldn't have made any other choice but to save Charlie. He'd never abandon a child in need. He wouldn't be able to live with himself, and his agony would be my agony."

"That's not what I'm apologizing for, although I can appreciate how difficult it must be to be apart from a new mate."

"What, then?"

Raven glanced away, toward Marius's feet. "The Council of Elders and I have recently learned of an uprising of citizens that want a return to the old ways. They want things how they were when Eleanor was on the throne."

"I've heard. They've been leaving flyers at the Silver Sunset where I work."

Raven frowned. "I'm sorry to admit that when I first learned you were spending time with Marius, I thought you might be involved with them."

"You thought I was stringing him along for information. You thought I was a spy."

"Yes."

"And now?"

"You're his mate."

"But am I still a spy?" Harlow scowled at her. Wherever Raven was going with this, it was insulting.

"No. I don't think so."

"I'm not. I never was."

"I'm sorry. I just thought... because of your parents' history with Eleanor."

Harlow sighed. "My father is an opportunist. He's not a bad man. He's someone who tries to make the best of the situation he's in. My mother goes along with whatever my father does. He never followed Eleanor because he liked her or even agreed with her politics. At home, it was clear he hated her. He just wanted the best for his family."

"He was complicit in allowing her to continue in power."

"Maybe so. Maybe the entire population of Paragon was too. I don't recall her closing the borders to keep citizens from fleeing. No one knew for sure what was going on up here. The press wasn't communicating the truth."

Raven gave her a stern look. "Do you think I was too hard on your family, taking away his business?"

"I think you were right to speculate my family was part of the uprising. When you leave people desperate, they do desperate things. I'm sure it is tempting for my father, honestly. He has nothing. But he hasn't, and he won't because he believes in Paragon and in you."

Raven frowned. "I am sorry, Harlow, but if Darium truly had nothing, he must take some responsibility. It's been a year. Your father is highly skilled. I'm sure if he wanted to work, he'd have no trouble finding a position."

Harlow scoffed. "Maybe, if he weren't blacklisted."

The queen scowled. "Who blacklisted him?"

"We don't know. All we know is that the Silver Sunset is the only business in Paragon that would give us the time of day. And I suspect Roosevelt only hired me because he saw me with Marius. No one wants a past supporter of Eleanor's on their payroll. No one wants to be associated with us."

Raven pondered that for a few moments. "But you had savings... connections."

"Our connections abandoned us the minute we carried a whiff of scandal, and our savings didn't last. That is my parents' fault, although in their defense, they had to deal with devastating change quickly. It threw them both into a horrible depression. They were slow to adapt, but understandably so."

Raven looked at her quizzically. "If your father hasn't been able to work this entire time, how have you survived?"

Harlow sighed. "I supported us by gambling in the pits. It's why I was so interested in Marius. I used to watch him fight as a young girl, you know. I had such a crush on him. And then when he came back... To be honest, I thought he was larger than life. I just knew he would fight again." She rubbed Marius's hand between hers. "I convinced him to let me train him, and the money he paid me kept us afloat. And now, because of him, I have a position at the Silver Sunset. We've learned to live modestly. We'll survive."

She felt Raven studying the side of her head. "Of course you will. The heirs of Paragon always take care of their mates."

Harlow scowled at her. "I'm not after Marius's support or yours. My family and I work hard. We always have." Her voice held an edge, and she knew she was pushing her luck speaking to the queen like this, but she couldn't stop herself. "Do you know that my father physically touched every door he produced? Unlike Adradys, who leaves all the work to his apprentices, my father believed in what he did. He poured himself into his art. And yes, he was wealthy, but he earned his money. Paragon is a less beautiful place now that he can't work."

Gabriel glared at her with fire in his eyes. She turned her gaze back to Marius. "I'm sorry for raising my voice. I'm exhausted and worried for Marius and Charlie."

"Don't apologize. For what it's worth, I didn't understand the fallout on your family. I expected it to be a punishment, not a death sentence."

Harlow said nothing. What could she say? It hadn't been a death sentence, just a horribly hungry and difficult year.

"Anyway, if you want to catch the New Order, find out who is charming those flyers they leave at the Silver Sunset."

"How do you know they call themselves the New Order?"

"I found one of the flyers. Roosevelt wanted me to throw it away, but I wanted to ask my parents about it in case they might have been approached. For all the reasons you mentioned, I thought they might be targets, and I wanted to give Marius any information I could get."

"And what did you learn?"

"The flyer itself must have been enchanted because a man came to me in the street. When I pressed him about who he was, he ran away. I was planning to tell Marius, but we were sidetracked with... this. I haven't had a chance to speak with my parents about it."

Out of the corner of her eye, Harlow saw Raven give Gabriel a long, hard look.

"Thank you for telling me," she said.

"You're welcome." She turned back to Marius. "His hands feel warmer now."

Raven repositioned herself at his ankles. "Come on, Marius. Make it home, and I swear I'll give you and your mate the royal wedding of a lifetime."

Harlow's pride made her want to say she could plan her own wedding, but she squelched that knee-jerk reaction. Who was she to turn aside Marius's family, after all? Glancing back at Raven, she raised an eyebrow and smiled.

CHAPTER THIRTY

Marius stood before the gaping maw of an ancient stone doorway, next to a little girl who was far more powerful than her child's body let on. She glowed softly beside him, her hand firmly in his, and stared into the darkness.

"Ready?" He tugged on her hand.

"Are there hunters inside?"

"I don't remember any. But there are other deadly things. It's constantly changing."

"Can I keep my light on?"

He shrugged. "I don't see why not. We're not going to slip by anything in this labyrinth, Charlie. Whatever we meet, we'll have to face it."

Her glow brightened. "I'm ready."

They stepped inside. The stone corridor narrowed and descended. He remembered this part. He'd made it this far before. Maybe once or twice. After a sharp left, the labyrinth presented them with a fork in the passageway.

"Right, straight, or left?" he asked her. "I went left

before... but I don't think I was successful." He stopped himself from admitting that he thought he died.

"It changes." She frowned.

"Yes, it does." She was a smart kid.

"Which way do you want to go?"

He hung his head. He didn't know which way, and the decision seemed impossible when a child's life was at stake. He was staring at his toes when he realized there were markings under the dust. He brushed the debris aside. An arrow pointed straight ahead.

A grin spread his lips. Had he drawn that arrow? Or maybe one of the others. "I think we go straight, kid."

She nodded, and they walked on. But soon, the passage ended at a stone wall. There was no visible way forward. A table lay set before them, candles burning, plates gleaming. Every manner of food was heaped upon golden trays at its center.

"I'm hungry!" Charlie lunged toward the table, arms outstretched.

"No, Charlie. You can't eat that. Don't ever eat anything in the underworld."

"Why not?" She pouted, staring longingly at the feast.

"It makes you forget why you're here. If you eat that, you'll never leave." He looked around the stone room for another clue, an arrow from a benevolent soul, maybe his own, with instructions on what to do next, but the floor was oddly clean of debris. Too clean. There should have been stones, dust. "This is wrong."

"Do we have to go back?"

"It's an illusion. Look how clean the floor is."

She shrugged her little shoulders.

"Trust me."

One of the candles flickered. "See that?" He pointed to

the candle. "Airflow. There's a way out. We just can't see it." He released her hand and rounded the table to examine the far wall. "Maybe we can feel it."

The room behind him grew darker. He looked over his shoulder. Charlie was using one of the teacups as a snuffer to put out the candles.

"Charlie... I'm not sure that's a good—"

The last candle went dark.

"They're bad," Charlie said.

With the candles extinguished, Marius saw immediately what she meant. By the light of Charlie's glow, the room was revealed for what it was. Skeletons sat at the table where no one had sat before, decaying in their seats. Skulls were stacked in every corner. The food on the table wriggled with worms. Thick cobwebs stretched across the room.

Horrified by the sight of the food, Charlie backed away and climbed off the table. A noise came from above, and she looked straight up. The cup she'd been using to extinguish the candles dropped from her hands and shattered on the floor. "Uncle Marius?"

Marius rushed forward, sweeping Charlie into his arms and drawing his sword. Above them, a spider the size of a small house dropped toward them, its fangs dripping. He tried to stab it, but the webs thickened around them. He could barely move.

He hacked at the webs, the spider growing closer. "Charlie, zap!"

Clap! Sparks flew into the thing's eyes, and webs burned and fell away from them. The spider skittered away, hissing. Slashing at what remained of the webs, Marius ducked beneath the table, bringing Charlie with him. Bad idea. The space was littered with bones. Charlie screamed as the arm of a decaying man slapped her shoulder.

But the webs weren't as thick here. He cut at the ones on the opposite side of the table between him and the far wall. "Look, Charlie! There's an opening."

A thump marked the spider's arrival. Marius stabbed around the edge of the table, managing to lop off one of the creature's hairy black legs. It screeched loud enough to hurt his ears, but he grabbed Charlie and bolted for the passageway. The space was narrow. He thrust Charlie through first and backed into it, stabbing at the flashing fangs that filled the doorway.

The spider couldn't fit through, but it could shoot its webs at him. Glossy threads wrapped around his sword and climbed his arms. The creature braced its legs on the wall and tried to pull him back into its lair. He dug in his heels. Zap!

The webs gave way, and he collapsed into the narrow passageway next to Charlie. The scent of singed hair filled his nose. He shook burned web from his hands. Empty hands. Goddess help him, his sword was gone. He couldn't complain too much. At least he was alive. But he mourned the loss of his last weapon, nonetheless. "Thanks, kid."

"What now?" Tears streamed down her cheeks.

He drew her into a hug. "It's okay. It can't follow us."

"I want to go home." Her lip quivered.

"Me too. Good news is, we're still alive, and there's only one way to go." He pointed down the long hall in front of him.

She wiped her eyes and took his hand. They started walking again.

After a long while, Charlie asked, "Are you going to marry Harlow?"

He choked on his own spit and coughed into his hand.

It wasn't the question itself that had set him off guard but the timing and the source.

"What made you think about that now?"

She shrugged. "Just wondering. I know you spend time with her sometimes."

Marius thought about the question. He was already mated to her. Marriage was the obvious next step. "I don't know. Haven't asked her yet."

"Are you going to ask her?"

"Maybe. If she wants me to."

"Why wouldn't she want you to?"

Marius shrugged. "Female minds are a mystery to me, Charlie, but I've learned it's always a good idea to get Harlow's permission before doing anything that involves her person."

Their feet crunched on the debris. "If you marry her, can I be the flower girl?"

"How do you even know what a flower girl is?"

"From Colin's wedding."

Marius thought back. His brother had married the elf scribe Leena in a small wedding in a court in Rogos. "I don't remember them having a flower girl."

"Oh, they didn't. But Mommy told Daddy that if they'd had one, I'd make the prettiest one."

"Hmm. Well then, I suppose there's no choice but to have the prettiest flower girl."

"But you need to ask Harlow," she muttered.

He grunted. "Not about this. This, I know she'd be absolutely behind. If we get married, you are our flower girl."

"How do you know? I thought you said her mind was a mystery."

"Sometimes, but the one consistency when it comes to

Harlow is her heart, and she loves you, Charlie. She insisted I come in here after you."

"But I've only met her once!"

Marius thought back. They would have met at the coronation. He beamed a smile down on her. "I guess once is enough."

Her face lit up. "Then I love her too."

"Harlow's easy to love." He stiffened when two silhouettes briefly appeared at the end of the hall. They were being watched. "Get behind me, Charlie. There's another test up ahead."

She did what she was told. Marius reached for his sword but then remembered he'd lost it to the spider. *Fuck.* He dropped into a fighting stance.

"It's about time you showed up, son. We need your help figuring out this puzzle."

Marius rose to his full height and strode forward, tugging Charlie along with him until her light illuminated the faces of the two beings he'd seen repeatedly in his dreams since he was resurrected. Killian's dark features stared at him from beside Brynhoff, whose shifting eyes and ratlike appearance hadn't changed at all since he'd been gone.

His father opened his arms and pulled Marius into his embrace. "I wondered if you were getting our messages. I knew you wouldn't fail us."

Brynhoff snorted. "Speak for yourself. Eleanor's spells aren't easily broken. The boy is here, but can he get us out?"

Marius hated the way his uncle referred to him as *the boy*. The man had always been useless, and his ongoing respect for Eleanor despite his circumstances grated on his last nerve.

Killian interrupted before he could take the bait. "Who

is with you, son?" His eyes fell on Charlie and lingered on her feather wings.

"Charlie." He offered no explanation. The sudden realization seized him that her very existence might fill both Killian and Brynhoff with terror. It was once a popular belief that the offspring of a witch and a dragon would destroy Paragon. In a way, Charlie had, but only the part that needed to be destroyed. It was too much to share. Too much for their minds to grasp.

"Hello," she said sweetly.

Killian's gaze fell on Charlie's satchel, heavy with their two hearts. Could he feel a piece of himself there? If he could, Brynhoff didn't seem to share that feeling. His arms were folded, and he was staring at the floor between them and the wall as if he were trying to figure something out.

"What do we need to do to open the passage?" Marius asked.

"Arrange the symbols in the slots." Killian pointed to six indentations in the side wall and a pile of stones painted with symbols. "We think the floor contains a clue to what the code should be, but we can't read it. We don't understand the language."

As happy as Marius was that this was a challenge of intellect, given he'd lost his sword in the skirmish with the spider, he was equally dismayed when he looked at the floor. The symbols weren't anything like Paragonian or the other languages he'd learned over his lifetime. They looked ancient.

"The one who passes here must prove their worth," Charlie read, edging her toes to the bottom of the last symbol. "Enter, thee, the name of thy soul's first guide."

"You can read that?" Marius asked her.

She nodded, her fist pressing into her lips.

"Did your mother teach you?"

She shook her head.

"Well, good luck for us." He ruffled the girl's curls.

"Sounds like gibberish to me. Worthy? Soul's first guide? It's impossibly obtuse." Brynhoff huffed.

Killian stroked his beard. "Charlie, can you spell *mother* with those stones?"

Charlie nodded. She went to work arranging the symbols on the floor, but when she was done, the word was too long.

"Try *heart*," Marius said.

Too short.

"*Mind*," Killian suggested.

Again, too short.

"First guide." Marius blinked at Killian. "I think you were onto something with mother. Maybe father?"

"Definitely not the first to guide a soul." Killian frowned.

Marius watched Charlie, his mind drifting to their earlier conversation. Harlow did love her, even without knowing her. It was that way with children, wasn't it?

"Try *love*," Marius said.

Charlie arranged the symbols. Exactly six. Marius began to plug them into the slots in the stone.

"Careful, boy. If you're wrong, it's the cave for us again," Brynhoff snapped.

Marius glanced toward Charlie. What would happen to her? Still, he had no choice but to continue. He slipped in the final stones.

The wall rumbled and then pulled aside.

Killian clapped his hands together and stepped into the next passageway. "Brilliant! This is the farthest we've come in a century."

"Which means we have one last challenge to face." Brynhoff grimaced. "And no weapons between us."

Killian growled. "Shut up, Brynhoff. Count your blessings. Look there."

The floor of the labyrinth was ascending, and at the top, a white glow beckoned them. Brynhoff increased his pace, his portly belly jiggling with his movements. "It's the temple! We're free!"

Marius moved to follow after them, but Charlie squeezed his hand.

"I feel weird." She grabbed her stomach.

"Weird how?"

"My tummy hurts, and my zap is in my blood." She tapped her torso with her fingers, imitating crackles under her skin.

Marius was feeling unwell himself, although his unpleasant sensation was in the general area of his heart. He rubbed his chest while she rubbed her tummy, wondering if the tug he was feeling there was because of Harlow. She needed him. They had to get home.

He gestured toward the light and the two men ahead of them. "There's only one way out, and that's through, kid."

Her face strained with worry.

"We've made a good team so far." He brushed her curls out of her face. "You've been very strong and brave. I think our chances are good."

Her eyes filled with tears.

"What do you think? Do we stay here in this passageway? Or do we try for home?"

"Try for home," she squeaked, but he'd never seen her so uncomfortable. Her palm was wet with sweat as they started up the ramp, and she panted as they neared the light. The temple, it seemed, was having an effect on her.

"Do you want me to take that satchel?" he asked. "Is it too heavy?"

She pulled it over her head, her hair damp with perspiration, and handed it to him. He hoped it was okay for him to carry it. She'd retrieved them from the past. Could he bring them into the future? He had no idea how Charlie's magic worked, or how the spell worked that had knocked him into this dimension. All he knew was that Charlie walked a little easier without the weight of the hearts. He took her hand again, and they were on their way.

Brynhoff was the first to make it to the end of the labyrinth. He did not look back before stepping into the light. His scream echoed down the passageway, but Marius couldn't tell if it was a scream of joy or of pain. It ended quickly. Brynhoff didn't return to the passageway.

Killian stopped and waited for them to catch up. "I couldn't see what happened. It's too bright."

"Maybe the temple sent him on," Marius said.

Killian grimaced. "Or whatever is guarding the temple killed him."

Marius swallowed hard. Together, they crept to the edge of the passageway. Charlie peered around the corner before Marius could stop her. After a quick peek, she leaped into Marius's arms, clutching at him and weeping.

"Charlie. What did you see?"

"They're like me, but *bad*. They're very bad!" She buried her face in his neck. Marius stroked her wings, trying his best to comfort her.

"What does she mean, they're like her?" Killian asked.

Marius stretched out on his belly and crept to the edge of the labyrinth. The same white marble temple he'd seen in every dimension was there, waiting to carry them away. All they had to do was make it through the wide columns of its pillars. But circling the temple were creatures that would strike fear into even the bravest heart.

They *were* like Charlie, but... more. Each was at least nine feet tall with platinum hair and white feathery wings that dragged on the ground when they walked. They wore white cloaks and scanned the area around them with glowing black eyes. Normally Marius wouldn't describe a thing as both glowing and dark, but somehow their eyes accomplished the feat. It was the guardians that put off the light, not the temple.

With horror, he realized a steaming pile of flesh to his left was what remained of Brynhoff. He wasn't dead yet. If he had been, his body would disappear and re-form in the cave. As if to prove his theory, the charred remains moaned woefully.

"How do we get past them?" Killian asked.

"No idea." Marius studied Charlie. It was possible they wouldn't kill her, looking like them as she did, and just as possible that they would. She also might be immune to their powers. But he refused to test that theory.

"They're bad," she said again.

He frowned. "What makes them bad, Charlie?"

She wiggled her fingers in front of her heart again. "On the inside. I can feel it."

Killian stared at the girl. "She's Gabriel's daughter, isn't she?"

Marius did a double take. "How did you know?"

"The eyes. She has his eyes. Not the same color— Gabriel's are hazel—but the shape. Who is the mother?"

Marius saw no reason to lie. "A witch named Raven. They've conquered Eleanor and now sit upon the throne. They're just rulers, Father. And Charlie is good. You can see that."

Killian stroked Charlie's hair. "I'm your grandpa, little one. Remember that your grandpa loves you."

He started for the edge.

"What are you doing?" Marius's eyes widened.

Killian smiled. "My time has come and gone, Marius. When you get back with that"—he eyed the satchel again—"free me. Brynhoff too. And be happy."

"No. Father, no!" Marius shook his head and held out an arm, but Killian was already stepping out into the light.

With one last look back at them, Killian yelled, "Run!"

CHAPTER THIRTY-ONE

Marius cried out, but it was no use. Killian ran from the labyrinth, waving his hands and calling to the guardians. Those strange, winged beings turned, their glowing eyes focusing on his father. Marius pulled Charlie into his arms and sprinted for the temple, using his wings to propel him forward, quicker than he'd ever moved in his life. Charlie clung to him, staring over his shoulder.

A flash of light ignited behind him, and Charlie screamed. "Grandpa! Oh, Grandpa!"

Marius did not look back. He leaped over stones and debris, flew as fast as his wings could carry him toward the stairs of the temple. His breath huffed in his lungs. He was going to make it. He was going to make it! His foot landed on the first step.

Pure energy plowed into his back. His body crashed onto the steps, and he threw Charlie toward the door. Everything hurt. On Ouros, only the goddess's tears were capable of inflicting this type of pain because only celestial magic could burn dragons. The guardians had to be made of the same stuff. Every nerve ending in his back felt like it was on fire. He crawled up another step, then raised his head to look at Charlie. Tossing the satchel toward her, he rasped, "Take this and run, kid. The door will take you home."

She climbed a few more steps toward the door, then turned around, her eyes filled with tears. "No! Get up!" She ran back down and grabbed his hand. "Get up, Uncle Marius! Get up now!" It was her mother's voice again.

He hauled himself up another step. Only a few more to go. A sound like static in the air told him why Charlie's eyes went wide. The guardians of the temple must be charging up again, focusing those deadly eyes on him. He tried to climb faster, but he couldn't get his feet under him. The crackle started again. "Run, Charlie!"

She didn't. She dropped into a fighting stance, crossed her arms, and bellowed like a dragon five hundred times her size. He heard the zap of celestial fire. Everything lit up like a sunrise. But when he looked back, all that bright light had stopped inches from his body, held back by some invisible shield Charlie was putting off. He cried out too, not that his howl would help her, but in reaction to the sheer power pulsing around him.

He only took a breath when the guardians ran out of steam.

Marius did not waste his niece's gift. Powering through the pain, he scrambled to his feet and swept her into his arms. Her eyes rolled back in her head, and she passed out. He hugged her to his chest.

"Hang on. Here we go." He leaped into the center of the temple, into the beam of light that pulsed there. Instantly, he was swept into the beyond.

Suspended in bright light with Charlie in his arms, all his pain vanished. It was, he realized, exactly as Avery had described it. He was in the bright place. The in-between.

The place between places. He knew instantly that if he chose, he could stay here. Not here exactly, but the next place. It would feel like this for all eternity. It would be bright and peaceful. He could rest. Everything would be easy.

But when he thought about moving on, something tugged, sharp and warm in his breastbone. There was someone he was forgetting. He sensed the child in his arms. Sensed because he was beyond sight. *Wake up, kid,* he thought to her. *What should we do?*

She did not respond. The weight of her seemed so slight in his arms.

The tug came again and then a voice. *Please, Marius, please!* Her voice. She was weeping for him. His hand felt warm. He looked down and could see it, where before his entire body had been washed out as if he were part of the light. He pulled on that hand and felt himself move.

Counterintuitive as it was to move toward darkness, toward cold, he understood *she* was there, on the other side of something. She needed him. Her name came to him, and he whispered, "Harlow."

Darkness rushed toward him, and then he collided with pain. He was on his back, something heavy and limp in his arms.

"Oh my goddess! Oh my goddess!" The weight was lifted off him. He was not strong enough to open his eyes.

"Marius? Marius?" Harlow cried. "He's hurt. Mountain, he's burned. His wings are... Mountain! What happened? What is this? I need the healer! She's fine, can't you see that!" Harlow was angry. The intensity in her voice made him try harder.

He opened his eyes to see Maiara leaning over him, the palace healer. She placed a shell around his neck. "Easy.

You have been injured but are healing. I am going to roll you onto your side."

He winced as hands moved him. Thank the Mountain, she was there, kneeling in front of him, holding his hands. "Harlow," he rasped again.

"I'm here." She kissed his temple. "You're home. You made it."

"Charlie?"

"She's fine. Tired, but awake. Uninjured. She has the hearts." Harlow blinked away tears.

"Good."

Something cool and thick spread across his back and eased his pain, and he closed his eyes.

"Maiara is putting a salve on your back and your wings. You're badly... burned." He understood her confusion. Dragons were typically immune to fire.

"Celestial," he said. "Like the goddess's tears."

Her eyes widened. "It's over now. You're home. You're already healing."

He did feel better, thank the Mountain. He grunted and sat up, allowing Harlow to help him. He turned to Raven and Gabriel, who were fawning over Charlie like she was made of glass.

"You okay, kid?"

Charlie blinked at him, looking far older than her seasons on Ouros. She nodded.

"Thanks for what you did in there."

Raven darted a glance between them. Charlie fidgeted, looking nervous.

"But we can talk about that later." Marius gestured toward the satchel. "Raven, we were right. They're still in there, and they need our help."

Raven dug into the satchel and pulled out the two

hearts, Killian's a navy-blue sapphire and Brynhoff's a dull agate. Each flickered as if a candle burned within it. She glanced toward Nathaniel, who moved to her side. Together, they uttered a series of syllables, raising the power in the room until the hair on his arms stood on end. They thrust it into the jewels.

The sound of a brisk wind sifted through the room. The lights in the gems went out.

Raven held the hearts up, inspecting them. "It is done."

But Marius could already feel that it was, like a deep ache had finally abated.

"Marius, your tattoos," Harlow said.

He looked down at himself. The symbols were still there, but they'd changed, no longer red and black but now silver, like old scars.

He closed his eyes and leaned into Harlow's embrace.

HARLOW HELPED MARIUS TO HIS FEET. "I'M GOING TO help him to bed."

"Wake me... never. Send food," Marius said as he hobbled toward the door.

Maiara raised a hand, a faint blush staining her cheeks. "My advice is to avoid strenuous activity for twenty-four hours."

Marius's lips pressed into the side of Harlow's head. She looked at him through her lashes. "Guess I'll have to do all the work," she drawled, low and sweet into his ear.

Miracle of miracles, she found out he could walk a lot faster. Relief washed over her when they reached Marius's chambers. He was healing, but he was weak, and she was worried about his wings. She feared his back and the webbing where they connected to his torso might be permanently scarred. But her deeper worry had to do with what might be happening on the inside. Marius had come a long way from the day they'd officially met. It had been obvious that he'd hated his appearance then. The symbols, the platinum hair. He hadn't felt like himself. It was why he'd started training again.

It would crush him if his injuries kept him from the pits. He'd just made the championship league. Would these injuries send him back to square one?

"What's bothering you, *mate*?" He ran his nose along the side of her neck, behind her ear, and planted a kiss in her hair.

She swallowed. "You were gone more than a day." She placed her hands on either side of his face and pressed her forehead to his. "I'm exhausted. Is it okay...? Can we sleep together? I mean actually sleep."

All she saw in his features was relief. She knew he wanted her, just as she wanted him. But he needed rest. He might not want to admit it, but he needed time to heal as well.

"Brilliant plan," he whispered.

She guided him to the bed and helped him into it. Carefully, she lay beside him, curled on her side, staring at the balcony where twilight again descended on Paragon. She scooched backward until she fit against his chest.

His breath felt soft on the shell of her ear as he whispered, "I came back for you."

"I know. I felt it." Warmth and pure happiness filled her at his words. "I love you, Marius."

His breathing had already evened out. He was fast asleep.

CHAPTER THIRTY-TWO

Paragon's dual suns blazed in a bright azure sky when Harlow woke. She slipped out of bed, careful not to wake Marius. He needed his sleep, and she was badly in need of a bath. She tiptoed into the bathroom and filled the tub, pouring in a selection of bubbles from the tray on the counter. The scents were decidedly feminine, and Harlow thought the soap must be common to all the bathrooms in the palace. It was more luxury than she'd experienced in over a year.

Stripping out of her dress, she sank into the tub and leaned her head back against the rim. The heat suffused her skin. She was surprised when tears poured from the corners of her eyes. But then, she hadn't allowed herself to cry yesterday. She'd stayed strong for him. Now she could finally let herself go.

The truth was that this mating had changed her irrevocably. Days ago, if something had happened to Marius, she might have gone on. But after yesterday, she knew that if he hadn't come back, she would have stopped existing regardless of whether her body was still here or not. She would have never been the same. Maybe she would have died of grief.

And wasn't that funny? After centuries of walls, of fortifying her heart and maintaining her independence, she could no longer survive without a man. She closed her eyes. Stupid, crazy, unexpected love. Everything was different now.

She sank down under the bubbles, scrubbed her face and hair, and then sat back up, smoothing the excess soap from her eyes.

"Mind if I join you?" Marius stared down at her. He was naked and hard. Unashamedly male. Her gaze scraped over him. All she could think was that giving up a portion of her independence was a small price to pay for this. This man was a god. This man was the sun.

She gave him a languid, lopsided smile. "Plenty of room." She pulled her knees to her chest, and he splashed into the space in front of her, facing her.

"You're so accommodating."

She used the sides of the tub to rise and straddle his hips, bringing her lips close to his. "You ain't seen nothin' yet."

His lids grew heavy, and he moved in to kiss her. "Hey, you didn't grunt when you got into the tub. And your wings are withdrawn!"

He shook his head and raised a brow. "It seems Maiara's salve worked."

"Let me see."

He turned in the water. Between the two crescent-shaped markings that indicated where his wings attached to his body, a white, star-shaped scar painted his back. She ran her fingers along it, marveling that all the symbols that were once there were gone. The ones on the rest of his body were still there, although they were lighter now, silvery. Almost as if all their magic had gone, leaving only a lingering impression in its place. She was totally okay with that.

"Show me your wings," she whispered.

He unraveled them, their diamond white whole again, although bearing the same starburst pattern as his back. "How's it look?"

"Perfect. There's a scar... a starburst... but no permanent damage as far as I can tell. It actually looks..."

"What?"

"Tough." She laughed. "You look... unyielding." She ran her fingers along the space between his wings, and he shivered at her touch.

Abruptly, he turned in the water and grabbed her hips, pulling her to straddle him again. She gasped as his hard length pressed between her thighs. "Let's put that theory to the test."

She loved that suggestion. Her mouth crashed into his. All the fear, all the love, all the need she'd felt in the past twenty-four hours, all poured into him where their mouths melded. Her mating trill thrummed in her chest. Her hand plunged into the water, wrapped around his cock, and stroked to the base. He moaned.

Electric sparks tingled through her veins, igniting her body with need. From the tips of her breasts to the tips of her wings, she wanted him. Needed him in her. She raised her hips to slide him in, but he wasn't having it. He lifted her and set her bottom on the edge of the tub. She had to grip the sides with both hands to keep from slipping over.

"Not going to rush this," he murmured against the space between her breasts. His tongue flicked over her right nipple, hard and taut from cool air on wet skin. Desire shot down her torso to her core. She tipped her head back as he laved and sucked at her breast, then bit, just to the point of pain. Goddess, she might come, and he hadn't even touched her below the waist yet.

His rough hands shoved against her thighs, spreading her wide. She didn't resist even though the cold teased her sensitive flesh. His head dipped, and a warm, wet tongue lapped along her folds. She moaned, but she could barely hear it over the deafening thrum of his trill and hers. The music they were creating echoed off the obsidian walls.

He licked at her slowly, focusing his attention on just the right spot. She was so close to orgasm her teeth hurt, and her inner dragon could barely be contained. Talons extended from her knuckles and scraped the sides of the tub. Her wings extended behind her, trembling. Scales danced along her skin and then disappeared under it.

"Marius..." Mountain, the way he looked at her—she wasn't sure who was enjoying this more.

His tongue dipped inside, and she called out at the intensity. Rhythmically, he sucked and thrust, his trill a heavy vibration against her clit. The orgasm took her hard and fast. She unraveled, giving herself over to the most intense pleasure she'd ever experienced. Wave after wave rolled through her until her arms shook and gave out. He caught her, held her through the aftershocks.

She hadn't even come down all the way before he was in her. He thrust his thick shaft inside, wrapped her legs around his hips. The feeling was so intense she wasn't sure if she'd had another orgasm or if it was the same one growing stronger again. She ran her hands down the corded muscles of his shoulders, dug her fingers into his pale hair.

His thrusts became wild and feral. She wrapped her arms around his neck and rode his hips, using the opportunity to play with his beautiful white wings. Her breasts rubbed against his chest with every tantalizing thrust. It was all her body could take. She tossed her head back again and cried out at the rush of pleasure.

Her inner muscles pulsed against him. His own release poured hot and wet into her. The feeling cast her over the edge again. Would she ever come down from this? Orgasm melted into orgasm until her thighs trembled and she started to slide back into the tub.

Their trills softened.

Time unraveled as he held her against him, until finally he whispered, "The water's getting cold." He helped her from the tub, wrapped a towel around her, and delivered a soft kiss to her nose. She felt full, claimed. Every inch of her... loved.

"Did you ever think it could be this way?" she asked without thinking. It was such an intimate question, a window into her soul. Considering where he'd been psychologically a year ago, maybe it was insensitive to ask. "I'd hoped for it one day, but I never expected it to actually happen."

He moved around her, picked up a brush from the counter, and started running it through her hair, teasing out the tangles. "I knew what mating was. I'd seen it in other couples. But my mother didn't have it. She was married to Killian. He was her royal consort. But they were never mated. In fact, it was common knowledge that she chose him for his family's long history of fruitful men. She needed children because Brynhoff had no interest in taking a mate. He had no interest in anything but himself. And one of them needed to reproduce to hold on to the throne. There was no love involved. Ever."

"That sounds like a difficult home life."

"Honestly, it was easy for me. Because I was the eldest,

they were the hardest on me when it came to royal expectations but also coddled me. I had to train harder than any other boy my age, but when it came to public matches, I always won. I always won because there were consequences for those who beat me. The only person to ever do it publicly was Xavier, and Killian punished him severely enough he never tried it again."

"By the Mountain." Harlow understood that people weren't black or white but shades of gray. His childhood had both been difficult and formed him into the perfect person he was today. His parents, just like hers, were capable of goodness and equally capable of evil. And wasn't that how all of them were? Every day was about doing your best to keep the darkness at bay.

"When I was resurrected, I felt sorry for myself. I missed all that I'd lost. And even though I knew I shouldn't challenge Gabriel for the throne, inside, I felt wronged, robbed of my destiny. Not because Raven and Gabriel ruled, but because I'd died. I'd missed three centuries. I wasn't special any longer. I wasn't preordained for greatness. And with all that gone—my looks, my position, my future—I didn't think I had anything left. I was useless, purposeless."

"That's not true."

He brushed her hair from front to back and fanned it out across her shoulders. "You saved me, Harlow. Even before we were mated. The moment you suggested I could try. The moment you saw in me what could be and not what was, was the moment I had hope for myself." His voice had grown soft. "So, no. I never expected to mate, especially not with someone like you."

She turned in his arms, took the brush from his hand, and set it on the counter. "Someone like me?"

"Goddess, woman, you have to be blind and deaf not to know that every man in the kingdom thinks you're an incomparable beauty. I'll never be worthy of you. I was never good enough. I got lucky that by some precious twist of fate, you fell in love with me."

She grabbed his face, touched her forehead to his. "Marius, only you would think it was lucky that a girl from the Swilton district, with a blacklisted family and barely two spencies to her name, would be his mate."

"Let's settle on we're both lucky. Come. I'm starving." He turned her by the shoulders and guided her from the bathroom.

"I should probably go. I'm supposed to work at the Silver Sunset tonight." She reached for her dress.

"I'm glad Roosevelt followed through."

"Hmm?" She looked at him, confused. "What do you mean?"

"Oh, that's right. I never had a chance to tell you... Roosevelt told me that it was Adradys who blacklisted you and your family. Said he'd make it difficult for anyone who associated with you. The doormaker's rich. No one wanted to piss him off, but apparently a little pressure from the palace was enough to make Roosevelt think again."

"That bastard!" Harlow had known Marius had helped get her the job, but she had no idea Adradys was behind their difficulty finding work. She'd thought it was simply loyalty to the crown.

"I was surprised how far Adradys was willing to go out of jealousy."

She scoffed. "He's not a man used to taking no for an answer." She pulled the dress over her head and had to catch her breath when Marius growled.

With a hard tug, Marius pulled her chest-to-chest with

him. He was hard again and looking at her like he wanted to fuck the memory of Adradys right out of her. She wasn't opposed to the idea.

"Thank you for helping me find work and for being the best mate a woman could want." She brushed her lips against his.

"There's one thing you can do to show me how grateful you are."

"What?"

He cradled her jaw in his palm, dusted his thumb across her lip. "Marry me, Harlow. Show the world you're mine."

CHAPTER THIRTY-THREE

Later that day, Harlow burst into her family home, her inner fire glowing bright. She'd never felt more alive or more optimistic about the future. Not even when they were rich and living in Firedrake. Back then, she had her needs met, she hadn't wanted for anything, but she wasn't happy. Not like this. Before, she wouldn't have been able to visualize the contentment she felt at this moment.

Her father rushed into the room and stopped short. "Oh, thank the Mountain." He rounded the table and pulled her into his arms. "Your mother and I worried something had happened to you. We haven't seen you in days."

Lemetria appeared from the kitchen. "Praise the Mountain. I hoped you were with..." She eyed Darium as if she wanted badly to tell him what she knew. "That man we spoke about, but I wasn't sure! I've been so worried."

"It's okay, Mom. We can tell Dad now. It is done."

"Tell Dad what?" Darium looked between them.

"I am mated," Harlow said. "And engaged."

"Finally!" her mother said.

"To whom?" her father added.

"To Marius." She beamed and pressed her hands over her heart. "I love him, Daddy. More than anything."

"Marius from…?" He gestured vaguely in the direction of the palace.

Lemetria was practically jumping up and down with excitement beside him.

Harlow grinned. "That's the one. He asked me to marry him this morning. We're going to have a royal wedding."

Darium frowned. "Will we be invited? Does he know who we are?"

Harlow laughed. "Yes, he knows. And yes, you'll be invited. I had a long talk with the queen. She harbors no ill will against you."

"But the blacklist—" He darted a glance toward Lemetria.

"Was not her doing." Harlow glared. "It was Adradys. He did it after I refused his proposal."

"That bastard," her parents said in unison.

"Yes, but it ends now. I won't use Marius's position to make things easy for us, but I can't help but think this wedding will improve our reputation."

Lemetria laughed. "It certainly will. I will enjoy seeing our old Firedrake friends eat crow over how they treated us."

Her father grew quiet. "There's something you both should know." He pointed at the table, looking serious. They both sat down.

"Why do I think I'm not going to like this?" Harlow asked. "Father, what have you done?"

"I beg your pardon!" He placed a hand on his chest. "I have done nothing!" He cleared his throat. "But I do know something, and considering the royals are to be family, I think they should know too."

Harlow had a bad feeling about this. Her father had that look in his eye, the one he always got when he was up to something shady.

"I started betting in the pits," he began, "just as you taught me, Harlow. It was all I could do, considering I couldn't find work."

Harlow nodded. "Did you win?"

"With your strategy, dear, I did. But my winning attracted the attention of Adradys, and he sat beside me one day. He told me that during the championship, I should place my bets on Dax. Then he said I'd be wise to value his ongoing friendship, considering your behavior, because soon things were going to change, and when that happened, I'd be glad I'd made the right sort of friends."

Harlow frowned. "You know, he said something similar to me. Something about that I'd be sorry when things changed."

Her father nodded. "After we had that conversation, he stood up and this was on the bench beside me." He reached into his vest and withdrew a folded piece of parchment.

"Is that a flyer about the New Order? Someone's been leaving them in the Silver Sunset." Harlow took the parchment, hands shaking with her building rage.

"There can be no question where it came from, Harlow. Adradys left it there for me to find. All that talk at dinner about working to make things how they used to be. He's behind this New Order. Mark my words."

Harlow frowned. "It makes far too much sense. Do you know what he said when I refused his proposal? He said I'd be sorry when things went back to the way they used to be and I was brought to heel."

"He did not say that!" Lemetria looked aghast on her behalf.

"He did. He also laid hands on me. I rather liked handing him his ass."

That made her mother smile.

"So what do we do?" her father asked. "I left him with the impression I might be interested."

"Daddy!"

"I'm not, darling, but you know me. I choose my words carefully and always keep my options open. It's how I've survived these many years."

Harlow read the flyer in her hands carefully. "By the Mountain! This one is different. He's left you a date and time for their meeting. It's tonight!"

Her father toyed with the neck of his shirt. "I suppose he trusts me. What reason would I have for favoring Raven and Gabriel?"

"As long as he doesn't know about my mating to Marius, there is no reason. Mother, you haven't told anyone, have you?"

"Not a soul."

"Keep it that way."

"But surely there will be a royal announcement!" Lemetria seemed visibly pained to have to keep the secret any longer.

"I'll make sure that doesn't happen." Adradys had seen her with Marius. He knew they had a connection. But considering he had entrusted her father with this, he must have assumed it was a fleeting fancy. She planned to keep it that way.

"But why, Harlow?" Lemetria tangled her fingers in her lap, totally put out.

"Because Dad is going to go to this meeting tonight." She waved the flyer between them. "He's going to find out the names of every supporter of the New Order, and he's going to report back their plans to the king and queen."

Her father gasped. "I'm to be a spy, Lemetria!" He preened a bit.

"I will let the king and queen know what you're doing. We are going to take this bastard and his entire entourage down."

That made her father smile in a way she hadn't seen since before the war.

CHAPTER THIRTY-FOUR

Marius sat across from Raven at the dining room table, so thankful to be back home he could hardly contain his joy or his hunger. He shoved another piece of bread between his teeth. He'd already eaten enough for a small army, but between his journey into the underworld and the demands of his mate that afternoon, he was ravenous. Now, with the suns having set over Paragon, it seemed he was making up for lost calories while he'd been in the underworld.

"I've asked Gabriel to take Charlie on a picnic on the grounds for dinner to give us time alone to talk." Raven glanced over at him.

"Sounds serious." Marius gave her his full attention. Up until that point, she'd been rather quiet, and he'd wondered when she'd get around to asking him the questions that must be on her mind.

"Thank you again for what you did. You must know that Gabriel and I understand that you are the reason our daughter is with us today."

"I can't take all the credit. Charlie is more powerful

than you know. She played a large part in helping us make it through to the temple."

Raven frowned. "About that. She won't tell me any details. Something happened near the temple—you mentioned it when you first came out—but she won't talk to me. It's almost as if she's ashamed."

Marius chewed pensively. The last thing Charlie should have been was ashamed. He didn't particularly care to break the girl's confidence, but this truth needed to be shared. Shame was a cancer he would not allow to infect his niece.

"When we reached the temple, there were *beings* guarding it. She's ashamed because those guardians were deadly and evil. They tried to kill us. And there wasn't anything human or dragon about them. They didn't seem to think or feel, they just killed."

"I don't understand. Why would she be ashamed about that?"

"Because the temple guardians looked just like her, Raven. Exactly like her, just larger. And they had her powers. Amped up a thousand times but still the same sort of abilities. Her power is celestial in nature. I'm sure of it. She shielded me from a blast that would have killed anyone who wasn't a god, goddess, or other celestial being. She shielded against at least four of them."

"Celestial." Raven released a deep breath. "Tell me what they looked like exactly."

"Seven feet tall. Platinum waves. White fluffy wings that dragged on the ground. Glowing white robes. They glowed like she does. It produces a halo of light above their heads."

"Charlie glows?"

Marius chuckled. "Like a light bulb. She can turn it on and off."

"What else?"

"The only thing different about Charlie and these guardians was the eyes. Their eyes had no whites. They were black as night but intense, electric, like the blackness gave off its own energy. I've never seen anything like it on Ouros. Charlie said she could feel them in her blood and that they were like her but bad. I don't know how she could tell."

Raven wiped a hand over her face. "Thank you for being so forthcoming."

He shrugged. "That little girl deserves better than to think she's related to those things even if there are physical and mystical similarities."

The queen held a hand to her forehead for a moment. Marius stopped eating. If anything, she looked *more* concerned than before.

"Why do I feel like this isn't good news for you?"

Raven smoothed her fingers along the edge of the table. "We have a name on Earth for celestial guardians. They're called angels, and until now, I didn't think they were real."

"Angels. By the tone of your voice, I'm guessing this isn't a label you want for your daughter."

"It's not about the label." She stood and started pacing the dining room. Marius thought she must walk several miles a day just in her pacing. He'd watched the queen pace like this all too often these past weeks. "When she was born, I thought she looked like an angel. Everyone did. But I knew she was Gabriel's and mine. She is half dragon and half witch. A hybrid."

"Nothing wrong with that," Marius said.

"Thing is, when I was researching your symbols, I came

across some ancient texts, and I was able to put some things together with Penelope's help. You see, she gave me access to some of Darnuith's sacred texts."

"What sorts of things?"

"Charlie isn't the first of her kind. Witches and dragons have mated and reproduced before, and their progeny are what we on Earth call angels. You've confirmed for me what I've suspected. Charlie is not witch or dragon. She will never shift. She will never cast spells like her mother. Her powers are celestial, of the gods. Zeus's lightning flows through her blood."

"She is extremely powerful." Marius paused, his brows knitting. "Wait, if there have been ones like her before, where are they now?"

Raven folded her arms as if he'd just now caught up with where she'd been the entire time. "It appears they are guarding temples in the underworld and likely those on Olympus as well. I only know as much from you, though. Their existence disappears from the books some hundred thousand years ago. It seems my daughter's existence in the here and now is unique."

Marius leaned back in his chair and studied the queen. He wasn't the type of man to tell someone how they should feel. In general, he lived by the law of live and let live. He'd been a selfish little prick during his first life, and then he'd been nothing, and now he was a mated warrior. These immortal lives they led wove together. They bent and braided into one another in ways none of them would suspect. Not even Dianthe with her second sight had seen his resurrection.

"So what?" he mumbled.

"Excuse me?" Raven's eyebrows rose.

"Charlie is one of a kind. She's an angel. So what?"

The queen's mouth dropped open. "I would think it was obvious, Marius! How am I supposed to raise her when I don't know anything about what she is? How fast will she age? How tall will she grow? Will she ever have children of her own? Will someone come and try to take her someday to wherever the rest of the angels went?"

Marius crossed his arms. "So. What." He shook his head slowly. "All of us travel the road of life blind to some extent. This mountain, this family, we like to think we have a preordained future because of our roles here, but I'm living proof that everything we know to be true can change in an instant. Immortal we may be, but we aren't guaranteed tomorrow. We wake up and study the road. We think we can see all its twists and turns, but once we start moving, they change. Every decision, every relationship, changes the path. Charlie is one of a kind. You'll have to take things day by day with her. How is that different from where we've all been before in this family?"

"I wanted it to be different!" Raven tossed her hands up and then covered her face with them. When she lowered them again, her eyes were red. "Ever since the day I met Gabriel, I've been navigating a sea of uncertainty. Would Crimson kill me? Would the baby in my womb survive? Would she be a monster? Would Eleanor kill us all? I wanted better for Charlie. I wanted her to have a more peaceful life."

"She does have a peaceful life because she's loved. She knows she's loved. That's more than a lot of people can say. What she doesn't have is a life without challenges. Then again, one could argue that a life without challenges is hardly a life."

The two stared at each other as the night stretched on between them. He continued eating.

Finally, Raven huffed out a deep breath. "Mating agrees with you, Marius. My goddess, you've become wise. I'm glad we had this talk. You've given me something to think about."

He finished what was in his mouth and bowed his head. "Happy to be of service."

A knock came on the door. "Who could that be this late?" Raven called out for the person to enter.

A guard ushered in Harlow and her parents, Darium and Lemetria.

"Harlow," Marius said, "I didn't think your parents would be joining us. I would have waited to eat if—"

Harlow raised her hand and turned toward Raven. "My father has learned more about the New Order."

Her father nodded vigorously beside her. "I've learned who's involved and where they're going to strike," Darium said. "And the best part is, we can stop them. Only, we'll have to act fast."

CHAPTER THIRTY-FIVE

Three weeks later...

Harlow stared down at the pit where Marius was dealing a match-ending blow to his competitor and found it difficult to hide her smile. He'd risen through the ranks with little effort. She'd like to think she had something to do with that.

"Looks like we've attracted some attention," her father whispered at her side. He offered her his bag of crispy fried wimble skins. She popped one into her mouth and looked toward the aisle. Sure enough, Adradys was making his way toward them.

"Darium, I'm so glad you've come to support the new champion." He stared down his nose at Harlow. "And it seems you've brought your daughter as well. Maybe she'll learn something today."

Fucking bastard. "Always interested in the pursuit of knowledge," she said, fluttering her lashes. Goddess, he made her want to vomit. "Perhaps you could tutor me on a thing or two after the match."

He glared at her with violent sexual need. "I could teach you many things, Harlow, if you are willing to learn."

Harlow swallowed down the bile rising in her throat and gave him a sweet smile.

"At least you came to your senses about Marius," Adradys murmured. "I'm relieved you saw the light."

Her father interrupted the exchange by clearing his throat and gave Adradys a smile so authentic Harlow might have believed it if she hadn't known the truth. "Well, I am certainly happy to be here today," he said. "After all your hard work, Adradys, you're finally going to get what you deserve."

Adradys crossed his legs and checked his pocket watch. "Yes. Everything is in place. Although Marius is an unexpected surprise. Who would have guessed he actually had any talent for the sport?"

"I did," Harlow mumbled.

"What's that?" Adradys asked, leaning across her father to hear her better.

"I said, I don't know. It's very unexpected," she filled in at a louder volume. In the pit, Marius finished his match and was declared the winner once again. "And look at that! It appears he will advance to the championship round."

Adradys narrowed his eyes on Darium. "You did deliver the elixir to him as you promised?"

Her father lied as smooth as silk. "Oh yes. Before the first of today's matches. Watched him drink it down myself. He thought it was a gift from that fire-breather from the Silver Sunset."

"It's certainly taking its time to kick in," Adradys muttered.

"Where did you have it made?"

"The witch who runs Aborella's old apothecary. He thought it was for me. Trouble sleeping, you understand."

"Brilliant ruse." Darium jiggled the bag of crisps in his hand.

"I've used him for a number of things. He never asks questions, but his magic can be temperamental."

"Perhaps it takes some time to work. If it was meant for you, he'd have been careful with the dosage."

"Hmmm. Yes. But I tripled it."

"In any case, I bet it is only a matter of time for it to kick in. I suspect this will be an easy win for Dax."

"Let's hope so. Our plan hinges on it."

The matchkeeper announced the championship match, and Marius and Dax entered the pit. They both bowed to the king and queen, who sat in the palace box with Charlie in the seat behind and between them. Harlow thought they were an attractive sight, all dressed in matching emerald green.

Raven held up the championship cape, embroidered with a dragon under a crown of stars. It would be awarded to the winner of this match, presented by the queen herself, who would wrap it around the champion's shoulders.

The fighters took their marks. Marius wavered on his feet.

"Ah, it appears you were right, Darium. The elixir seems to be taking effect."

Harlow slanted the man a shallow smile. "And there goes the flag."

Even Harlow was surprised at the brutality with which Dax collided with Marius. There was no mercy in the exchange of blows until, with one punch that wasn't nearly enough to rattle Marius, Dax caused her mate to stagger back and collapse. He stayed down to the count of ten.

Harlow swallowed, her stomach tightening at the sight of Marius as still as death on those pebbles. But she remained outwardly impassive as Dax's arm was raised and he was then escorted toward the platform beside the royal box.

Queen Raven stood, the champion's cape in her hands. She strode toward the platform, the epitome of grace and aplomb.

Beside her father, Adradys grinned like he was about to receive the cape himself. He glanced at his watch again. "Right on schedule," he murmured.

Around the arena, his supporters readied themselves, their hands going to the weapons they'd smuggled in inside their boots.

The song of crowning began to play, and a fog of purple smoke licked the platform. Dax took his place at the center. The look of pride on his face turned Harlow's stomach. Raven stepped toward him, the cape offered with both hands in front of her.

In one movement, Dax drew a blade from his boot and swung it toward her neck. His aim was true, and if that dagger had met its mark, the queen would be dead. Harlow watched it bounce harmlessly off an invisible barrier. Thanks to the symbols sewn into the cape Raven was holding and Nathaniel's spell circling Dax's ankles, the brute was frozen in place.

Adradys and his supporters were already on their feet. The plan had been to storm the contingent of guards once Raven's head rolled. But Raven was very much alive. And the number of soldiers in the stadium had tripled in the blink of an eye.

Next to her father, Adradys glanced at the two soldiers

who had silently appeared behind him and were holding silver rods toward his sides. "What is the meaning of this?"

One of the guards grabbed his arms and cuffed him. "Adradys, you are under arrest for treason. We are escorting you to the dungeon by order of King Gabriel."

Colin appeared in the aisle and gestured with his hand. The guardsman wrestled Adradys toward him.

All around the stadium, guardsmen, some in uniforms and some in plain clothing, were arresting New Order supporters, fishing out the weapons hidden in a panel of their boots exactly where her father had indicated. The arrests were swift. Already a dozen men and a handful of women were being hauled toward the doors along with Dax, who'd been tranquilized with Nathaniel's smoke.

Harlow leaned back in her chair to get a better look. The shock on Adradys's face as he was ushered up the aisle was pure gold.

"What are you doing? Do you know who I am?" he protested to the guards.

She laughed. "I do enjoy learning new things," Harlow called to him. "And today, you have taught me something. I learned that I was right, and my father is definitely smarter than you."

Adradys shot a look of disbelief in Darium's direction.

"Enjoy Paragon's brand new dungeon, Adradys," her father said with a smile. "I know that you'll make the best of it. You always do."

Harlow leaned her head against her father's shoulder as Adradys and every single one of his supporters were ushered from the arena. Below them, Marius had gotten to his feet and was brushing the pebbles off his fighting uniform. It had all been a ruse. Her father had never drugged him, and Dax's hit was not enough to knock him out. Now he turned and bowed to the royal family.

Queen Raven returned to the awards platform and raised her wand to amplify her voice. "It gives me no pleasure to tell you that the men and women who were escorted from the arena moments ago were part of a failed assassination attempt. Dax planned to kill me and then Gabriel, leaving Paragon without a ruler. The New Order didn't want a ruler; they wanted a tyrant. Their intent was to replace us with someone more like Eleanor."

A gasp rose up from the crowd. People cried out their support of Raven and Gabriel.

"They might have succeeded if not for the kindness and bravery of Darium and Lemetria. Darium learned of the nefarious plans of the New Order and shared them with the king and me, giving us time to enact a plan to counter them. Please join me in thanking Darium and Lemetria for their role in the protection of Paragon."

Her mother and father stood and bowed as the stadium clapped along with Raven.

When the applause finally died down, Raven gestured to Marius. "Marius agreed to throw this match so that Dax's murderous ways could be outed publicly. I am pleased to give you your true and rightful champion, Marius!"

CHAPTER THIRTY-SIX

Two cycles later...

"I still can't believe you won the championship," Colin whispered. "The last time we trained together, I thought you had a bright future as towel boy."

Marius smirked. "It doesn't feel quite right considering Dax was disqualified."

"Vilt fodder. There's no longer any law or suggestion that anyone should let you win. On the contrary, most of those guys wanted to kill you." Colin adjusted the strange clothing he was wearing. "You won fair and square. Besides, you'd already proved you could beat Dax when you faced him in trials."

"Fine, I deserved to win." Marius folded his hands in front of his hips.

"And now you have a lifetime to thank the woman who taught you how to fight." Colin jutted his chin toward the aisle and the empty space where they'd been told Harlow would appear.

After winning the championship, Marius had

announced his mating and engagement to Harlow. Everything changed the second it went public. Based on their service to the crown, her parents were reinstated as the official doormakers of Paragon and soon moved back into the Firedrake district. But Harlow had never once slept under their new roof. She was his and now shared his chambers in the palace.

Not that the relationship had curbed her independence one bit. She continued to work, although she'd left her job at the Silver Sunset to take a role offered by the queen herself—community outreach ambassador. She'd been charged with improving conditions in the poorest areas of the kingdom, a role she took on passionately.

Queen Raven had helped them plan an Earth-style wedding, an exotic affair where he could fulfill his promise to Charlie to allow her to be a flower girl. The oreads had set up row after row of white folding chairs in the garden. It seemed like every dragon in the kingdom was there, surrounded by the most beautiful blooms in all of Ouros.

In the first row, the entire Treasure of Paragon, aside from Colin, who was serving as his best man, and Avery, who was Harlow's matron of honor, sat with their mates. Tobias and Sabrina, Rowan and Nick, and Nathaniel and Clarissa had returned from Earth for the affair. Sylas and Dianthe, along with the three fairy children they'd recently adopted as their own, had traveled from Everfield as well. Leena sat in the front row, scrawling everything that was happening on a roll of parchment.

The music started to play, and Charlie, dressed in a white dress with a red sash, walked slowly toward him, sprinkling red flower petals as she did.

When she reached him and turned, he whispered, "The most beautiful flower girl ever."

Her eyes twinkled with her smile before she continued on and took a seat next to the king and queen.

Then Harlow appeared at the head of the aisle.

Marius had trouble staying upright. He'd seen Harlow every day for months. They shared a bed. But seeing her in the red ball gown she'd selected for the occasion, her gold wings sparkling in the sun... Her beauty was almost blinding.

"Breathe," Colin said, elbowing him in the side.

He parted his lips and took a hungry gulp of air. She was his equal, his perfect partner. Funny that saving Charlie had been something he'd done for the child and her parents. He'd done it out of love. But what he'd received in return was all his. He felt at home in his own skin for the first time since his resurrection.

He was brave. Selfless. A champion. And he was worthy of this woman.

She was beautiful. Cunning. And loyal. And she was everything he'd ever wanted.

When she finally reached him, he took her hand in his own and followed the strange, elaborate ceremony. It was a human-style wedding with candles and singing to the goddess of the mountain. As they exchanged their vows, the wind picked up and sent white petals drifting through the air, showering them in soft, fragrant blooms.

Pronounced man and wife, dragon and mate, he pulled her into his arms and kissed her like there was no tomorrow to the applause of their guests. A banquet followed, and something called a wedding cake that Harlow enjoyed but was too sweet for him.

Later, when they were enjoying a drink at the bar and watching Raven twirl Charlie around by her arms on the dance floor, Harlow glanced up at him. "I never thought I'd be this happy."

He gave his head a firm shake. "Never. A kingdom at peace, a beautiful mate. Not even when I thought I would be king."

"For centuries, we all feared her... the idea of her..." She pointed her chin at Charlie. "And she was the answer, the key to a better Paragon."

He snorted. "I guess that's true."

"So I suppose if one little girl can bring such joy to the kingdom, another child can only bring more."

Marius's brows squeezed together as he tried to think which of his siblings would be having a whelp. Sylas and Dianthe had adopted three children weeks ago, but he hadn't heard them speak of taking in more. It was rare for dragons who'd mated outside their species to have children. Charlie was the only one he knew of, and none of his siblings had mated dragons except... He did a double take when he saw Harlow's impish grin.

"You're..."

"Yes." She ran a hand over the subtle mound of her belly. "Don't look so surprised, Marius. We are two dragons who've made good practice at all manner of mating."

There wasn't room for all the joy he felt in his diamond heart in that moment. He swept her into his arms and spun her around, thanking the Mountain for every blessing and the life that was to come.

And that night, when they returned to their chambers, they found a gift from her mother and father. Darium had created a custom door with swirls of diamond and amethyst at its center and all of the jewels representing their families branching out straight to the edges of the heavy, gold-encrusted wood. To his delight, there was space left near their stones in the pattern. Plenty of space. He placed a hand on Harlow's belly and hoped one day to populate every square inch.

EPILOGUE

Perched above the palace, Aitna, goddess of the mountain, watched the festivities below and smiled. Although the ceremony was strange, all the fanfare was done in her honor, and she found it quite pleasing. Her creation brought her such joy. And she could feel the love wash over her in waves.

"Do you think he knows?" her cousin Circe asked from beside her. She sipped from her goblet, her hair wild around her head. Her hair was always wild. As wild as her soul.

"Zeus?" Aitna laughed. "What would he care? I have been no concern of his since the beginning of the beginning."

"His loss," Circe said. "He has never known love. Never been part of creating it."

Aitna clinked her glass against her cousin's. "Not like us. We created creatures who are masters of it."

Zeus had once been her lover, but even when they were together, he never brought her the joy she was experiencing now. Her island home was her greatest pleasure, and the work of her hand, the dragons she'd cut from the fabric of the universe, made into their soma forms by Circe, had proven a worthy project. The sounds of laughter floated up to her. Her name, spoken in gratitude, fell from the lips of many. They adored her, and she was utterly content.

"What about the girl? Do you think they will come for her?"

She focused on the child, the angel. A guardian she was, but her mother needn't worry. Aitna had heard her prayers and would not allow anyone to harm her. Her wings would guard only this mountain. Her heart would know only peace.

"As long as I have power over this mountain, they will not."

Circe nodded. "Zeus still protects Ouros. They may never know what she is. They may never know she exists."

"I plan to keep it that way." Aitna's dress, made of liquid fire, sizzled with her energy.

"You have much to be proud of, Aitna, and I am happy for you." Circe stood. "I should get back to my prison."

"You know you are always welcome here. The angel isn't the only thing I can hide."

"You are, as always, the kindest heart."

Aitna bowed her head, and Circe was gone.

The goddess returned her gaze to the family dancing in the garden at the base of her mountain. They were her bounty, her ultimate prize, her treasure. And in the shelter of her protection forevermore, they'd shine.

Thank you for reading THE LAST DRAGON. If you enjoyed this book and this series, please leave a review.

Reviews help other readers find books they love and feed an author's soul.

In the TREASURE OF PARAGON, the witch queen of Darnuith is a legend and her true story is lost to history. Learn the truth behind the folklore in The Three Sisters Trilogy. Book 1, THE TANGLEWOOD WITCHES is available now! Get your copy, or continue on to read an excerpt.

DON'T MISS THE TANGLEWOOD WITCHES

Flip the page to read an excerpt of the action-packed prequel to the TREASURE OF PARAGON, THE TANGLEWOOD WITCHES!

THE TANGLEWOOD WITCHES

ORIGINS: CHAPTER 1

Alexandria, Egypt, 30 BC

"Unhand me. I demand to know what this is about!" Alena grunted as the guard's palm rudely connected with the center of her back and thrust her into the stone cell with no regard for her ongoing protests.

This morning had gone from bad to worse. At the crack of dawn, a team of Egyptian soldiers had hauled her out of her meager lodgings and dragged her to Cleopatra's palace. The soldiers had offered no explanation for her arrest. That was bad.

But if the experience had warranted the label of worst day since she'd come to Egypt, her current situation trumped that epithet. She found herself in a crowded room that smelled of limestone and dark spices, and judging by her company, the guards had made a terrible mistake.

She rubbed her sleepy eyes and took in the others around her. It wasn't just her tattered, filthy garments that made her stand out like Zeus's lightning bolt; she was the only woman in the group, and based on appearances, these

305

men were important. *Sau* priests if the leopard skins draped over their shoulders was any indication. Powerful magicians. Each was completely shaven of all body hair, as was the custom. Dressed in light linen, they sparkled from their bald heads to their bare toenails. She'd never been that clean in her life.

Suddenly she realized the source of the scent she'd noticed when she arrived. Not dark spices but anointing oils. The priests gave her a disapproving look, and she moved away from them to huddle on the far side of the room.

She did not belong here. Not only was she not a priest, she wasn't even Egyptian. Alena hailed from Crete, Greece, a commoner who had taken to the healing arts. She'd only made the perilous journey to Egypt to study in the library of Alexandria. Herbs and pharmacopoeia were her passion, and she wished to learn what knowledge the books and scrolls there contained. The library had almost burned down once. It was her life's dream to investigate what it had to offer before some other disaster challenged its stacks.

Her father had begged her not to go. He'd become dependent on her in many ways, the least of which was to fill the hole that had been left when her mother died. But two seasons ago she'd realized she would never leave Crete or realize her potential as a healer if she didn't seek passage to the greatest source of knowledge her generation had ever known.

Thank the gods her talents had proven lucrative. Quickly she had taken to tending the sick and acting as a midwife. News of her competence had traveled far and wide and earned her the sobriquet of Healer of the Nile. And although it was dirty work and she was rarely paid in coin, her calling had provided a suitable dwelling and a full belly.

At least the presence of the priests in this stone room meant she wasn't in any real danger. Why would Cleopatra imprison her own sorcerers? This was either a misunderstanding or some sort of royal request for services. Perhaps the pharaoh was in need of healing. She tried to remain calm and take comfort in the fact that she was in the company of important men, not criminals.

"Well, well, well. If it isn't the Healer of the Nile," a man said from behind her.

Her spine stiffened. She knew that voice. She hated that voice. She closed her eyes and sighed before turning to face him.

"Orpheus, the louse charmer." She shot the man a slanted glance. Like her, Orpheus stood out from the others in the room, although his clothing was also of far better quality than hers. His thick black hair and short beard contradicted the clean-shaven heads of the others, and he was certainly *not* a priest. A smooth-talking charlatan maybe, but not a priest.

By profession, he was a popular barber, one who claimed the rare distinction of successfully ridding heads of vermin without having to shave them. The skill was all but unheard of, and people came from everywhere for his services. Truly, it was a shame a man of such talent and wealth had the personality of a pimple on the ass of a diseased rat.

"Why the hostility, Alena? You're not still mad about what happened between us?" He flashed his most disarming smile.

She silently cursed as her insides reacted with a reflexive rush of lightning. The man was devastatingly handsome with the tawny glow of one blessed by the gods. In other circumstances, she would feel quite honored to have garnered his attention, she'd give him that. Dark-haired and blue-eyed, he had a mouth that seemed locked in a permanent smirk. She'd made the mistake of kissing that mouth, an act akin to drinking sweet poison.

An exasperated sigh tore from her lips. "Did *you* have something to do with this? You did something stupid, didn't you, and then likely threw out *my* name as an alibi!"

"No!" He scoffed.

She spread her hands and gestured toward the priests, who were doing their best to ignore them properly. "Then why are *we* here?"

"No idea, but we are the only ones in this room not employed by Cleopatra. These men are magicians, sorcerers, priests. They tend to the gods. It seems odd they've summoned us as well."

"My thoughts exactly." Alena hated to agree with Orpheus about anything, but she was hard-pressed to come up with any explanation.

Their conversation was interrupted by the heavy grinding of stone on stone. Alena whirled to find soldiers sliding a heavy slab into the doorway, completely sealing off the exit. With no windows or alternate ways out of the tiny room, Alena instantly felt choked off.

"Stop! What are you doing?" She lurched toward the door, but Orpheus caught her by the arms.

"Those swords aren't for show, Alena. Whatever they have in store for us, you won't avoid it that way."

"But... but... we're trapped in here." Pain flared in her chest, and her breath came in ragged pants.

"Easy." Orpheus rubbed her shoulders. Her wild eyes

found his and he guided her through some deep breaths. "Keep your wits about you. We're going to need them."

Slowly her panic abated. Despite being a rake and a scoundrel, Orpheus was an important man in Alexandria. Surely she was safe here among the priests and him. A half dozen torches mounted above their heads bathed them in flickering shadows.

"I can't even make out the door we came through," Alena said.

"Odd that." Orpheus grimaced, showing a mouthful of suspiciously straight white teeth. No other man, Greek or Egyptian, sported such a perfect smile. She wondered for the hundredth time what bargain he'd struck with the gods to maintain his impossibly good looks.

"Can't you charm a louse to squeeze through the walls and get us out of here?" Alena said through her teeth, annoyed by his nearness. She crossed her arms between them and tapped her foot expectantly in his direction.

"If there was a louse among this hairless crew, yes I could."

"I have hair."

He arched a brow. "And we both know that thanks to your herbal concoctions, there isn't a single louse on you either. Although what a tiny insect could do to open a stone door anyway, I have no idea. Unfortunately, there isn't a single living thing in this room that would be any help in getting us out of it."

She shook her head. "As expected, a bastion of self-importance but completely useless in a crunch."

He recoiled from the insult but recovered soon enough. "What about you, Alena? Don't you have anything in that bag that could help us?" He glared at the satchel at her hip.

She didn't go anywhere without her apothecary basket,

and she'd felt fortunate when the guards had allowed her to bring it. Inside, she stored a wide variety of herbs and elixirs in small glass jars or wrapped in parchment.

She placed a protective hand over it. "Only if we all come down with fever."

Nonchalantly, he leaned a shoulder against the wall and crossed his legs at the ankle. "As expected. Asserts to raise the dead but completely useless in an emergency."

"I never said I could raise the dead! Oh, you're a child." She turned her back to him, a welcome surge of anger and frustration driving out her previous fears.

"Frankly, I'm surprised the soldiers allowed you to bring your apothecary," he murmured thoughtfully.

She turned back to him. "It was unusual. At the time, I assumed someone in the palace needed healing, but clearly that's not why I'm here." Her eyes narrowed on him.

"Why are *you* here anyway? Didn't you tell Cleopatra's guards that you're an archon of Athens, invited here as an advisor by the pharaoh herself?"

His face fell at her reference to the lie he'd used to try to take advantage of her. "I never said I was an archon. You assumed."

She clenched her teeth. "Only because you had suggested as much on the boat to Alexandria. The elaborate clothing, the food, the servants. It all seemed to indicate you were an important government official, a leader."

"As I recall, you benefited frequently from my generosity."

She couldn't deny it. He had been generous, and at the time that generosity had meant everything to her.

"The crew of the vessel said you were the eponymous archon of Athens. Who would have told them such if not you? And you did not refute it, although you must have heard the rumors."

"Is it my duty to correct every wagging tongue? Athens has a council of archons, not a single magistrate. You should have known it was a falsehood."

"You knew and you allowed me to believe it. It was under that presumption that I allowed you to woo me within a hair's breadth of your bed, only to discover in the most embarrassing way that it was all a lie."

For weeks he'd pursued her, bringing her gifts, sharing long walks, even doing his best to bump into her at the market. But then he'd invited her to a feast at the home of a prominent Alexandrian. It was there that a group of elderly wives had pulled her aside and told her the truth. He was the louse charmer—their name for the barber—and she was one of many women he'd wooed under false pretenses. He was a cad, a rake, and a scoundrel. The old women had wasted no time sharing their deep regret that her reputation among the elite was already scarred by arriving on his arm.

"I pursued you because I enjoyed your company." He gave her a wicked half smile. "Not only to bed you."

"He flirts with every woman in the city," she said, mimicking the voice of the old women. "He's a scoundrel, a cheater. Allow him between your legs and it will be the last time he gives you any attention whatsoever."

"Untrue. You can't believe such things." He raised an eyebrow.

"Oh?" She planted her fists on her hips. "And the woman I saw coming out of your abode on the last moon?"

He opened his mouth but stopped short. His gaze lifted toward the ceiling. "Not that I don't love debating the history of our meeting and my scandalous behavior once again, but does it appear to you that the smoke is gathering?"

Alena glanced upward to find a thick cloud building above them. "The torches. There's no ventilation." The small, windowless room was growing warmer as well. Already her eyes stung, and the air appeared cloudy between them. "There isn't enough space and too many mouths breathing. Orpheus, if this keeps building..." She gave him an ominous look.

He inhaled deeply and muttered something inaudible under his breath.

One of the priests tested the door. As she suspected, it was sealed. Alena couldn't even see the outline of the opening in the stone. Another priest pounded on the walls and cried for help. Still another tried to scale the wall to put out one of the torches, but the brace was set too high and caged in iron. Worse, Alena noticed more smoke coming through the stone up above.

"They're doing this on purpose!" she cried, gathering a loose bit of fabric from the neck of her cloak and pressing it around her mouth and nose. Did Cleopatra mean to kill them all?

The smoke thickened by the minute. The walls were too close, the air too tight. True fear pulverized her resolve to stay calm, and the shaking in her knees spread to the rest of her body. Orpheus tugged on her hand, gesturing for her to sit. Considering her knees were about to give out anyway, she dropped to the rough, mercifully cool floor. The air was cleaner there, and she drew in a panicked breath.

"Alena, it's a test," Orpheus said with utmost certainty.

She stared at him with stinging eyes, willing her addled brain to understand what he was talking about. To her surprise, he didn't seem to be struggling to breathe at all. Nor was he panicked as she was.

"What kind of test?" she rasped. "One to see who can hold their breath the longest? I fear we will all fail. Cleopatra may be the reincarnation of Isis, but the rest of us are only human."

"Are you?" Orpheus's eyes crinkled at the corners.

"Aren't *you*?" Alena's gaze connected with his through the smoky air.

One of the priests banged on the wall in earnest now, his pleas for release growing as he struggled for air, while still others slumped or crawled on their bellies, anything for a small measure of comfort. She lowered her chest to the floor. Orpheus followed, although the smoke didn't seem to be bothering him anyway.

"Haven't you noticed that everyone in this room has a reputation for magic?" he asked.

"Not everyone. I do not advertise myself as such." She coughed into her cloak.

"Ah, but it is known, Alena. You are the healer they say can make a tonic to cure any ill. Some call you a hedge witch."

She coughed violently. "Those who wish to be healed should stop making up names for me."

"But they aren't wrong, are they?"

A priest who'd balanced on the shoulders of another to try to extinguish one of the torches fell unconscious to the stone floor. His head cracked near her hand. Blood ran from his fractured skull, scoring a deep crimson river in the stone. Alena shuffled away from it. Her instinct was to dig in her basket and find something to try to heal him, but she could hardly breathe herself. They were all doomed. All but Orpheus, who hadn't coughed once.

"You believe this is a test of our abilities? Someone is trying to prove we have... magic?"

His lips pursed and he gave a curt nod. "It would be a particularly gruesome horror to watch a woman as beautiful as you die. I'd much prefer your company under sweeter circumstances. I enjoyed our time together up until those crones ruined everything with their lies. More than I can say." He grabbed her arm and gave her a hard shake. "Come on, Alena. Think. Tell me you have something in that bag you can use. How hard can it be? All you have to do is survive."

Her throat and eyes burned and her lungs spasmed with their need for air. She cursed. Why wasn't he as affected as she? He still wasn't coughing, and his eyes glowed an arresting shade of lapis in the dingy room. She shook her head and concentrated. He was right. She was a powerful healer. There must be something she could use to protect herself from the smoke if she could calm herself long enough to remember how to use it. Digging in her basket, she drew a length of aeras lily root and wove a braid of Nile grasses around it. Muttering a spell, she formed the resulting mask into a shallow bowl and cupped it over her mouth and nose. Instantly, she could breathe again.

"Aeras root. I hadn't thought of that."

"I developed this spell for a boy in the village who has trouble breathing during the dry season. I wouldn't have thought to use it if you hadn't..." She stopped. She wouldn't give him the satisfaction. "What did you use?"

"Containment spell. I'm inside a sophisticated barrier. Although, to be honest, I didn't think it through. The air is getting thin in here. If this test goes on much longer, I may be joining our friends." He gestured to the priests who were now writhing on the floor, either coughing or limp and unconscious. "I can't renew the spell without any fresh air to seal around myself."

Alena could see it now, how the smoke never seemed to actually touch Orpheus. It curled away from his flesh. Genius, she thought. She'd love to ask him about that particular spell if they ever got out of this room.

"How long have you known about me?" she asked.

"Since the feast. When I kissed you, I knew you were magic. Couldn't you sense it in me?"

She searched his face. The kiss had sent tingles through her body, but it wasn't as though she'd had anything to compare it to. Weren't all kisses like that? She shook her head.

Orpheus shrugged and started to cough. "Hades, it seems my spell is wearing off. And no closer to finding out what Cleopatra wants from us, other than to die."

No one could claim to know the mind of Cleopatra. Far above the commoners of Egypt, her will was a maze of secrets known only to her. Alena had always thought it would be lonely to be a pharaoh; perhaps that was why it wasn't hard to believe the rumors that Cleopatra's obsessive quest for power had made her a killer. Some said she'd murdered her own brother for the throne.

Orpheus pressed his face into his hands, body stretched out on the floor. She had to make a difficult decision. Did she assume this trial must have one winner and allow the smoke to overcome him? Or did she help him and risk inviting the wrath of Cleopatra?

In the end, there was no decision to make. It was bad enough to live with the knowledge that she could do nothing to help the other men who'd collapsed in the room. Refusing aid to Orpheus when he was the reason she'd thought to build the mask in the first place would be a black mark on her soul she could not abide.

Alena took a deep breath and then moved her mask to cover Orpheus's nose and mouth. His body eased beside her, his breathing evening out. He took three long breaths, then moved the mask back to her face. They survived together, sharing the mask, until the smoke was so thick she could no longer see the walls of the room, only his deep-blue eyes.

And then the stone-on-stone rumble filled the room again. Not the door this time. Like a dream, one entire wall of their cell slid away. Cool air wafted around them. The smoke rose up and out in a billow of gray. Light cut through the foggy air. Orpheus had her by the shoulders and was helping her to her feet.

She blinked rapidly. Through the dispelling haze, she could make out a vast hall ahead of them with brightly painted columns. Colorful tapestries draped the walls, and a long red rug led to a dais. She squinted to make out who or what was on that platform at the other end of the room, but her eyes still stung from the smoke, and their watering blurred her vision. Alena leaned into Orpheus, and together they hobbled along the aisle. Fire burned in a series of great gold bowls lighting their way. Alena blinked and blinked again.

Dread filled her heart when she realized who it was on that platform, sitting on her golden throne. Not some soldier or priest or counselor as she'd expected but Cleopatra herself.

Her hair was as black and shiny as the Nile at midnight, and her clothing was solid gold. Everything about her was fashioned to intimidate her subjects, from the robe made to resemble the feathers of Isis to the headdress of horns that framed a large red disk that reflected the light of the flickering torches in a way that seemed supernatural.

Alena swallowed hard. This woman ruled Egypt. She truly might be a goddess for all Alena knew. She definitely held their lives in her hands. It was said she was beautiful, but Alena didn't see beauty, only power. She radiated it like a deadly, burning sun.

Orpheus tugged her shoulders as they arrived at the base of the dais, and she followed his lead, dropping to her knees beside him.

An elderly man who stood beside the pharaoh announced, "All hail Cleopatra, the embodiment of Isis, sister to Horus and Ra, and queen of all Egypt."

Alena lowered her forehead to the floor and prayed to all the gods whose names she could remember that the worst was already behind her.

Continue THE TANGLEWOOD WITCHES wherever you buy books!

ACKNOWLEDGMENTS

It is with mixed emotions that I scrawl a tentative *The End* on this the ninth and final book in the TREASURE OF PARAGON series, THE LAST DRAGON. Tentative because after devoting more than three years of my writing life to this royal family, I'm not sure it's possible to completely leave them behind. As I write this, I'm about to embark on the final book in the Three Sisters Trilogy, Tanglewood Legacy, and then the full story will be told.

To me, this story was always far more than a shifter series or a witch series. It was an epic fantasy about a royal family who crossed paths with a magical family and, through love and destiny, changed their world forever. Thank you, Tanglewoods. Thank you, Treasure of Paragon. Your stories live on in my heart and the hearts of my readers. It's been a beautiful three years.

I would like to again thank Anne at Victory Editing for her work on this novel and this series. Anne edited every book in the Treasure of Paragon, and the series wouldn't be what it is without her. A huge thank you to Lisa Hollett, Silently Correcting Your Grammar, for her editing skills and story bible. Nine dragons plus mates and supporting characters is a lot of moving parts. Lisa kept everyone's hearts and rings the right color and ensured consistency across books. I can't thank her enough.

Another big thank you to Deranged Doctor Designs for

the fabulous cover art. They captured the look I was going for with this series perfectly.

A special thank you to author Sara Whitney who helped me put the finishing touches on THE LAST DRAGON. Her help and support were critical as I carried this one across the finish line.

And finally, thank you, readers, for trusting me with the hours you invest in my books. I strive to give you a memorable experience and hope you enjoyed every one.

USA Today bestselling and multi-award winning author Genevieve Jack writes wild, witty, and wicked-hot paranormal romance and romantic fantasy. She believes there's magic in every breath we take and probably something supernatural living in most dark basements. You can summon her with coffee, wine, and books, but she sticks around for dogs and chocolate. Her novels feature badass heroines, fiercely loyal heroes, and fantasy elements that will fill you with wonder. Learn more at GenevieveJack.com.

Do you know Jack? Keep in touch to stay in the know about new releases, sales, and giveaways.

Join my VIP reader group

Sign up for my newsletter

- facebook.com/AuthorGenevieveJack
- twitter.com/genevieve_jack
- instagram.com/authorgenevievejack
- bookbub.com/authors/genevieve-jack

www.ingramcontent.com/pod-product-compliance
Lightning Source LLC
Chambersburg PA
CBHW010549170726
48285CB00011B/2823